# Sha'Daa

# Zombie Park

CREATED BY

## MICHAEL H. HANSON

FEATURING

## ERIC S. BROWN
## GUSTAVO BONDONI
## JASON CORDOVA

MoonDream
PRESS

AN IMPRINT OF COPPER DOG PUBLISHING, LLC

# The Sha'Daa Series

Published by Moondream Press, an imprint of Copper Dog Publishing, LLC
537 Leader Circle
Louisville, CO 80027

Visit our Web site: www.copperdogpublishing.com

Credits:
Cover and Interior Design: Helen Harrison
Edited by Michael H. Hanson
Sha'Daa™: Zombie Park created by Michael H. Hanson

978-1-943690-30-5

First Edition: October 2020

Printed in the United States of America

# Contents

This book is dedicated to:

*Those who love us and have given us the space and time to write and dream.*

# ACKNOWLEDGMENTS

*No man is an island, entire of itself.*

—*John Donne*

'D LIKE TO TAKE THIS OPPORTUNITY TO THANK the folks who are responsible for this shared-world anthology making it into print:

Novelists Eric S. Brown, Gustavo Bondoni, and Jason Cordova for jumping on board the very first Sha'Daa Novella Anthology.

David Robbins for writing the Introduction to Zombie Park, the seventh volume in the Sha'Daa saga.

Catherine Van Sciver for helping to format the book.

Copper Dog Publishing Editor-in-Chief Edward F. McKeown whose fierce drive and professionalism has kept this long-running project on track through some very tough times.

Copper Dog Publishing Creative Director Helen Harrison for another one of her excellent Sha'Daa Covers.

From the depths of my heart, I thank you all.

Michael H. Hanson
Sha'Daa Creator
Louisville, Colorado
October 2020

by David Robbins

# MASTERS OF MAYHEM

**K**ICK BACK AND THRILL TO THE APOCALYPSE. Everyone says we're in for an end-times scenario. The Mayans. The BIBLE. (Too many denominations to list.) Islam has its Day of Judgment. Nostradamus jumped on the bandwagon. So did Christopher Columbus. (Yes. The guy who 'discovered America'. He wrote something called his *BOOK OF PROPHECIES*. He thought the end time would take place in 1656.) Isaac Newton also got into the act. (Yes. The guy who "discovered gravity." He gave a number of dates. The earliest he mentioned is 2034. So we're getting close.)

The Hermetic Order of the Golden Dawn thought it would be 2010. (You're probably never heard of them but they have such a cool name, I had to throw them in.) Jeane Dixon predicted it. Hindu cosmology teaches that after something like 300 trillion years all matter returns to the state of Prakriti. (Which may not constitute an Apocalypse in the truest sense. But hey.)

A lot of books and movies have delved into various aspects of the end times.

Which brings us to *SHA'DAA: Zombie Park*. An immensely entertaining entry that will have you on the edge of your seat.

If you think you know Apocalypses, you haven't seen anything---or read anything---quite like the mayhem fueled bloodbath that descends on Central Park. Or ascends, as the case may be.

Four authors lend their talents to this energetic tale of humans and otherwise who battle for supremacy with the fate of the world at stake.

Eric S. Brown, Gustavo Bondoni, and Jason Cordova contribute the three main elements, respectively, with their stories linked by interludes provided by Michael H. Hanson.

Since a book entitled *Zombie Park* clearly includes the hungry dead, you might think you've seen it all before where zombies are concerned. You haven't. The four authors inject new slants that lend fresh perspective and keep you on the edge of your seat.

One of those slants involves a mysterious someone who keeps showing up out of nowhere, adding another layer to a tale that is far more than another "zombies eat people" gorefest.

Which brings us to a word of warning. You might not want to become too attached to the protagonists. Just when you do, here comes the gore.

It should be noted that the book is part of a series, so if you like what you read, you might pick up the others.

David Robbins

2020

# The Watcher

by Michael H. Hanson

*"All that we see or seem, is but a dream within a dream."*
— *Edgar Allen Poe*

AN AGELESS, COSMIC BEING OF UNIMAG-inable powers, hovered unnoticed in the darkness a full three miles above Manhattan's Central Park. He made for a rather macabre apparition, a tall slender man wearing a black fedora hat and shrouded in a long dark trench coat whose ends rippled and flowed with the winds. It was midnight, twenty-four hours before the beginning of the Summer Solstice. He had waited ten thousand years for this most improbable of events, the mother of all apocalypses which had occurred across the breadth and span of time once every ten millennia. The reasons for his own involvement in this hideous yet majestic set of circumstances were lost in antiquity, but his purpose remained true, and his mission, unwavering and uncompromised.

Why this particular locale had drawn his attention was a mystery even to him. Portals to various Hell dimensions, numbering in the hundreds, were slowly beginning to come to life all over the planet. If even just one of them fully opened, it spelled certain doom for all humanity, perhaps even all life larger than bacteria.

Barely perceptible waves of gravitic distortion began emanating upward from the park. His eyes, two dark pools of blackness from which no light escaped, opened wide as he began to understand the abomination that was growing beneath him.

There was a Hell portal here, one deep underground, and the very nature of the arcane energies about to begin emanating from it would not only unearth a host of horrors upon the city but would radically alter the underlying fundamental nature of reality itself in a six-mile circumference.

Battling this particular breach in the quantum walls that surrounded Earth was going to require far more effort, resources, and human lives than he had ever imagined…but the fate of the human race was at stake, and ever the ultimate pragmatist, he steeled himself to face a sheer hurricane of death and suffering that could no longer be put off. Wish as he might, he could not directly interfere in the terrible events about to occur. His was a curse of mighty restraint, though he had long ago discovered a small but precious defect in the deific decree that nearly crippled his cause. He now looked down upon the Earth with all the creative focus of a Chess Grandmaster or a Nine Dan Professional Go Player.

His mouth stretched into a wide, bitter grin, momentarily exposing a single bright, shiny gold tooth, his left lateral incisor, set amidst an otherwise perfect set of glistening, white enamel.

Twelve hours passed and Noon struck New York City.

A gargantuan explosion of pale jade light flashed through the heavens to smite the Earth like a forbidden whisper.

The Sha'Daa began…

# Showtime

## by Eric S. Brown

*"There are things in the universe that are simply and purely evil. A warrior does not seek to understand them, or to compromise with them. He seeks only to obliterate them."*

—Grand Admiral Thrawn (Timothy Zahn, Star Wars)

AGENT LANNING GLANCED AT HIS WATCH. Its digital display clicked from Eleven Fifty-Nine eastern time to Twelve PM, noon. He sighed and looked over at Eastman and Driggle, shaking his head. The three of them were stationed inside Central Park's historical "Blockhouse" as the locals called it. It was the only remnant of an old fort, constructed long ago to fend off invading British armies or some such crap. History wasn't really Lanning's area of expertise. His talents lay in saving the fragging world. He was second in command of Taskforce Augur. Lanning wasn't overly fond of the name but hey, it fit. Taskforce Augur was composed of the most powerful psychics in the United States and a few on loan from other countries. Among their numbers were those who could see the future, read other people's thoughts, move things with their mind, and so much more.

"It's showtime," Lanning told the others.

Eastman pumped a round into the chamber of the shotgun he held. Driggle just nodded.

"Any idea how this is supposed to play out?" Eastman asked.

"Frag if I know," Lanning grumbled. "Sawyer just saw this park as being Hell central today. The end of the world is supposed to start here."

"Got to admit that "end of the world" is pretty vague," Driggle snorted. "That could be anything from the start of a vampire plague to a nuclear strike."

Eastman cocked his head towards the Blockhouse's locked gate. "I don't hear any screaming out there yet."

"Give it time," Lanning assured Eastman though he felt more than a bit uneasy himself. The unknown was a dangerous thing in their kind of work. Unknowns got folks killed. A few years back, the government had dumped fifty billion dollars into creating Taskforce Augur to deal with threats to the country and the world that more conventional agencies and the military weren't equipped to handle. Based on what little Lanning knew, it was all to prepare for something called the Sha'Daa. Who or what the Sha'Daa happened to be was above his paid grade. Taskforce Augur had cut their teeth chasing down monsters straight out of Old-World legends, staking vampires, stalking werewolves, exorcising demons, trudging through sewers after albino alligator infestations, and battling the stuff of nightmares. All of that was just prep work, preparing and hardening them for today. Whatever the Sha'Daa was, it was here now, and Taskforce Augur was the first line of defense against it.

Ben Sawyer was Augur's best and brightest pre-cog. The vision Sawyer had of the future came true over ninety percent of the time. His visions were usually spot on. If Ben told you it was going to rain, you'd dang well better be grabbing an umbrella. As good as Ben was, the man was still human and sometimes his visions could be a bit …unclear. That was the case with today. Ben had told them that the end of the world would begin promptly at noon, eastern time in Central Park and the entire place would become a bloodbath, a full out war zone between the forces of good and evil. Beyond that, Ben hadn't been able to tell them anything else so Taskforce Augur wasn't taking any chances.

Director Stevenson had mobilized not only every member of Taskforce Augur but had enlisted the military and national guard's aid as well. While he, Eastman, and Driggle, along with a few other small squads, had been sent on into the park to be his eyes and ears there, Director Stevenson was in route with enough agents and soldiers to surround the entire massive park in attempt to contain whatever was about to be unleashed within its borders. Central Park was around two point five miles long and half a mile wide. Though preparation for today had begun months ago, the deployment of that level of a containment force was still no easy thing especially when it all had to be done as covertly as possible until the last few hours and even then made to look as it were only some kind of training exercise.

In theory, Lanning and the squads under his command were to do what they could to hold the line in the park and prevent as much of the coming loss of life as possible. That's why Harrison and Shandra were among the other squads already inside the park. Both of them were power houses in terms of their abilities but even so, you were talking about nine people, with all three squads combined, covering an area large enough to be a small town unto itself. There was only such much ground they cover and so much that they could do until Director Stevenson's force arrived. If they knew what to look out for or where it was all going to start in terms of an exact location within the park maybe things would be different…but they didn't. All they could do was wait for hell to break loose and try to deal with it as it happened.

The gate of the Blockhouse creaked as Lanning opened it and led the others out. Eastman was right about there being no signs of trouble yet. Lanning hoped that meant whatever was about to happen would be a slow building event and give the others time to get on site before the worst of it all broke loose. Regardless, it was time to get moving. They wouldn't do anyone any good staying where they were.

Larry jogged along one of the running paths on the Northern side of the park. The day was hot and the sky a bright blue above. Larry was beginning to "feel the burn." but he was feeling good about himself for finally getting off his couch and trying to make something of both himself and his life again. Things had been hard since Stella had left. Her leaving had nearly been the end of him. It had taken months to pull himself back together even to the point of where he was now. Larry supposed he should have seen it coming but he hadn't. Her sudden demand for "space" and moving out had hit him out of the blue. She claimed that they had just drifted apart and none of their problems were his fault. Larry knew better though. They say that hindsight is twenty/twenty and looking back, Larry was forced to admit that he hadn't fought hard enough to keep her. He couldn't remember the last time the two of them had a date that was more than watching a movie on the couch followed by stale, passionless sex in the bedroom before turning in for the night. The sex was just as bad or maybe even worse for Stella. It was more than just those things Larry figured but they were sure a big part of it all. Whenever she tried to talk to him, it always seemed to be at the worst possible moment and more often than not, Larry had blown her off completely about the things she tried to tell him.

The track wasn't very crowed today in the section of it that he was in. Larry was glad for that. His belly bounced with each stride he took. A picture of health, he wasn't. His skin was pale and sweat dripped from the wet mop his hair had become. His breath came in ragged gasps. Still, Larry pushed on.

Without warning, the entire park shook. The ground moved under his feet. One of Larry's ankles twisted as he tried to catch himself and keep his balance. Larry hit the pavement hard with a loud grunt. The impact jarred him to the bone. His head whipped about at the other folks close by. Most of them too had been knocked to the ground by the tremor. People were panicking as they got to their feet. They were running for cover even though from the looks of them they were as clueless about what had just happened as he was. Larry's best guess was that the tremor had been a small earthquake. That didn't make much sense. This was Manhattan not L.A. Larry checked his ankle. It was bruised but not broken. As he got to his feet, he saw something moving just beyond the bushes at the side of the track. The ground had been partially torn up in that area by the small quake. Larry stumbled toward the movement to see if there was someone there who needed help. As he drew closer, Larry saw a man emerging from the dirt. The fellow appeared to be pulling his body up and out of the ground. Had the quake been bad enough to actually swallow people up? Larry wondered in shock and horror. If so, he had been dang lucky to get away with nothing more than a bruised ankle. Then the man's head rose up to where Larry could see his face.

Fat, writhing maggots crawled over and through what was left of the man's checks. His nose was mostly gone. Larry could see the white of bone gleaming in the rays of the hot midday sun. Larry gagged as the stench of the man's rotted flesh reached his nostrils. The man heaved his body free of the dirt and rose to his feet. Larry stared at him, feeling sick. The man was clearly dead, long dead, but somehow, he was moving.

In the wake of the quake, there had been some scattered screams from around the section of park that Larry was in. Instead of dying down, Larry heard them rise in volume and intensity. He didn't dare turn his head to see what the cause was. His gaze was fixed entirely on the dead man that had begun to limp towards him.

"Hey buddy," Larry said., stretching out an open palm at the dead man as if to ward him off. "You just stay where you are, and I will go get help okay?"

A low growl rumbled up from the dead man's rotted lungs. His eyes appeared to flash a bright shade of green as he lunged at Larry. Staggering backwards, Larry avoided the dead man's grasping hands. The man kept coming though.

"Back off!" Larry yelled but the man didn't seem to hear his words at all.

Left with no choice but to defend himself, Larry jerked back a fist and slammed it into the side of the man's skull. The blow sent the dead man sprawling onto the running path. Larry looked down at his knuckles. They had scraped away part of the man's rotted flesh which clung to them. There were maggots on his hand too. Larry shook it, flinging the maggots away. That was all he could take. Collapsing onto his knees, Larry threw up. Heaves rocked his bent over body as his breakfast splattered onto the pavement in front of him. As the heaves stopped, cold hands took hold of his shoulders from behind him. Larry spun about, grabbing the dead man's arms to pull himself free. The man's head jerked forward like a rabid dog's as teeth snapped at his face. For a guy who was dead, the man was crazy strong. Using all his strength, Larry held the man back away from him, getting to his feet. The two of them were locked together in a desperate struggle. The dead man relentlessly trying to press closer to him and Larry fighting to keep him at bay. Larry kicked the inside of the dead man's right leg with all the force he could muster. Bone cracked as his foot made contact just below the man's knee joint. A jagged shard of white tore through the skin and tattered pants of the man's leg. The man dropped giving Larry the advantage he needed to finally break free. As Larry back peddled, he kicked at the man again. The tip of his shoe smashed into the underside of the man's chin, driving his head skyward. Larry heard a sickening popping noise as the man's neck broke from the impact. The man toppled over, laying on the pavement. Breaking his neck had finally taken the fight out of him but impossibly, somehow the man was still...alive. His eyes were darting about inside their sockets, following Larry as he continued to retreat. The man's teeth were still snapping though his body from the neck down remained motionless.

Larry managed to tear his eyes away from the dead man to look around. He almost wished he hadn't. There were people running everywhere and things like the dead man he had just put down were chasing after them.

Caroline sprinted along the walkway towards the small restroom building. There were screams coming from every direction. To her right, she saw a man wearing an expensive looking business suit trying to fend off a woman in the remains of what looked to be a wedding dress. The woman was missing an eye as well as several teeth but that wasn't stopping her from trying to sink what was left of them into the man. Her decayed flesh was a grayish hue in the bright light of the midday sun. She snarled and growled as the two of them fought. Not far away, a mother had been taken to the ground by two men who were ripping her to shreds. The carriage holding her baby sat nearby. Her baby was crying and squealing at the top of its lungs. Caroline's heart broke for the child but there was nothing she could do to help it. If she stopped, one of the dead things that had risen up out of the ground would get her too. She knew that sticking to her plan was her only hope.

Reaching the restroom building, Caroline flung its door open, hurling herself into the Ladies Room. A quick look about assured her that it was empty.

All the stalls were open and there was no one in sight, dead or alive. She had no means of locking the main door to the bathroom. There was nothing to wedge it closed with either. All Caroline could do was dragged the heavy trash can next to the door over in front of it. Once that was done, she headed for one of the empty stalls. Locking it, she climbed up onto the toilet there, pulling her legs up to her chest so that her feet couldn't be seen from beneath the stall's door. Her cheeks were wet with tears and her breath came in ragged gasps between bouts of whimpering. Caroline fumbled her cell out of the pockets of the shorts she wore, dialing Nine-One-One. As she raised the phone to her ear, all she heard was a dull, ringing tone. Her phone was dead. It was more than just a lack of signal. Something was really wrong with her service. She had seen a movie where someone had used a military grade jammer once and what she was hearing from her phone reminded of her that scene. It was like the signal of her cell was being blocked or jammed somehow.

In a fit of fear and rage, Caroline slammed her phone against the side of the stall, shattering its screen. As soon as she had done it, Caroline realized how stupid she had been. The phone was her only lifeline to help…and now she had smashed it.

Something crashed into the door of the bathroom, shaking the heavy trash can she had scooted into front of it. Caroline dropped her phone. It clattered onto the floor next to the toilet she cowered on. She held her breath, listening, as whatever had struck the door rammed into it again. This time, the heavy trash can turned over, crashing onto its side, contents spilling out of it and someone or something entered the bathroom with her. Caroline prayed that it was just someone else trying to escape the hell outside but then she heard a low growl that accompanied the footsteps of the person who had broken through the door. No sane, normal human would make that kind of noise. A chill ran through her as Caroline pulled her legs tighter to her chest and did her best to be as still and quiet as she could.

The footsteps staggered from one stall to the next. As the thing reached each stall, it pounded on their doors with its fists until they gave way, crashing inward. The dead thing was working its way down the line of stalls. Caroline knew she had only a few moments until it reached hers. She could hear her father's voice in her head, telling her how unsafe the city was and that she should get a concealed carry permit. Caroline had always argued that getting such a permit in New York was nigh impossible but there was just no getting her Texan father to accept that. He was a firm believer in people's rights to defend themselves. New York's *duty to retreat stuff* was crap to him created by liberals who wanted nothing more than to oppress freedom. Right now, Caroline wished she had listened to her dad and carried a pistol even if she had been forced to break the law to do it. As it was, all she had on her was a can of mace. Caroline hastily dug out the small can and got it ready to use.

Rotting fists banged against the door of the stall next to hers. She heard its wood splinter from blows the dead thing rained upon it before it finally smashed inward. Caroline flinched. The muscles of her entire body tightened up in a fight or flight response though there really was nowhere to run to. Caroline was trapped inside the stall where she hid. All she could do was wait for the thing to reach her there. Caroline gritted her teeth as her fear turned to anger. Her father hadn't raised her to give up without a fight. As soon as the first blow of the dead thing's fists hammered into the door of her stall, Caroline kicked outward with both legs. The door broke loose from its hinges, being driven forward and outward. It thudded into the woman there, hitting her with such force that she reeled away from the stall's entrance. Caroline sprang to her feet, darting out of the stall. Her head turned as she saw the dead woman. Half the woman's face had been eaten away by worms and maggots. Her body was completely naked and withered. The long dried up wound of where something had slashed open her chest left the woman's rib cage exposed down her left side. Her breast there was gone as was most of her flesh in that area. The woman's eyes glowed a hot, burning green.

The dead woman recovered from being hit by the door faster than Caroline would have thought possible. Snarling, she charged at Caroline. Everything inside of Caroline told her to get out of the woman's path, make a run for it, but she didn't. Caroline stood her ground. She met the woman head on, grabbing her. With a twist of her body, Caroline used the dead woman's own momentum against her. She brought the woman's head down into the side of one of the bathroom's sinks. Its edge shattered. The woman's skull caved inward with a sickening crunching noise. Caroline let go of her as the woman fell onto the floor and lay there twitching. She body flopped about like a fish out of water slinging gore from the smash in wound on the side of her head. Caroline felt sick covering her mouth with her hand. All that mattered was that the woman was down and not coming after her anymore she told herself, turning to run for the bathroom's door.

The monkey was dead. It had to be. A chunk the size of full-grown man's hand was missing from its side and the animal's hair was drenched in blood. Derrick stood staring up at the thing where it sat on the tree limb above him. He had escaped the chaos engulfing the park by fleeing into the Ramble. It was a thirty-six acre *wild garden* and he had run deeper and deeper into its expanse where there were only trees and rocks. Derrick had managed to convince himself that he had found a safe haven within the nightmarish hells-cape of the park at last coming to a stop. That was when the monkey shrieked at him. He was pretty dang sure there weren't supposed to be any monkeys in it, much less dead ones with glowing green eyes. Sweat dripped from Derrick's hair as he waited on the thing to make the first move. He spotted a piece of wood washed up onto the rocks to his right and did his best not to show that he had seen it.

Derrick knew that there was a zoo in the park. More than one zoo really. The monkey had to be one of the Snow Monkeys he had read about. Somehow the thing had gotten loose, whether from the quake or the carnage that followed in its wake, didn't matter. The monkey was here now and his problem to deal with if he wanted to keep breathing. The worst thing about the dead animal in the tree above him wasn't its evident wounds or even its snarling, half parted black lips. It was the red splashed doll that dangled from its right hand. Derrick felt sick as his heart broke and he imagined the fate of the doll's previous owner.

Screeching, the monkey dropped the doll, leaping from the tree. Derrick snatched up the piece of wood, swinging it around to meet the monkey. The half-rotted wood smashed apart as it made contact with the side of the monkey's skull sending splinters flying. The impact knocked the animal off its path towards him. The animal thudded onto the bank of the small stream above its water line. Before it could right itself, Derrick moved to drive the remainder of the piece of wood into the animal's chest. The makeshift spear plunged through the monkey as Derrick tried to pin it down. Even as he recoiled in horror, backing away, the monkey tore loose of the wood, sliding its body up and off of it. Despite the fresh hole Derrick had put in the thing's body, it rushed him in an impossible burst of speed. Derrick lost his balance, toppling over into the water behind where he stood. The dead monkey was on him instantly, its claws tearing at his flesh. Derrick screamed as long strips of his skin were raked away, but he managed to wedge the flat of his right arm under the monkey's chin keeping its teeth from reaching face and throat. The monkey was too strong to hold off in such a manner though, so Derrick rolled, flinging the animal off of him as he scrambled onto his feet. Rivers of red flowed from the mangled slashed up flesh of his wounds as Derrick sprinted up the stream's bank. He had barely made it a few steps before the monkey got its claws into him again. The thing pounced onto his back. Its claws dug deep into the muscles of Derrick's shoulders. Derrick's hands shot up, reaching to try to pry the dead monkey off of him.

Suddenly, something grabbed hold of the monkey and ripped it loose from his back. Derrick toppled onto the ground. Rocks scraped at the palms of his hands as he landed on them. Rolling over, Derrick saw the monkey floating in the air. Some invisible force beyond his understanding held the dead creature there. Its arms and legs were rigid and stretched out away from the central mass of the monkey's body. The monkey's head was free from whatever was holding its limbs tight. Glowing green eyes burned with anger as the thing's head whipped from side to side searching for the source of the power that held it. A gun shot rang out. The monkey's skull exploded in a shower of bone fragments and gore. Whatever was holding the dead creature released it. The monkey's corpse flopped onto the bank of the stream next to where Derrick lay.

Derrick looked in the direction the shot had come from. He saw the woman that had shot the dead monkey. The barrel of her revolver was still smoking as she lowered it. Two men flanked her. All of three of them were wearing some sort of light, military style body armor. One of the men was carrying a heavy shotgun, the other a P-90. But it was the woman that took Derrick's breath away. Red hair blazed atop her head spilling down over her shoulders. The pupils of her eyes were a bright yellow unlike any he had ever heard anyone having before. Her body was sleek despite the armor she wore. She was an image of beauty and lethalness intermingled into a near perfect being.

"A thank you would be nice kid," the older looking of the two men growled at Derrick as the other moved forward to offer him a hand up.

"You okay?" the younger man asked.

"Do I look okay?" Derrick snapped before he could stop himself.

"Gary, get the kid's wounds tended to before he bleeds out," the woman ordered. "And quick. We can't stay here."

"Roger that," Gary nodded, shrugging a backpack from his shoulders and opening it up. He sprayed Derrick's wounds with something and then started getting them bandaged.

"Who are you people?" Derrick asked.

"We're the ones saving your butt kid," the older man told him. "That's all you need to know."

The woman raised her wrist close to her face. On it was a communications device.

"Lanning! What the hell is happening?" the woman shouted into it. "We got zombies everywhere."

"We do too Shandra," the voice from her comm. device answered. "On the upside, I would say it's pretty clear what we're dealing with now."

"Just had to be fragging zombies didn't it?" Derrick heard the older man mutter.

"Copy that," Shandra said. "Where the hell is Stevenson?"

"Still in route," Lanning's voice replied. "ETA in less than thirty."

"That's not going to be soon enough," Gary said. "Not with the way those dead things keep coming up out of the ground."

"I heard that," Lanning's voice snapped. "Our orders stand people. We're to save everyone we can until they get here and seal off the park. In the meantime, I think we're going to be better off if we meet up at a rallying point that we can hold until they get here. What's your current position?"

"We're somewhere in the Ramble," Shandra said.

"Belvedere Castle isn't far from here," the older man suggested.

"We'll meet you there. Try to send as many of these creatures that are popping up back to whatever hell they crawled out of on the way. Lanning, out!"

"The castle? Really Harrison?" Shandra frowned at the older man.

He shrugged. "Why not? It's dang well better than being out in the open like we are now."

"Can't argue that," Gary agreed finishing up the last of the bandages he was putting on as Derrick winced at how tight it was around his left arm.

"What about the kid?" Harrison asked.

"I'm not a kid!" Derrick yelled. "Stop calling me that!"

"Just call them as I see them kid," Harrison smirked. "You're what? Twenty?"

"That's fragging right old man!" Derrick spat. "My name is Derrick!"

"Well?" Harrison asked looking over at Shandra while completely ignoring his outburst.

"He comes with us," Shandra sighed. "We can't leave him here. Those things out there will tear him apart before he even makes it out of the Ramble."

Derrick was getting ticked that these people were barely paying attention to him. Sure, they had saved his life and patched him up but…he didn't have a freaking clue who they were or why they were armed to the teeth.

"You okay to move Derrick?" Shandra asked him, her yellow eyes burning into his soul.

Derrick swallowed hard. "Yes ma'am," he nodded.

"Then try to keep up. We're going to be moving fast and God only knows what is waiting out there for us. You fall behind and get yourself killed, that's on you. Got it?" Shandra warned.

"Uh. . ." Derrick stammered. "Can I ask what is happening out there?"

"Hell if we know kid," Harrison snorted. "We sure didn't come here expecting to go up against an army of dead folks."

"Then why are you here?" Derrick asked.

"We're here to save the world," Shandra told him as if that explained everything then turned her attention to the men with her. "Harrison, you've got point. Gary, keep anything that comes our way off our tail. I'll keep an eye on our new friend. Now let's get moving people. It looks like we've overstayed our welcome!"

A pack of dead men and women were racing up the stream towards their position, their faces twisted in horrid snarls and their green eyes glowing. Gary laid down cover fire, hosing the men and women with his P-90 on full auto. Derrick watched for a moment as Gary's fire tore into the ranks of the dead. Bullets punched holes in their bodies causing some of them to stagger. Others were hurled from their feet splashing into the shallow water. He could see that Gary's bullets weren't really stopping the dead men and women but rather just slowing them down. Derrick felt Shandra's hand clamp onto his shoulder as she yanked him out of her way.

"Run you idiot!" she yelled at him raising a hand outstretched towards the approaching dead. Her forehead creased up in concentration as her yellow eyes burned like mini fusion reactors inside their sockets. The very air itself around Derrick seemed to shift and change. A fraction of a second later, all of the dead were smashed down into the stream as if a heavy weight had dropped onto them.

"Frag me," Derrick whispered under his breath and then said, "What did you do to them?"

"Didn't I tell you to run?" Shandra barked. "What I did isn't going to hold them long."

Without waiting for him, she turned and sprinted away in the direction the others had gone. Derrick followed after her.

Agent Lanning and his squad had gotten moving before the quake had hit the park. They had been moving south when it struck, and all hell broke loose as the dead started crawling up out of the ground. Lanning stood among the trees of the section of the park known as the Ravine. He could hear the splashing of its waterfall not far away. The Ravine seemed the best option of places to duck into in order to avoid the chaos of the rampaging dead and the poor bastard civilians the things were chasing down one by one. There was a hell of a lot ground to cover between their current position and the rally point at the castle he had set up with the other squads. Shandra's was the closest to the castle and he was counting on her to reach it first and secure the place by the time the other squads, including his own, arrived. Lanning knew that the North Meadow lay between him and where his squad needed to reach. There was no way they could go straight through that place. It had to be swarming with the dead and people trying to stay alive. He and his men couldn't get bogged down in all that crap. Lanning figure their best route was to head towards *the pool*, swing around it, and keep as close to the perimeter of the park as they could in order to avoid the meadows.

Tapping the comm. he wore on his wrist, Lanning said, "Come in Alpha Division. This is Gamma 1. I need to be patched through directly to Director Stevenson."

"Roger that," the voice of a tech answered him over the comm.

"Stevenson here," a deep, rumbling voice announced.

"Sir! A quake hit us here and it seems to have opened up the gates of hell. We've got deaders all over the park," Lanning blurted out using Taskforce Augur's code name for zombies. "The whole place had become a giant buffet for the blasted things. We need back up A.S.A.P."

"We're still in route Agent Lanning," Director Stevenson informed him. "ETA in less than twenty."

"I am rallying all units already deployed within the park to the castle. The plan is to hole up there with any civilians we can pick up along the way," Lanning told him.

A moment of silence ticked by before Director Stevenson responded. "Understood. Once we're in place, I'll dispatch troops help you hold the castle."

"Thank you, sir. Any chance of air support in the meantime?" Lanning asked.

"Negative Gamma 1. An energy field is forming above the park. The atmospheric EM pulses the thing is generating are off the charts. Can't risk sending anything into that mess until we know more about it," Director Stevenson said. "Just get to that castle and hold the place. We'll have back up your way as soon as we are able. Stevenson out."

"He's in a mood," Eastman quipped having overheard what was being said.

"Can you blame him?" Lanning gritted his teeth. "Even with the advance warning Sawyer gave us on the apocalypse starting here and the preparations we made, we're totally screwed right now."

"Hey, no one could have known it was going to play out like this," Driggle pointed out. "Swayer didn't say squat about a freaking army of zombies."

"We should all be grateful that shooting them in the head still seems to work at least. Those things are fragged up big time. They ain't your run of the mill deaders," Eastman said. "Did you get a look at the eyes on those bastards?"

"Yeah, I saw them," Lanning nodded. "Whatever pulled those things up out of the ground isn't viral in nature like with the deaders we've came across before."

"Sure as frag isn't. I can tell you that much with one hundred percent certainty boss," Driggle agreed.

Lanning, unlike most of the agents pre-positioned inside the park, wasn't a PSI. He was just one heck of a hard-assed soldier. Driggle though, he knew, was a *Detector*. His talent gave him the ability to sense other sources of psionic energy and sometimes even mystical based energies at work around him. The closer the source, the better he could *feel* it.

"So then, what are we dealing with here Driggle?" Lanning pressed him.

"Magic sir," Driggle frowned. "I can feel it all over the park and especially inside of those dead things that are running about killing folks."

"Any ideas on how to shut it down?" Lanning moved closer to Driggle as he spoke, towering over the shorter man.

"No sir," Driggle shook his head. "It's the blackest, foulest magic I've ever felt. The stuff has an edge to it too sir. Like it isn't even supposed to exist in this world."

"We got company heading our way," Eastman interrupted them, gesturing to the north with the barrel of his shotgun.

Lanning looked in that direction and almost wished he hadn't. A group of deaders with glowing green eyes was closing in on them fast. The things were sprinting through the trees at a breakneck pace, snarling as they came.

"Move!" Lanning shouted, breaking into a run. "Don't stop for anything until we're clear of the Ravine!"

He knew they would be heading onto Park Drive but there wasn't a fragging thing he could do about that. They were just going to have to take their chances and hope that it wouldn't be the nightmare he expected it to be.

Agent Wagner and his squad, under the command of Agent Sherry Taylor, had been positioned in Sheep Meadow. They were doing their best to blend in with the hundreds of people enjoying their afternoon there. Thankfully, it was New York after all so folks made a point of keeping their distance from the trio in the heavy trench coats that concealed the light body armor they wore.

There were couples making out on blankets, people sunbathing, and others sprawled out reading both physical books as well ones downloaded to various devices. A few scattered families and couples were picnicking. Frisbee throwers and ball tossers were about too as well those just strolling through the area walking their pets or getting in some exercise jogging or doing yoga with their mats spread out on the meadow's grass. All of it had been so normal, just another day for the park's patrons.

Then the quake hit, the ground opened up, and the dead rose. Corpses heaved themselves up from the ground. Some were fresher looking than others. Those still had most of their flesh and meat attached to their bones. A few were little more than skeletons with glowing green orbs of energy contained within the sockets where their eyes had once been. All of the things stunk to high heavens. The sheer number of them polluted the air of the Sheep Meadow with the stench of rot and decay. Agent Wagner gagged at the smell of it. The corpses flung themselves at anything breathing within their reach, nails tearing at skin and teeth sinking into it. People were screaming everywhere. Some as the things tore into them, others in outright panic as they tried to make a run for it though Agent Wagner wasn't sure where they thought they were heading for. The dead were rising as far as he could see, and they were an *army*!

Agent Taylor had immediately ordered their squad to engage the monsters. That had been a mistake. Her PSI talent tended to impair her judgement when restraint was the better course of action. She was hot tempered and the sight of the dead preying upon the people around them was too much for her to stand by and do nothing.

"Take 'em!" Agent Taylor yelled, casting aside her trench coat. She carried no weapon. Sherry Taylor was a weapon. Fire burst into being around both of her hands, engulfing them. A deader wearing the tattered remains of an old fashion police uniform came charging at her. Agent Taylor met the monster with a burst of fire from her right hand, so intense and hot, that it burned away the top half of the dead policeman's body. His charred bottom half collapsed into the grass of the meadow. A stream of fire leap from her left hand, washing over two more of the dead. Their snarls became moans as the flames melted away their flesh and set their clothes ablaze.

Agent Markham, the other member of their squad, joined the battle. He was a pale man, his skin so white it reminded Wagner of the snows of winter. Markham clutched an automatic pistol in his left hand but it was with his right that he struck at the deaders around them. A wave of cold, solidifying into ice as it sprang forth, shot from his extended right hand, freezing a deader solid to its very core.

Wagner refrained from bringing his own power into play instead using the pump action shotgun he had been concealing beneath his coat. He brought the weapon up, chambering a round, as he picked his target. There was sure fragging enough to choose from. The dead already seemed to be everywhere with more and more of the creatures emerging from the ground with each passing second. His shotgun thundered as Wagner blew a gaping hole in the closest deader's chest. The dead woman shrieked, stumbling backwards away from the young couple she had been chasing. Her attention was fully on Wagner now as she swung herself about to engage him. Wagner pumped another ready and took aim. He remembered from the horror movies he had watched as a child and his training that deaders could usually only be truly stopped by a shot to their heads. The dead woman was faster than he expected her to be though. She reached him before he could get off his shot. Her cold, rotting hands closed on the barrel of his shotgun, trying to rip the weapon from his grasp. In desperation, Wagner squeezed the shotgun's trigger. The blast that exploded out of its barrel struck the dead woman point blank. She lurched backwards, looking down at the strands of intestines sliding out of what remained of her mangled stomach. Her head jerked up, its glowing green eyes locked onto him and burning with unadulterated rage.

"Stop messing around and kill her!" Agent Markham shouted at Wagner. Markham's automatic pistol roared as he let loose with a burst of rounds that splattered another deader's skull into pulp.

Wagner sighed, channeling his will into using his own power at last. Beams of crackling blue energy shot from the centers of his eyes. They vaporized the dead woman's head, leaving only the smoking stump of the top of her neck below where it had been. Wagner swept his gaze around, letting his eye blasts continue in continuous streams, as he cut several more deaders apart at the waist with them. The pieces of their bodies twitched in the grass, taken out of the fight but from being truly dead.

The deaders in this section of the meadow took notice of the three Task-force Augur members and the damage they were doing. Zombies…deaders… whatever you wanted to call the things they weren't supposed to be smart but these things sure had mind enough to realize who the primary threat to them was. The deaders closed in on the squad members in waves. Taylor yelled at the top of her lungs as she unleashed twin geysers of flame from her hands into the thickest mass of the creatures. Two of them went down instantly, cooked to a crisp. Another one reeled about, pounding at its own face, trying to put out the fire burning there as what was left of its fatty tissues popped and cracked beneath its skin. The remaining three burned as they came but pressed on, closing the distance between them and Agent Taylor. Her hair was now aflame too as the full force of Agent Taylor's power flowed through her body. One of the three burning deaders burst apart like an exploding popcorn kernel in a shower of boiling fat and shattering bone. The remaining two had closed in and hurled themselves at Agent Taylor. The hands of one melted as it reached for her, burning a bright orange and then into nothingness. Still the monster kept coming. It lunged forward as the deader next to let loose a moan of pain from what was left of its face. Agent Taylor went down with the two deaders atop her. Teeth the plunged into her next dissolved in the heat of her blood but none the less broke her skin before they were gone. Agent Taylor's blood ran down over the side of her neck beneath the wound, boiling there as the bodies of the two creatures pinned her to the ground. She struggled against their weight even as they cooked away into ash and pools of bubbling goo.

"Taylor's down!" Agent Markham shouted.

*No, really?* Wagner thought. *Do you think I'm blind?*

He and Agent Markham drew closer to each other, Markham trying to keep the deaders at bay with both his pistol and pyrokinetic blasts. Wagner had spent the energy of his eye beams and was back to using his shotgun. The weapon thundered as he blew apart the midsection of an approaching deader before pumping another round ready and firing it into the monster's head. The thing's decapitated body flopped over into the grass.

Nearby, the flames covering Agent Taylor's body had gone out. Tendrils of smoke rose from her corpse towards the sky above. Wagner could see the nasty wound the deader that had taken her out had inflicted upon her neck. It was clear that Taylor was dead. That meant he was now in command of their squad.

"We can't stay here!" Agent Markham yelled at him. "We've got to fallback!"

Wagner completely agreed. The only problem was he couldn't see a means of breaking through the growing number of deaders around them. Gone was any hope of saving all the people in the Sheep Meadow. Wagner didn't even know how to save the two of them.

"Markham! Can you clear out these things around us?" Wagner shouted.

"I can try! Get down!" Markham answered.

Wagner threw himself flat as Markham grunted, pushing his power to its limits. Spikes of ice erupted from his body, flying in all directions. Wagner grabbed a deader's corpse, pulling it over him at the least second. Even with using the deader as a shield, he wasn't spared injury. A shard of ice entered his leg just below his knee. He screamed as the cold of the ice pierced his flesh. The next thing he knew, Markham was yanking him up from the ground.

"That bought us a few seconds!" Markham's frantic voice told him. "But we have to move. Now!"

Wagner looked around as Markham got him onto his feet. The explosion of ice had cut all the deaders within forty feet of them to shreds. The ones with bodies that were still mostly intact looked like writhing pincushions in the grass, moaning, as they rolled about, trying to get up. Markham was even more pale than usual and looked on the verge of passing out from the strain he had just endured.

The two of them ran as fast they could for the northern edge of the Sheep Meadow. Wagner limped along, half dragging his injured leg. Markham staggering along at his side, firing wildly with his automatic pistol at any deaders who came sprinting in too close. The fact that the meadow was so full of easier prey was all that really saved them. The deaders who had been so focused on taking them out had been finished by Markham's burst of ice spikes. The others were busy with the poor bastards that were being held to the ground and eaten alive or chasing down those who hadn't been caught yet.

As they ran, Wagner spotted Le Pain Quotidien, the famous restaurant, up ahead. Many of its outside tables were overturned or smashed. Chairs and bodies covered the area in front of its main doors. Several deaders were tearing at and feasting upon a few unlucky souls that they had overrun. The restaurant's walls were made of brick and looked tough as hell. Wagner knew they had to get inside of it and out of the open. If they could bar themselves up inside of it somehow, maybe they could get a breather from their mad flight long enough to come up with a real plan of action.

"In there!" Wagner ordered Markham, pointing at the restaurant.

Wagner pulped the face of a deader that looked up from the body of a woman it was feeding on as he ran past it with a blast from his shotgun. Markham dispatched another that leapt up, leaving its own meal behind, to come after them. His automatic pistol roared as the rounds it spat tore into the thing's forehead. Brain matter and bone fragments blew out of the backside of the deader's skull. Then they were inside the restaurant. There were only a few deaders scattered about the place's interior. Wagner's eyes scanned the wide room searching for somewhere they could duck into. There was no sign of an office or enclosed kitchen area from where he was. All he could see were the restrooms. One of them would have to do. Markham followed as Wagner dove into the closest one. He slammed the door shut behind Markham and reached to pull a heavy trashcan in front of it.

"We can't hold them here," Markham told him.

"I know," Wagner agreed, altering his plan on the fly as he spotted a window at the rear of the restroom. "We're going back out over there!"

Markham made it to the window first, smashing out its glass with the butt of his pistol. It was too small for them to fit through but that wasn't a problem. Markham created a wedge of ice inside the window's frame, expanding it. The wood around the ice cracked and gave way as the window's opening grew wider.

"After you," Markham urged him as Wagner got a running start and jumped through the broken window. He landed in the grass outside, rolling to his feet. Markham landed roughly next to him only seconds later. There were still deaders about on this side of the building too but not as many. They could run through them…or at least Wagner hoped they could. The two of them made a mad dash away from Le Pain Quotidien.

The APC with Director Stevenson aboard it rolled into position on the western side of Central Park. It was far from alone. Other units, both additional APCs and numerous transport trucks, took up defensive positions all around the giant park. Troops dismounted from them, forming up firing lines. Scattered among the gathering defenders of the city were several Abrams tanks. As vast as the park was, Director Stevenson only had true line of sight with a few of the units that accompanied his own, but video feeds streamed onto the screens in the rear of the command APC from units all around the park. Already, bursts of gunfire were ringing out up and down the line forward of where his unit had rolled to a stop.

"We've engaged the hostiles at several points along the perimeter we're setting up around the park sir," his second in command, Major Flint reported.

Director Stevenson hadn't wanted to believe Agent Lanning's reports of what they were up against. Zombies, or Deaders as Taskforce Augur labeled them, could sometimes be the worst. They weren't as tough as demons, vampires, or werewolves, but their numbers often made the blasted things nigh unstoppable. He and his people had months to prepare for today and yet despite all their efforts it seemed the odds were still stacked against them.

"Any more information on the quake that hit the park?" Director Stevenson asked.

"Not much sir," Major Flint answered. "Flannigan confirms that it wasn't a natural occurrence though."

Director Stevenson snorted at the major's answer. Flannigan was the best of Taskforce Augur's Geo-psychics. A Geo-psi could feel disturbances, both natural and otherwise, that affected the planet through a connection with its Leylines. The quake had been too timely, too aligned with the Sha'daa for Director Stevenson to have really believed I was a natural occurrence anyway.

Outside his command APC, a battle was being waged to keep the Deaders moving towards the borders of the park pushed back. There were currently only a handful of the monsters and the troops under his command were making short work of the things. M-16s and M249s chattered and roared, pouring fire into them. So far, it looked like the dead were for the most part content to remain inside the park, perhaps focusing on finishing off those trapped within its borders with them. Director Stevenson knew that wouldn't last much longer. More likely sooner rather than later, the dead would run out of victims and make a real effort to break out of the park and reach the city beyond its borders. He couldn't allow that to happen. Sawyer, the best pre-cog the Task force had, warned that if it did, then it was game over for the human race. New York would fall first and then the surrounding cites as the deaders spread like wild fire eventually consuming the entire United States and then the world. The weight of responsibility he carried on his shoulders would likely have broken a lesser man, but Director Stevenson had trained his whole adult life for this day. He and his men were both the world's first and last line of defense against the ancient and alien forces that were manifesting inside Central Park. Director Stevenson knew this was not the first time the Sha'Daa had tried to break through into the world of man. They had been stopped before and that meant he could stop them now too. All he had to do was hold on and keep the dead inside the park until either the time of the alignment that allowed the Sha'Daa their access to the world passed or a means of closing the portal or portals they had entered through were found. From a tactical standpoint, Director Stevenson had to admit he was impressed by the Sha'Daa's choice of where to strike. Central Park was a vast area that gave them plenty of ground to run amok and gather their forces inside of. And once they were ready, one of the most heavily populated cities on Earth lay just beyond its borders for them to flood into.

None the less, Director Stevenson had hoped the entities breaching the barriers between worlds to be a much smaller but super powerful group of demons. That was why he had positioned Lanning 's and the other squads within the park, to face them head on from the moment they appeared. That clearly wasn't the case and he found himself bloody glad he had brought a fragging army with him. Every single soldier, every single round they carried with them was going to be needed to keep the demons of the Sha'Daa contained within the park.

Major Flint's voice ripped him away from his thoughts, returning his focus to the present.

"All units are in place and holding," Major Flint assured him.

"Good," Director Stevenson grunted in response. "We can't let those things out of the park. If even one gets out. . ."

"I am well aware of the stakes sir," Major Flint reminded him. "The local authorities have been informed of the situation as well. The N.Y.P.D. and National Guard are ready behind our lines and throughout the city to deal with any that do."

"We'll have to hope that it's enough," Director Stevenson sighed. "Any word from Lanning and the others?"

"Not since Lanning ordered them all to converge on the castle sir," Major Flint shrugged. "That was good thinking on his part."

"Assuming the other squads can reach it," Director Stevenson pointed out. "And that they can hold it."

"If anyone can, it's Lanning sir," Major Flint said. "That man is the toughest S.O.B I've met but I think we have to face the fact there is a lot more at stake here than just Lanning and the squads deployed inside the park."

"It's not so much about saving their butts Major as it is saving ours," Director Stevenson frowned. "Lanning and those squads may be our only hope of locating and shutting down the Sha'Daa portal that's allowing whatever is reanimating all the zombies into our world. They are the only people we have that are already inside. Take a look at those video feeds Major."

Director Stevenson gestured at the multiple screens on the console in the rear of the command APC. Each one showed images of their soldiers firing into groups of the dead as they approached the barricades being set up around the park.

"Getting anyone else deep into the park now is going to be costly," Director Stevenson told Major Flint.

"If that's even possible sir," Major Flint shook his head.

"It's going to have to be Major," Director Stevenson said as he continued to watch the growing number of engagements being fought around the perimeter of the park on the monitors.

Caroline came bursting out of the restroom she had taken shelter in directly into the path of two armed men wearing body armor. She collided with the first of them. They hit the pavement, a mess of flailing arms and legs.

"Shoot her!" the man she had accidently ran into screamed.

The other man's pistol was aimed at her head. Caroline's eyes were wide as she stared up, into its barrel.

"Can't," the man with the pistol snapped. "She's alive!"

"I am!" Caroline cried out. "I'm not one of those things!"

The man on the pavement with her stopped his mad struggling, turning his head to get a better look at her.

"Who the frag are you?" the man yelled.

"Doesn't matter who she is!" the man with the pistol shouted. "We gotta get out of here Wagner!"

Wagner leaped up with Caroline stumbling to her feet next to him.

"I'm sorry," Caroline started, "I didn't mean to…"

The man named Wagner grabbed her by the arm. "Looks like you're with us now. Come on!"

There were deaders closing in on them from all directions. The snarls and moans of the dead seemed to be coming from everywhere around them. Only a handful of the creatures were really close enough yet to be a real threat though. Wagner wore a pistol on the belt of his armor. Caroline grabbed it before he could stop her. The weapon slid free of its holster as she back peddled away from him, pulling free of his grip on her arm.

"Hey!" Wagner glared at her, swinging the barrel of the pump action shotgun he held level with her chest. "What the frag?"

"No time!" the other man shouted, and he was right too. There was no time for Wagner to argue with her. They all had to get moving or they were dead.

Wagner's shotgun boomed as he fired into a dead woman, knocking her out of their way as the trio started northward.

"Where are we heading for?" Caroline managed to get out though her mind was reeling from the insanity around them to the point of being on the verge of her passing out.

"Belvedere Castle," man with Wagner answered. "Our people are rallying there. Agent Lanning thinks we can hold the place until help arrives."

Caroline didn't know who Agent Lanning or the men were but sticking with them was her only alternative to being alone with the growing army of hungry dead rampaging through the park.

"Head for those trees!" Wagner ordered. "Maybe we can lose them there!"

As they entered the wide, wooded section of the park known as the Ramble, a pack of dead men and women met them head on, running out of the trees into their path.

"Markham!" Wagner yelled.

Caroline looked in Markham's direction as she felt the air around her grow colder. Markham's eyes flashed a frigid shade of blue as he raised the hand that wasn't clutching his pistol towards the cluster of the dead. A cone of snowy wind erupted from it, freezing the dead in place. Their rotting flesh froze solid, their muscles locking up. Caroline's eyes bugged as her breath caught in her throat and her heart skipped a beat. What Markham had just done was like something out of a comic book, but he sure didn't look like any superhero Caroline had ever heard of. Besides, superheroes weren't real! People didn't shoot beams of cold out their hands! But then, the dead weren't supposed to crawl out of their graves and eat people either were they? She wanted to stop, to yell *what the hell are you?* at the man named Markham. Caroline couldn't though. Not if she wanted to stay alive. Markham had taken out the zombies directly in their path but there were dozens more of the monsters on their heels. The zombies weren't slow like they were in the old movies. They were deadly fast. The one she had killed had been strong too. Caroline prayed that the things were only in the park and that her family, far away, were safe.

Wagner was leading the way as they sprinted through the Ramble. Caroline clutched the pistol she had taken from him in a white knuckled grip. The weapon brought her little comfort. Caroline knew that if she stopped to use it, the zombies would overrun her. It seemed like everyone who was in the park when the quake hit, were dead now and part of the army of the dead that was so intent on adding them to its ranks.

Markham stumbled over the roots of a tree that protruded partly out of the ground. He landed hard, his face smacking against the dirt. When his head rose up, blood was pouring from his nose and he looked half out of it. Caroline came to an abrupt stop, whirling about to go to his aid. Markham stared up at her as she grabbed hold of him, straining to get him back onto his feet. A zombie reached them with black lips parted in a fierce snarl. Caroline leveled her pistol at the creature's face and blew a gaping hole through its head. Its body flopped over backwards into the grass. Others of the creatures were almost on them as she got Markham moving. Wagner appeared at her side. He dropped something onto the ground where Markham had been lying and yelled, "Come on!"

As the three of them ran on northward through the woods of the Ramble, the grenade he had left behind for the zombies detonated. Caroline imagined she felt the shockwave of its blast though rationally she knew that was impossible. They were already too far away.

Caroline didn't know how long they ran. Seconds ticked by like hours to her. Legs aching with each step, breath coming in ragged gasps, she pushed herself on. Markham's nose was still bleeding but the man appeared to have otherwise recovered from his fall.

"There!" she heard Wagner shout. The castle they were heading for had come into view up ahead. Below it was the park's weather station. A fenced in area containing all sorts of machines that Caroline had no idea what it was they each actually did.

Wagner raced up to the weather station's gate and found it was locked as he struggled to open it. Caroline could see his plan was to get them inside the fence as it would offer them at least some protection from the dead that were gaining on them. They would never be able to reach the castle ahead of the monsters without a moment to catch their breath and regroup. Caroline watched in utter astonishment and disbelief as beams of energy shot from Wagner's eyes slicing the lock open. As soon it was cut away from the gate, Wagner slung it open. She and Markham followed him through the gate inside the fenced off area. There was a small shed among the machines, and they took cover in it, Wagner wedging his body against the door after they were all inside. All of them held their breath and waited, listening to the howls and snarls of the zombies in the distance. They had just enough of a lead over the monsters to be able to enter the shed without being seen. Caroline knew that was what Wagner had to be counting on, that the zombies would pass them by as they hid within its walls.

The shrieks of the zombies drew close and then began to go quieter and more distant. They had lucked out and they all knew it. Wagner slumped where he was against the door.

"Thank God," he breathed. "I think we're good at least for a little bit."

"It's about time we caught a break," Markham smirked darkly. "I figured this was our last rodeo for a while there."

Caroline found herself staring at Markham and just how pale his skin was. She hadn't really noticed how almost inhuman he looked until right now, but it was starting to sink in. Her head whipped around towards Wagner as she blurted out, "Just who are you people?"

Both Markham and Wagner laughed. That only served to put her even more on edge. She had to remind herself that she was still holding a pistol and knew how to use it if either of them proved to be a bigger threat than the monsters they had just escaped.

"What's your name again?" Wagner asked.

"Caroline. Caroline Gibson," she answered.

"I bet you're wondering if we're even human right?" Markham chuckled.

"That's about the size of it," Caroline told him, her southern accent fully coming out as she spoke.

"We are," Wagner told her. "I'm Agent Joseph Wagner and that guy over there is Agent Ryan Markham. We're part of a…let's just call it special ops unit named Taskforce Augur."

"The powers that be knew that something bad was going to be happening in the park today and we were deployed here to stop it before it started," Markham explained.

Caroline snorted. "You really screwed that up then huh?"

Grinning Wagner shook his head and sighed while Markham glared at her though he couldn't argue what she had just said.

"I guess we did," Wagner admitted. "You're right about that Caroline. You see, we didn't really know *what* was going to happen here in the park today, just that we had to stop it. Everything went all pear shaped after that quake for any of us to do anything about it."

"Any of you?" Caroline questioned Wagner.

"Any of us," he nodded. "There were three of our squads positioned inside the park. We thought we were ready for anything that came our way, but we weren't. Now we're on the run, trying to stay alive just like you."

"But the rest of our taskforce and some big-time support are supposed to be surrounding the park to keep the crap happening here from getting out of it even as we're talking," Markham said.

"That's why we're heading for the castle. The agent in command of our squads inside the park radioed for those of who could make it to come there. I'd wager the plan is to secure it and hold there until help can reach us," Wagner did his best to give her a reassuring smile.

"So, you're government agents," Caroline frowned, "That doesn't explain…"

"The things you saw us do," Wagner smirked.

"We're psychics," Markham chuckled.

"Never heard of psychics that could shoot beams out of their eyes or freeze things solid," Caroline challenged the two agents.

"Maybe that's the wrong word," Wagner smiled. "But it doesn't change the fact that our powers are psychic in nature. We're still human, just like you are, except that we were born with talents that most people don't have."

"Uh, yeah. Sure," Caroline didn't know what else to say.

Wagner turned, cracking open the door of the small shed. There was no sign of the dead beyond it. "I think the coast is clear."

"Good," Markham sounded even more relieved than Caroline felt.

"I'd say this is our opening," Wagner told them. "Best we make use of it and get onto the castle while we can."

Larry ran faster and harder than he ever had in his life. His clothes were drenched in sweat and the foul blackness that passed for the blood of the creatures that were seemingly everywhere. The second one that got its hands on him had come even closer to killing him than the first. It hit him out of nowhere, jumping out of a patch of bushes along the jogging path. Its gnarled fingernails dug into the flesh of his arms as the thing had tried to eat him alive. If his reflexes had been a hair slower, he would be dead now. Larry managed to jerk the creature around and throw it onto the path at his feet, diving to snatch the lid off a nearby metal trash can. As the thing tried to get up, Larry went at it, knocking the dead man onto his back with the lid wedge between his chin and chest. The lid crushed the man's throat but with him being dead already, that wasn't enough to stop him. The man didn't even appear to feel any pain from the damage Larry had done to his throat. Larry leaned on the lid, pressing the weight of his body down onto it. The dead man's head separated from his body in an explosion of black pus and gore, popping loose. His body stopped fighting Larry as his head bounced further up along the path.

Wiping at the black goo that had splashed over his arms and cheeks, Larry had left the dead man's corpse where it lay and kept right on running.

Right now, Larry was focused on staying ahead of the fat zombie behind him. The thing made him look skinny in comparison. Its rolls of belly fat bounced and shook, jarred about by each step it took. Larry knew he couldn't outrun the thing forever. It was dead and wasn't going to get tired and he was already pushing his body past its limits. Much more and he would have a heart attack based on how hard his heart was hammering against the backside of his ribs. It was getting harder and harder to breath. Larry was proud of himself that he had dispatched two of the monsters but knew that stopping to take on this one was a sure loss. The fat, dead man would tear him apart like a sumo wrestler would crush a little, high school math nerd if he tried. Larry zagged, altering his course, darting off the main path into a wooded section of the park as he heard the sound of gunfire ring out from that direction. If someone had a gun that meant that meant they were fighting back. He hoped they were winning too. Surely, whoever was shooting in the park had to be either its security personnel or the cops. He desperately needed help and hoped he would find it up ahead.

A group of people, real people, not dead ones, came into view. There were four of them. A beautiful, red headed woman and two men dressed in combat armor and another guy that didn't look as if he belonged with them at all. He was younger and wore only shorts, running shoes, and a black shirt. The younger man was bandaged up. Red was seeping through the white of his bandages.

The red head was carrying a pistol and clearly knew how to use it well. Larry watched as she blew out the brains of a zombies with a shot that he never would have been able to make even on his best day. One of the two armored men carried a heavy shotgun and the other some sort of machine gun looking weapon that roared on full auto as it blazed away at a pair of snarling, dead women. The bandaged-up kid was unarmed.

"Hey!" Larry yelled, waving his arms above his head. "Over here!"

Larry's attempt at getting their attention almost got his own head blown off as a shot from the woman's pistol whistled through the air passed him. He could see from the woman's expression that she had realized he was alive too late to hold back her shot. Or at least that's what he thought until Larry heard the fat, dead thing behind him grunt. Looking over his shoulder, Larry saw that her shot had smacked into the center of the thing's chest, punching into its sternum. The fat dead man was thrown off balance by the bullet hitting him and got tripped up. His overweight body crashed, face first onto the ground.

"Come on!" the older of the two armored men shouted at him, waving Larry on towards their group.

A fresh burst of adrenaline flooded Larry's system as he pushed himself even harder, closing the distance between himself and the others. "Who are you people?" Larry blurted out, knowing they wouldn't have the time to answer him. They didn't. Not the three in armor anyway. He fell into their loose running formation next to the wounded kid.

"I'm Derrick!" the kid told him. "Who are you?"

"Larry," he grunted in response, barely managing to get his own name out.

"We're headed for the castle," Derrick said. "There's supposed to be more people like them there that can help us."

"The castle?" Larry asked.

"Yeah," Derrick nodded as they ran side by side. "It's not far from here."

Larry hoped the kid was right about that. His legs burned to the point where there were tears streaming from his eyes, sliding down over the curves of his cheeks.

"Watch out!" the guy in armor behind them warned as a dead woman with blonde hair on half her head and the rest of it exposed bone burst out of the trees at them. Derrick deftly avoided the charging woman. Larry had no idea how the kid could still move so fast as hurt as he looked to be but he had. Derrick stepping out of the dead woman's path left on her a direct line for him as Larry scrambled to get his body ready for her to hit him as there was no chance of him pulling off a move like the kid had. Larry screamed as the charging dead woman plowed into him. Despite his exhaustion and pain, Larry was able to brace himself so that she didn't knock him over. His hands shot up and out to grab the woman's wrists as she tried to sink her fingernails into his face. Out of instinct, Larry flung his head forward, smashing it into the woman's. The bone of her nose crunched against his forehead. Black pus covered his face as he jerked his head back. His eyes locked with the woman's. Her eyes glowed an eerie green as Larry stared into them. Just what in the hell was she, he wondered. She sure wasn't human anymore. That much was for sure.

The others kept going without him as he struggled to keep the woman's snapping teeth away from him. The red headed woman whirled around and snapped off a shot that struck the woman in the back. Thankfully the round didn't penetrate all the way through her, or it would have hit him too. Larry could see that was all the help he would be getting from the others in the group as the red head spun about and started running to keep up with the rest again. Larry's heart broke at that realization. For the little thing that she was, the dead woman was strong as hell. Ripping her wrists free of his hold on them, she tackled him. This time, she did take him to the ground. Larry landed on his back with her on top of him, clawing at his eyes. He yanked up an arm to protect them from her jagged fingernails and let out a yelp of pain.

Her nails raked across the side of his forearm, tearing open the skin there. Larry twisted his body trying to roll out from under the dead woman. All that did was expose more of him to her fury. Her head came down as the woman's teeth bit into him just below his right arm pit. They tore a good-sized chunk of meat from him as he rolled back towards the woman, his balled-up fist smashing into her cheek. Bone gave way beneath what remained of the rotting skin that was stretched tight over the structure of her face. Teeth and black gore sprayed from the side of her mouth. His blow rocked the dead woman and allowed Larry to shove her away. He pushed himself up onto his feet just in time to see the other dead people closing in on him.

"Frag me," Larry muttered knowing he was dead as two dead men and another dead woman reached him. They took him to the ground again, piling onto him, their fingernails clawing at his body. One of the dead men bit a chunk out of his left arm. The other found his throat with its teeth. Larry felt the warmth of his own blood spraying out of him as he struggled against the dead, thrashing about and trying to break free of them. His vision blurred and Larry's world went dark, but he could still hear the dead's smacking lips as they made a meal out of his chubby body.

Agents Shandra, Harrison, and Gary, along with the civilian kid, Derrick, they had picked up unintentionally in route, reached Belvedere Castle. The sky had gone dark. Shandra checked her watch. It was only Four PM. The blackness of the sky wasn't normal. It was supposed to still be daytime with the sun burning bright above them. Whatever force had raised the dead was apparently blocking the sunlight as well. That kind of power left her in awe as she thought about it. Taskforce Augur had faced many monsters over the years but this. . .the Sha'Daa…it was unquestionably the worst and most powerful thing they had ever gone up against.

The chubby jogger hadn't made it despite her risky attempt to help him at the edge of the Ramble. She had paused long enough to take a shot at the deader that had been wrestling with the jogger hoping to give him a chance of breaking away from the thing. That was all she had been able to do. Anymore and she would have been swarmed by deaders herself.

The lights in the castle were on and Shandra could see that its main entrance was closed as her squad approached it. With any luck, Agent Lanning and his squad were already inside the castle and had secured it. The scattered bodies of the dead that lay about in front of the castle's door gave her hope that they were.

She spotted Agents Wagner and Markham racing towards the castle from the east. She was glad to see that the two of them had made it too. There was a young woman with them that looked to be civilian but there was no sign of Agent Taylor. Shandra wondered if the woman's hot-headed rashness had finally gotten the better of her. It took a calm, level head to survive something like what was happening in Central Park today.

There were only a handful of active deaders between her squad and the castle's entrance. Harrison's shotgun boomed as he took a shot at one of the things, blowing open its stomach. The deader stumbled backwards, strands of black slicked intestines toppling out of the wound Harrison had dealt the thing. Agent Wagner finished the monster with a shot from his pistol that splattered the deader's brain matter into the air.

"Thank God you guys made it too!" Agent Markham grinned as their squad came up alongside her own.

"Frag am I glad to see you," Agent Wagner told her. "Taylor is dead."

Gary's P-90 barked as he hosed two deaders near the castle's door with a spray of fully automatic fire. The deaders jerked about like puppets dancing on invisible strings as the bullets ripped through their rotting bodies. His shots didn't kill the things of course, it took a hit to the head to do that, but they did take the monsters out of action at least for a bit and slow them down.

"Any word from Lanning?" Shandra snapped at Wagner as their two squads and the civilians with them formed a defensive circle in front of Belvedere Castle's entrance.

Wagner shook his head. "Not since he told us to come here."

Shandra frowned. "Harrison, the door?"

"It's locked!" Harrison answered her, having tried it already.

"Great," Shandra snarled. "Anybody got a plan on how to get it open?"

"No, but we better come up with one soon. We're starting to draw a crowd out here," Markham shouted.

And he was right. Dozens of deaders were coming out of the woods and up the various paths that led to the castle's entrance. The number of the things seemed to be growing with each passing heartbeat. Everyone was pouring fire into their ranks but there were just too many of the blasted things to stop them all. For each one that fell with the eerie green glow gone from its eyes, two more appeared to take its place. Shandra knew she could use her power to make the door so heavy that it collapsed upon itself or that Markham could freeze its lock and simply force his way through it but anything that damaged the door would leave the entrance to the castle open and they would need it sealed as soon as they were inside.

"Gary!" Shandra yelled.

"On it!" Gary answered, apparently reading her mind despite not being a telepath. He was on the radio in seconds. She heard him calling out into it.

"Lanning! We're at the front door!" Gary shouted. "We need inside. Now!"

The only answer Gary got was the crackling noise of static coming back at him through his radio.

"God help us," Shandra heard the girl that had come with Wagner and Markham shriek. A trio of fragging grizzly bears were swaggering up the walkway towards them and the castle's entrance. Their eyes glowed the same bright shade of green as that of the human deaders that came with them.

"You've got to be kidding me!" Markham cried out, pointing up into the sky. "Not the fragging birds too!"

A massive flock of undead pigeons were flying in from the south, a cloud of winged death with glowing green eyes. Shandra couldn't even guess at how many of the birds there were but she knew it was too many to deal with at least with conventional weapons.

"Concentrate your fire on the bears and the deaders with them!" Shandra barked at the others. "I'll deal with the birds!"

Shandra shoved the pistol she carried into the holster on the belt of her armor and raised both her hands up in the direction of the quickly closing pigeons. She sucked in a breath, exhaling it slowly, as she found her center. Reaching deep inside, Shandra focused her psionic talent on the birds. At first only a few of them fell from the sky, dropping like rocks to crash onto the ground, their bodies suddenly far too heavy for their wings to keep aloft.

"You're going to have to do better than that," Shandra heard Harrison say before she blocked out the sound of his voice and sunk every ounce of her will into using her power on the birds. Shandra grunted from the amount of effort it took but she managed to get the job done. Every single one of the pigeons fell like dead weights from the sky.

Markham, Gary, and the girl, who had somehow gotten a Taskforce Augur machine pistol, were all shooting at the grizzly bears and the deaders that were picking up speed as they charged their way towards the position of her and Wagner's combined squads. Deaders were falling all around the bears but the bears themselves were just too tough in their undead state to be bothered by the rounds ripping at their flesh. One of them roared, lunging ahead of the others. Shandra slumped onto her knees, too spent from dealing with the pigeons to do anything about it. It was up to the others to stop the bears before they were all torn apart.

Agent Wagner stepped out of the defensive circle the two squads had formed up into, directly into the path of the bears. He screamed in pain and desperation, his eyes ablaze with crackling blue energy. Beams of that energy shot out them, almost vaporizing the lead bear entirely. What was left of its charred form lay with smoke coiling upwards from the randomly scattered bit of it that were still somewhat intact. Wagner's eye beams swung to slice the next bear in two then sputtered out. Hands jerking up to cover his eyes, Wagner stumbled backwards. Markham grabbed him, supporting his weight, keeping Wagner on his feet.

Harrison's shotgun thundered three times in rapid succession before clicking empty. Each shot slammed into the dead grizzly's body. They didn't do crap in terms of stopping it or even slowing the monster down. The heavy slugs just looked to make the bear angrier than it already was. Gary and the girl that had showed up with Wagner's squad were emptying their own weapons into the deaders accompanying the bear, somehow managing to hold them back. Harrison reached down and drew twin knives from the sheathes strapped to the boots of his armor. He threw them upwards into the air, taking hold of them with his telekinetic talent. The blades spun end over end with impossible speed as they flew at the grizzly. They tore into its head like helicopter blades, cutting and slicing through the bear's skull all the way to the upper end of its neck. The grizzly's charging body fell and skidded to a halt just short of the position of the two squads gathered outside the castle's entrance. There wasn't much left of the bear's head atop its neck. The creature's head was an unrecognizable, mangled mass of shredded and pulped meat.

Suddenly, the door leading into the castle opened. Agent Lanning and a man that Shandra didn't know, dressed in a N.Y.P.D. Uniform, were there, ushering them all inside. Lanning and the cop were both armed with M4a1 rifles. The two of them laid down heavy cover fire as she and the others scrambled through the entrance into Belvedere Castle.

The area of the perimeter where Director Stevenson's command APC had taken up position was under heavy attack by the deaders pouring out of the park. The creatures came in waves, six or seven deep at a time. His men were holding the line. A cacophony of gunfire raged around him mingled with the shouts of the military officers that were currently under his command barking orders. Director Stevenson had given up the relative safety of the command APC to join the battle. They all needed every man on the line that they could get. With the butt of M4 braced against his shoulder, Director Stevenson fired a burst of shots that sent a dead woman wearing an Eighteen Hundred's style dress back to hell. His bullets punched into her face, crunching the bone there, and sent brain matter bursting from the back of her exploding skull.

"More animals incoming!" a voice down the line from him yelled.

Director Stevenson looked to see a pack of Snow Leopards rushing forward amid the ranks of the human dead. The sleek cats moved incredible grace and speed considering that they were dead. He knew the things were on the endangered species list but frag it, they were already dead, and it was the job of his taskforce and the soldiers with it to make sure the damned things remembered it. Director Stevenson swung his M4 around to target one of the cats as he shouted, "Don't let those cats close on us! We'll be in for hell if they do!"

The math didn't add up with the numbers of deaders they were facing. Director Stevenson had a fairly good estimate of how many people were supposed to be inside the park when the time of the Sha'Daa began and there was already a hell of a lot more deaders than that figure accounted for. But then, supposedly anything was possible during the Sha'Daa when the barriers between worlds were weaker and the evils of Hell itself flowed over into the world of man. Based on the intel Director Stevenson was getting, some of the deaders wore clothes centuries out of date or bits of them at any rate. He had personally blown the head off a deader dressed like a British soldier from the Revolutionary War. How the dead man's uniform was so intact could only be explained by the use of magic. Each wave of the deaders were more intact and stronger than the ones before it as if the magic that was powering was growing more and more intense as the portal or portals created by the Sha'Daa event were apparently stabilizing and settling into place. Director Stevenson wished to God that he knew where openings were centered so that he could attack it directly and maybe find means of shutting the Sha'Daa down.

The Snow Leopard that Director Stevenson was gunning for darted along among the ranks of the human dead, swerving between their legs on its path towards the firing line. The thing was using the other dead as cover. That impressed him. Clearly, the thing could think and reason at least on some level. He wondered if the dead Snow Leopards were a higher class of the deaders in the park. Their eyes glowed a bright green just like those of the human dead. Director Stevenson finally got a clear shot at the Snow Leopard he was focused on. Squeezing the trigger of his M4, the rifle bucked in his hands as he fired a burst at the thing's head. His shot missed its intended target but still pegged the dead cat sending it rolling sideways through the grass with huge chunks of flesh and meat blown from its upper leg joint on its right side. The Snow Leopard tried to get up, but he had done too much damage to it. The leg beneath the damaged joint gave out when the cat put its weight on it. Director Stevenson fired again, this time hitting his target. A burst of rounds punched open the right side of the cat's skull spraying foul, black blood and brain matter into the air in an explosion of gore. The cat fell then and didn't move anymore.

"Sir!" A soldier coming up behind him yelled.

Director Stevenson glared over his shoulder at the young man approaching him. "What the frag is it?"

"You're needed in the command APC as soon as possible!" the soldier looked frantic and far more scared of his anger than the dead that were attacking the firing line.

"Take my position here," Director Stevenson snapped at the young soldier, moving out of his way so that he could.

"Yes sir," the young soldier barked, slinging the M-16 that hung from its strap over his shoulder into his hands and readying the weapon.

Director Stevenson raced for the command APC. It sat a good distance behind the firing line. He could see that its door was open. Two more soldiers stood at their posts outside of it. The senior one nodded at him as Director Stevenson bounded between by them into the vehicle. He had been expecting Major Flint to be waiting on him inside. Instead, he found the APC dark and empty. Its interior lights were dimmed and the glow of the screens showing the camera feeds of the battles raging all around the perimeter of the park was sharp in the darkness. What the hell? Director Stevenson thought. He didn't have time for games or screw ups. Taskforce Augur and its military support were in the fight of their lives. As he whirled about to head back out of the APC, Director Stevenson froze. There was a man sitting in the chair of the comm. console as if he had appeared there out of thin air. The man wore a dull black suit that reminded Director Stevenson of one that an undertaker at a funeral home might wear beneath an equally dark trench coat. The man's shoes were black as well. Atop his head was a black fedora hat. Even with the man sitting down, he could tell that the man was tall. His hair matched the clothes that he wore. The features of his shadowed face that Director Stevenson could make out were sharp and angular. The man smiled at him showing perfect white teeth that nearly sparkled in the dimness of the APC's interior lights. One of the man's teeth, his left lateral incisor, was shiny gold. The thing looked entirely out of place. His skin was pale in contrast to almost everything about him in its coloring.

"Director Stevenson," the man said in a voice that was deep and resonated with untold power.

Despite the level of power Director Stevenson could feel seeping out of the man, he kept his cool and demanded, "How the frag did you get in here?"

Whoever this guy was, Director Stevenson could sense that he wasn't human, at least not entirely.

"Well now, that's an interesting question to begin with Director," the man smirked. "The answer is a simple one. I convinced your guards that I needed to see you and they let me inside. All it took were some choice words and gentle mental suggestion of just how important it is that I speak to you before things out there get any worse."

"Is that so?" Director Stevenson growled, towering over the seated man in black.

The man nodded. "The Sha'Daa is a deadly and strange time Director Stevenson. Almost anything can happen during it."

"And just what do you know about the Sha'Daa?" Director Stevenson challenged the man knowing that all information about the event was classified except to the highest levels of rank and clearance.

"A great deal more than I would like," the man sighed then looked up at him, "And far more than you."

"I doubt that," Director Stevenson snapped.

"You've yet to ask who I am or why I am here," the man in black pointed out.

"Guards!" Director Stevenson bellowed. "Get this whacko out of here!"

He could see the two soldiers standing just beyond the APC's open door. Neither of them appeared to hear his words. The two of them remained as they were with no indication that anything was wrong, whatsoever.

"They can't hear you Director Stevenson," the man in black told him. "This time is ours and ours alone. The space we are existing in during this moment is what you might call an alternate, pocket dimension and we will remain inside of it until our business is concluded."

Director Stevenson leveled the barrel of the M4 in his hands at the man in black. "I don't need them to put a stop to this insanity," he warned.

The man in black laughed. "You would shoot me. I can see that about you in your eyes Director. However, you need me so I wouldn't advise doing it."

"And just why in the devil would I need you?" Director Stevenson challenged the man.

"Because Director without me, you lose and the things inside this park get out into the world," the man chuckled. "I can offer you the power you need to contain them where they are."

Director Stevenson took a breath and forced himself to lower his M4. Somehow, he knew deep inside that if this man in black wanted to harm him, he would be dead already. Then it came to him, a memory of something he had read in the files of the Sha'Daa that he had access to. That was a man, a phantom, that appeared each time the event happened. Nothing really was known about the shadowy figure except that he wasn't a direct player in the events. As if reading his mind, the man winked at him.

"Since you still haven't asked Director, my name is Johnny. I am a salesman of sorts and I have within the pocket of my coat exactly what you need to accomplish your goal here around this park."

Johnny reached into his coat and produced a black diamond that was almost the size of the hand that held it. The jewel seemed to pulse with evil energy. The waves of dark power coming off the thing made Director Stevenson sick at his stomach. Johnny laughed.

"Yes, this diamond is evil," Johnny grinned once again showing his teeth. "But its power can be used for good purposes. The diamond has the power to bend reality, reshaping it to certain extents. And you have the psychics at your disposal to use it. If we can come to an agreement, then perhaps you could have one of them use it to create an energy shield surrounding the park to keep the flowing into this world contained…at least for a time. I know your men are stretched thin and even now aren't truly able to secure the perimeter of this vast place. As the Sha'Daa goes on, I can assure you that your containment lines will be breached without its power. The number of the dead attacking them will only grow with the passage of time as the Sha'Daa continues and the barriers between worlds becomes weaker and weaker."

"Okay Johnny, if that's even your real name. . ." Director Stevenson snarled. "Let's say that I believe you. Just what the hell is it that you want for that diamond?"

"I think that the pin in the pocket of your uniform might make a fair trade for it, don't you?" Johnny smiled.

Director Stevenson blinked, taken aback by what Johnny apparently knew about him and the pin the salesman had mentioned. The pin was a simple thing, a pair of U.S.A.F. wings that his father had earned during his time in the Air Force and given him before passing away. The pin was worthless to anyone but himself but to Director Stevenson, it was his rock, the foundation of his will. His father had been a proud and tough old bastard. He had been hard on him on growing up. Compliments and words of praise were things that weren't given by his father, ever. Yet, as his old man had laid there in the hospital bed, straining for each breath he took, he had passed on the pin to him. Director Stevenson had carried the pin with him ever since that cruel day that took his father away when his smoker lungs had finally betrayed the old man. There was no reason in the world for the strange man in the fedora to want the thing.

"Why?" Director Stevenson frowned. "Why would you want that?"

"It's my price. That's all that matters Director Stevenson," Johnny said.

"I…I can't give you the pin," Director Stevenson shook his head. "It's all I have of my father."

"What I ask is not negotiable," Johnny the Salesman frowned. "If you want the tool you need to fight the battle ahead of you and stand a chance of winning it..."

"How do I know that thing will even do what you say it will?" Director Stevenson raged.

"Come now, do I look like the type of person who would try to play a man like yourself?" Johnny chuckled. "Taskforce Augur is not a group that even someone like I would take less than seriously knowing the varied, shall we call them talents, at its disposal."

"Surely there is something else that you want," Director Stevenson pleaded. "My resources are vast. I can you get so much more than the pin in my pocket. It's of no use to anyway. It's just a tiny, worthless..."

Johnny stopped him there. "We both know that pin is not worthless. You hesitate when I offer you the hope of saving the entire world rather than trade to me. That pin is your core, your heart, perhaps the most human piece of you. And it is a part of you Director Stevenson, in the here and now and the past. Without it to steady you, would you be in charge of Taskforce Augur today?"

Leaning back in the chair in front of the comm. console, Johnny relaxed, clasping his hands behind his head, beneath the rim of his hat. "It's your choice Director. The world or your father's pin?"

"Fine!" Director Stevenson shouted, yanking the small pin out of his pocket and throwing at the dark man.

Johnny's hand shot out like lightning, snatching the pin from the air. His lips parted in a wide smile, getting out of his chair, already heading for the APC's door.

"It was nice doing business with you sir," Johnny laughed. "And good luck to you in the battle that lies ahead."

With that, the mysterious salesman stepped through the APC's door and vanished into nothingness.

Director Stevenson was left staring at the piece of black diamond the salesman had left on the communications console. He could see the energy crackling about inside of the thing. Now, he just needed to find someone who could use the damn thing.

"This is some high-grade evil sir," Warren told him as Director Stevenson watched the mage inspecting the black diamond that Johnny the Salesman had traded him. It had taken less than an hour to get the mage on site. All of Task force Augur's personnel had been relocated to the city of New York in preparation for the Sha'Daa. Most of them were either part of the containment lines around Central Park or among the squad that were inside them. A few though remained in their temporary base of operations in the city itself. They were mostly administrative personnel or psychics with talents that weren't combat oriented. Warren didn't fit either of those categories. He was one of the task force's rare magic users. Director Stevenson couldn't stand mages. More often than not they were either arrogant bastards or incompetent fools. Warren was closer to the latter than the former, but the higher ups insisted that the task force keep a number of magic users on hand. Today, that protocol had paid off whether Director Stevenson wanted to admit it or not.

"I am aware of what the diamond is Warren," Director Stevenson grunted. "The question is can you make it work? I can't spare the PSIs to power the thing."

"Oh sure," Warren shrugged. "What do you want it to do sir?"

Director Stevenson gritted his teeth. "I need a shield around this entire park. One that keep those dead things coming up out of the ground trapped here."

"That shouldn't be too hard to make happen," Warren said, "I'll need some time to get the rituals to secure the diamond's energies in place and then. . ."

"We don't have time for that crap Warren," Director Stevenson was doing his best to keep the frustration and anger boiling inside of him in check but there were limits to what a man could endure. "I know you saw what we're up against on the way in here."

"The gunfire was rather disturbing sir," Warren frowned. "There was so much of it."

Director Stevenson rubbed at his forehead. "There was so much of it, Warren, because we're under constant attack by thousands of reanimated corpses kid. We'll be overrun eventually unless we can get that shield up and in place."

"But sir, the rituals. . ." Warren stammered.

"The man who gave me the diamond assured me that it would work. He didn't mention any kind of threat from using it. Just trust me and assume that diamond is good to go as is. Got it?"

"That's not protocol sir," Warren challenged him.

"If anything happens, it's on me not you.," Director Stevenson restrained himself from punching Warren in the face.

"That's not what I meant," Warren shook his head. "I meant this thing could fry my brain or worse if something goes wrong with it."

"The whole world is at stake here Warren, all of existence as we know it. You're a part of this task force so stop being a baby and do your blasted job! You knew the risks that came with this job when you signed up for it."

"Yes sir," Warren looked scared out of his mind and on the verge of tears but nonetheless, he went to work. With the diamond in his hands, Warren took a seat in a cross-legged position on the floor of the command APC and began to concentrate on the jewel. The energies of the diamond flickered brightly and spun about wildly inside of it.

The door to the command APC was open and Director Stevenson was close enough to it to see the ripple of reality wrapping energy that sprang into being, shooting across the blackness of the sky. As far as Director Stevenson could see in both directions, a wall of shinning, nearly transparent yellow energy leaped up from the ground, surging over fifty feet into the air. It spread upwards from there engulfing the park within it.

"Sir. . ." Warren croaked, opening his eyes. They were as black as the diamond itself now and his voice was hollow sounding as the young mage spoke. "The shield is up."

"Good," Director Stevenson smiled and almost slapped Warren on the back to congratulate him before catching himself at the last moment. Such a slap might have disturbed Warren's concentration on the shield and Director Stevenson was glad he hadn't inadvertently taken that chance. "Can you keep it up?"

"For now, Director," Warren told him. "But not forever."

"Can you give me something a bit more specific than that kid?" Director Stevenson demanded.

"Maybe a day sir. Two at best," Warren managed to answer him though it was clear that doing so took effort on the young mage's part.

"That's good enough for me," Director Stevenson nodded and turned to his staff. "Somebody get me Major Flint on the line!"

"Patching him through to your personal comm. now sir," one of them responded.

"Flint here," the major's voice came over the comm. unit strapped to Director Stevenson's wrist.

"We've got the shield up Major," Director Stevenson told him. "Nothing is getting in or out of this park now without us letting it."

"That's fantastic sir," Major Flint answered.

"The bad part is we're trapped in here too. Your people will have to continue to hold their positions however the presence of the shield does allow us some freedom now. I want you to put together a small group to make a push inward towards Belvedere Castle. I've got several of my squads trapped there and they need relief as soon as possible."

"Copy that sir. Consider me on it," Major Flint assured him.

"Keep me posted of your progress in that regard Major," Director Stevenson ordered and then ended his transmission. They were almost nine hours into the Sha'Daa event now and it was nothing short of a miracle that things hadn't gone worse than they had. But with the appearance of the Salesman, things had certainly taken a turn their way and Director Stevenson sure as Hades planned to make the most of it while their new-found luck lasted.

Agent Lanning looked up from stealing a glance at his watch to see the others watching him closely. All of them were there. Wagner, Markham, Driggle, Eastman, Harrison, Gary, and Shandra. Only Agent Taylor was missing. Markham had reported her loss again upon arriving at the castle having already let him know via comms while in route. They stood atop the castle looking out at the park and the giant, shimmering barrier of energy that filled the sky above them in a dome shape that spread downward to from their viewpoint to enclose the entire park.

"What's up with that stuff in the sky?" Shandra asked.

"It's sure putting off a heck of magical energy," Driggle commented.

Lanning shrugged. "Has to be something Director Stevenson came up with to help with containment. Even with all the military support together, there's no way he could have realistically hoped to hold this place through the entire length of the Sha'Daa."

"What exactly is it?" Markham wondered aloud, staring up at the shield in awe.

"Your guess is as good as mine," Lanning answered. "Driggle would be better suited to answer that one than me."

Driggle looked uncomfortable as everyone turned in his direction. "That thing is magical in nature. That's about all I can tell you."

"Stevenson hates magic," Wagner frowned. "You have to wonder just how desperate things are if he's resorted to using it."

"Enough about that shield," Lanning ended the discussion. "We need to focus on us at this point. It's up to Lanning to hold things together out there."

There hadn't been a real organized or massed attack by the dead on the castle yet. Lanning was grateful for it but…It begged the question - why? The dead had to know they were inside the castle. Small groups did assault its walls at random intervals. When he, Driggle, and Eastman arrived at it they found the place already being secured by the survivors of a S.W.A.T. Unit that had been in the park for an unrelated terrorist threat. The unit had lost half its number reaching the castle but upon making it there put the castle hardcore into lockdown mode. With them were around two dozen civilians under their protection. Lanning had flashed his Task force Augur ID and taken command. The survivors of the S.W.A.T. worked for him now. They didn't have a problem with that either. Being S.W.A.T. The men and women of the unit realized that sticking with someone of his rank and importance was the best hope they had of getting out of Central Park alive. Lanning ordered them to dispense what weapons that they could afford to the more capable of the civilians. Every gun that could be brought into play for the castle's defense counted. The mixed group of S.W.A.T. armed civilians were standing guard at various weak points so that he and his people could have the meeting that they were now.

"That was so lucky, I mean you finding a S.W.A.T. Unit waiting here for you to help out," Shandra smirked.

"Owe that one to Eastman," Lanning gestured his way. "He claims not to have a psi-talent but we all know there's an angel watching over him."

Before Eastman could say anything in response, Markham spoke up. "It's going to take more than the group of us and eight S.W.A.T. Officers to hold this castle if the dead out there decide they want to break in and really come at it in force."

"He's right," Wagner agreed. "We're out numbered thousands or more to one. Likely a lot freaking more based on how things look out there."

"We ain't got no choice Wagner," Lanning said. "But on the upside, we only have to hold this place until Director Stevenson can either get reinforcements to us or find a means of getting us out."

"You would think he would have sent Jane by now," Shandra pointed out.

"Psycho-portation is a tricky thing Shandra," Eastman turned to face her. "Whatever energies the Sha'Daa is releasing, not to mention that shield thing, likely make it where she can't port in and out of park. For all we know, she's already tried and failed."

"Holding this castle is our only options folks," Lanning reminded them. "Best we come up with a plan on just how to do that eh?"

"Shandra, Wagner, Harrison, Markham, you four are the only ones among us with combat-oriented power. We're going to need to split you guys up and get you in place to defend the most vulnerable parts of this castle," Lanning look from one of them to the next. "The rest of us...we'll just be playing back up to you guys."

"This Sha'Daa event is supposed to last for forty-eight hours," Eastman said. "That's what Lanning and Sawyer claim anyway. We're over twelve hours into it and we're still alive. I'd say that's something we can take hope from."

"Yeah," Markham nodded, "And Lanning will surely get help to us long before that much time passes."

"Again, we can't count on that," Lanning shook his head.

"So, where do you want us?" Shandra said getting right down to what needed to be done.

"Thankfully, there is still a lot of work being done to this place. Most of it is currently sealed off for that and a good number of the windows have bars in place over them. The rest of reinforced glass that could take a bullet and hold together. The city has really been working on them. That leaves us with only two weak points to where there's no option but for us to hold the line and they are the main entrance and the entranceway at the bottom of the structure next to the tower we're standing on."

"Thank God for that," Eastman's relief was clear in his voice.

"Shandra, I want you and Markham on the main entrance," Lanning told them. "Wagner, you've got the lower one. I'll give you half of the S.W.A.T guys and Harrison as support."

Harrison grunted at being called support. He was a high-level telekinetic powerhouse and wasn't used to being referred to in such a manner.

"What about the civilians?" Gary asked. "Do we really have the right to ask them to be putting their lives on the line like we are?"

Lanning snorted. "Son, if it weren't for us and that S.W.A.T. Unit, they would all be dead and out there with the rest of those things, snarling and trying to eat us, already. So yeah, I dang well intend to make use of them. You got an issue with that?"

"No sir," Gary lowered his head like chastised school kid who had been called down by his teacher. "I guess not."

"That's it then people," Lanning said, "Let's get to it already."

As the group headed back into the castle, Lanning called out, "Hey Wagner. Wait up a second!"

Wagner paused. Lanning waited until the two of them were alone before saying anything more.

"Tell me you've got some surprises tucked away in that mind of yours," Lanning said.

Lanning knew what Wagner's talent was. The man was what Task force Augur called a *Loader*. To date, Wagner was the only one they had ever came across and they had been bloody lucky to recruit him. The type of psi that Wagner was got the name Loader because an individual with his power could duplicate the powers of other psychics and store those powers inside of them. Wagner was supposedly capable of carrying the limited use of up to three psychic talents and any time with a fourth that served as his primary. Lanning knew which talent Wagner was packing as his primary- bio-energy generated eye beams capable of slicing through the armor of a tank. He didn't know what others were tucked away within the man though and that was knowledge Lanning needed.

"Sir?" Wagner looked at him questioningly. "Are you asking me what powers I am loaded up with?"

"I am son," Lanning nodded. "We're in a dang bad spot here as you know. I was hoping. . ."

"That I might be carrying a way out?" Wagner asked.

"I am asking if you've got anything beyond those eye beams that I know you loaded up with as your primary for this mission. Anything at all that might make a difference given the mess we're in."

"I've got Traci's psycho-metabolic healing, Chev's tracking ability, and Mike's energy absorption sir. None of them are combat talents so I have stuck with using Brent's eye beams," Wagner shrugged. "They seemed to be the best choice considering our circumstances."

"How long does it take you to switch out again?" Lanning cocked an eyebrow as if an idea had just occurred to him.

"Not long sir. A few minutes at worst," Wagner told him.

"And if I remember correctly, the fewer powers you carry, the stronger each is right? And say that you only have one you're loaded with. . ." Lanning stared Wagner.

"Then it's boosted beyond that of the psi I copied it from," Wagner finished for him.

"I'm not ready for you to let loose of Traci's healing yet son but there may come a time when having Harrison's telekinesis working for us at a boosted level may save all our butts. You get what I am saying?"

"Is that why you put the two of us together at the lower entrance?" Wagner met Lanning's eyes.

"Load up with a copy of his power son and be ready to drop the others just in case son. That's an order," Lanning said firmly.

The approach to the entrance of the castle that Shandra and Markham were assigned to, had an advantage to it. Outside, stone walls extended both sides of the doorway for many yards. They limited the number of deaders that could come at the door and would essentially trap the monsters in a small kill zone after the doorway was smashed open and the castle's defenders no longer needed to be concerned about damaging it. There was no if about that. The things would get through the door. It was just a matter of time once their assault on the castle began in earnest. Shandra ordered Markham to reinforce the door with a thick layer of ice acting an additional barricade behind it. The ice formed from the water vapor in the air however was constantly melting due to the summer heat and wasn't as strong as she wished it was.

Greg, the commander of the S.W.A.T. Unit holed up in the castle with them, kept his people alert and ready for the first sign of trouble at the doorway. Shandra had taken an instant liking to Greg. He was rather gruff in his demeanor and certainly lacked her experience in dealing with things like the deaders outside but seemed more than competent enough to truly be useful once the crap hit the fan. Most of his unit were armed with AR-15s but Greg himself carried a M4 carbine. All of them wore a secondary firearm of some sort, mostly Glocks, holstered on their belts.

They were almost fourteen hours into the Sha'Daa which meant it was nearly Two AM. The sun was gone from the sky. The day had been as dark as the night before it. The only light outside was the eerie glow of the energy field around the park that Lanning assumed Director Stevenson had managed to somehow erect. There had been no word from the Director or anyone else. None of the comms. was working. They were cut off inside the castle with no means of knowing when or even if help was coming.

"Ma'am…" Greg said, walking over to where Shandra stood. "There's something happening outside."

"I can see it Greg," Shandra assured him though it was hard to through the layer of ice between them and the door. Everything outside was clouded and distorted.

"Everybody get ready," Markham warned the others despite Shandra being the one in command.

Shandra let the affront slide as Markham was right in doing so.

Suddenly the door and the ice behind it blew apart, shattering inward. Shandra barely managed to save herself from being shredded by the shards of ice that flew into the area behind the doorway like shrapnel. Her right hand jerked through the air adding enough weight to the debris that the pieces of it coming her way thudded onto the castle's floor. Markham protected himself by forming a circular shield composed of ice on his left arm. The S.W.A.T folks dove for cover. Not everyone escaped the shrapnel though. One of the S.W.A.T. Officers died as a shard of ice imbedded itself in her throat. Blood bubbling out of her mouth, she collapsed. Two of the armed civilians were taken out as well. They fell backwards looking like human pin cushions with numerous, jagged pieces of ice protruding from their bodies.

The door and the barrier of ice were utterly torn into rubble. Only Shandra and Markham were still on their feet as the deaders came pouring through into the castle. Markham shot icicles from the fingertips of both his hands into their ranks as Shandra focusing the full power of her talent on the fastest of the creatures crushed those three into bloody pulp that smeared the floor in front of her. The commander of the S.W.A.T unit and his two remaining officers that were present scrambled to their feet, weapons blazing. The charge of deaders ended as quickly as it had begun. Beyond the shattered doorway, hundreds more of the monsters were waiting but they made no move towards the castle. Between them and it stood a trio of rotting figures with glowing green eyes. The clothes they wore were pristine and each had an aura of power about them that even the S.W.A.T. Unit members seemed to be able to feel.

Shandra instantly realized what they had to be. The things were liches, reanimated psychics and wizards that had been loosed from the depths of Hell by the Sha'Daa.

"Humans," the center lich purred through withered, rotting lips. "Your time is at an end."

"I don't fragging think so!" Greg shouted, taking aim at the thing's head. His M4 roared as took his shot at it. The female lich to the right of the one that had spoken raised a hand and a shimmering shield of energy appeared to block the M4 rounds. The bullets stuck it, bouncing away harmlessly.

The lich cloaked in dark robes to the left of the one that had spoken shed them, revealing its misshapen, sickening form. Two sets of twisted arms rose upwards from its side, the fingers of all four of the lich's hands crackling with green energy as they wiggled in the process of casting a spell. The lich charged forward directly at Shandra.

One of the S.W.A.T. Officers moved between her and the thing. The woman's AR-15 chattered as she blasted at it on full auto. Her bullets ripped into the lich's rotting flesh, tearing chunks of it from the thing's body. The lich wasn't even slowed down by the woman's efforts. Its lower right hand slashed outward, plunging into the woman's stomach. The officer grunted in pain and then coughed blood that shot out over her lips. It ran down her chin as her wide eyes stared in horror at the lich. Its upper left hand closed around the woman's throat, removing it from her body with a quick twist that tore it free from her neck.

The woman's sacrifice gave Shandra time to act. She let loose a concentrated beam of solidified gravity into the lich's chest. The beam picked the lich up from where it was by the sheer force of its impacted and flung the dead thing backwards. It landed, hard, on its back. Shandra sprang forward, pressing her attack, before the lich could recover. Sweat beaded on her forehead below her hair as she strained to crush the dead monster where it lay, increasing the weight of the very air above it, pressing it downward. The lich squirmed and twisted beneath the pressure Shandra was pouring onto it. Wriggling an arm up just enough to get it pointed at her, bolts of crackling, lightning like energy leaped from its fingertips. Shandra flung herself out of their path, narrowly avoiding the lich's attack. Doing so broke her concentration though and the lich was able to free itself from the field of gravity that had been pinning it down.

Meanwhile, Markham found himself facing off with the leader of the three liches as the dead thing spoke again.

"Humanity's time is over!" the lich snarled. "Can't you see that?"

The lead lich raised its arms. They grew outward towards Markham like snakes, threatening to wrap about him. Markham turned the palms of his hands sideways, one at each of the snake like arms of the lich. Blasts of super intense cold erupted from them freezing the lich's arms solid. The lich wailed as it tried to recoil its arms and they shattered into thousands of tiny pieces of frozen, rotted flesh. Markham brought his hands up and together, firing a single large bolt of cold at the lead lich's body. The bolt struck a shimmering shield of energy that sprang into being, protecting the thing from the devastation he had intended to inflict upon it. The shield had been created by the female lich. She came running at Markham, gleaming claws growing from the fingers of her hands as she ran. Her rotted lips were parted as she hissed her fury at him.

Greg and the other S.W.A.T. Officers saved Markham's life. They all targeted the female lich, their weapons blazing. Dozens of rounds punched into her body, jerking it about as they entered it. The lich woman staggered but didn't fall. Her eyes glowed a brighter shade of green as she jumped at the closest of the officers. The claws of her right hand sliced across the officer's face, mangling his eyes and nose. The officer collapsed to his knees, dropping his weapon, as his hands came up to cover the mess his face had become. He was still wailing in pain as the lich drove the claws of her right hand into the top of his skull, ending him.

"Don't let her get near you!" Greg yelled, warning the other officers.

The lich woman blinked out of existence, reappearing behind Greg. Before he even realized she was there, one of her hands caught him by his hair, yanking his head back to expose the softer tissue of his throat. Her other hand darted around Greg, claws raking over the front his throat. Blood exploded from neck as her claws opened it up.

"No!" Markham screamed, watching the S.W.A.T. Leader die. There wasn't a fragging thing he could about it though. The lead lich had regrown its arms and was out of his blood. Its arms, legs, and neck all extending from its body the lead lich pounced at him. In the fraction of a second before the dead thing landed on top of him, Markham glanced up into its glowing, furious, green eyes. The lich took him to the floor beneath it, the thing's body engulfing Markham. Not a single part of the ice wielding psychic could be seen as he thrashed about inside the lich's form. Markham's thrashing ended quickly. When the lich slithered off of him, all that remained was blackened, charred bones that looked as if they had been dipped in acid.

Shandra hammered the lich in the back with a gravity bolt as it slithered away from Markham's remains. The bolt tore through the central mass of the thing's twisted form. The lich howled, either in rage or pain. Shandra wasn't sure which but she hit it again. A second gravity bolt reduced the lich's skull to pulp and shattered bone fragments. Its body flopped onto the floor of the castle and didn't move again.

*One down, two to go,* Shandra thought as she saw the female lich glaring at her. She met its eyes, looking into them. The witch thing was going to pay for Markham's death and all the others she had caused. Shandra was going to make sure of it.

Another two S.W.A.T. Officers died as the four-armed lich released blasts of energy that ripped into their armor and their bodies beneath it, burning holes clean through them. Shandra realized in that moment that she was now alone with the two remaining liches. Everyone else around her was dead, killed by the undead monsters she was engaged with. The army of deaders outside the castle's entrance continued to hold their position, waiting for the liches to finish her.

Shandra raised herself up, as straight and tall as she could, a determined look of righteous anger on her face. It was up to her to hold the castle's main entrance now. There was no one else with her left alive to help get the job done.

"You bastards," Shandra growled as she marched towards the two lichs. The four armed one snickered at her while the female lich hissed with renewed fury. Shandra's hand snapped up, gravity bolts exploding from them at the four-armed lich. It met her bolts with crackling blasts of energy. The two met in an explosion that shook the entire section of the castle they stood in. Cracks formed in the walls and pieces of the ceiling above them broke loose, collapsing. Shandra screamed as she put every ounce of willpower within her into the bolts she was firing. They pushed through the crackling energy beams that had been keeping them from reaching their target to strike the four-armed lich. The undead thing's body blew apart in a shower of gore and black pus.

The female lich had disappeared again. Shandra's shoulders slumped from the level of effort it had taken to slay the four-armed lich but her eyes whipped around searching for the female lich. There was no sign of the dead woman. Shandra shivered and then shook herself to clear her head. Where the hell had the lich gone to?

A drop of putrid, black blood dropped into her hair. Shandra's head jerked upwards just in time to see that the female lich had been clinging to the roof of the room above before the thing's body fell onto her. Shandra cried out, blood popping like exploding tears from the corner of her eyes, as inverted gravity and slung the dead woman back upwards into the roof that the lich had dropped from. The lich slammed into the ceiling with enough force to bring the rest of it down. Both of them were crushed and buried by the weight of the falling rubble.

Agent Lanning and two armed civilians had been on their way to reinforce Shandra and the others at the castle's main entrance when the ceiling ahead of them caved in blocking their path. The hallway was filled with a cloud of dust from the ceiling's collapse.

"Frag me," Lanning muttered. His knuckles went white from the pressure of his grip on the M4 carbine he carried.

It was enough to break the nerve of one of the two civilians with him. The kid named Derrick turned and ran back the way they had come from. The young woman though, Lanning thought he remembered her name being Caroline, held her ground beside him. She's got some balls on her, Lanning smirked, impressed by her courage.

As the dust cleared above the rubble filling the hallway ahead of them, Lanning saw a mass of deaders closing in on them. The things were crawling over the top of the masses of shattered stone and broken wood.

"It's do or die time kiddo," Lanning told Caroline. "We have to stop these things here. If they get fully into the castle, we're dead. There will be nowhere left to run to that they can't find us."

"Copy that," Caroline said, in a gruff voice. Lanning could see that she was putting on a brave face for his benefit.

The two of them raised their weapons at the approaching deaders as the monster drew closer and closer to their position crawling over the rubble.

"Hold your fire until you're sure you can make it count," Lanning ordered.

The first of the deaders made it through the rubble and dropped to the floor several yards from where the two of them stood. Lanning blew the thing to hell with a burst from his M4 that splattered the insides of its head everywhere.

It was like the gates of hell itself gave way and opened up as the thing's body toppled onto the floor. Dozens more of the deaders sprang from where they climbed through the rubble into the hallway with them. Lanning had given Caroline a pump action shotgun. It bucked in her hands as it thundered. Her first shot punched through a deader's chest, sending it stumbling backwards into those behind it. Lanning's M4 hosed the front ranks of the deaders with a stream of fully automatic fire. Bodies of the deaders piled up on the floor in front of the debris as he and Caroline cut them down as fast as they came. Caroline had emptied her shotgun and switched over to an AR-15 that she had been carrying swung over her shoulder by its strap. The hallway filled up with gun smoke and the stench of spilt and ruptured intestines.

Lanning knew they weren't going to be able to hold the monsters. His M4 clicked empty. As he popped the weapon's spent magazine, shoving another into place inside of it, Lanning yelled, "Fall back!"

Caroline put a final burst of fire into the ranks of the hungry dead and then made a run for it with Lanning following after her. The two of them fled deeper into the castle. The shrieks and snarls of the dead behind them echoed along the corridors.

"In here!" Caroline shouted as they came upon a room in the middle of being remodeled. The room was torn apart and there nothing in it but tools and lumber. However, it had a door that could be closed after them as they entered it. Lanning didn't have the time to argue with Caroline even though he knew sealing themselves in the room was a mistake. They were in it with the door slammed shut behind them before Caroline seemed to realize too that her actions had just trapped them with God only knew how many of the dead outside. The door to the room shook in its frames as the fists of the dead pounded against it.

"Great" Lanning spat. "Now what kid?"

"I was hoping you could take it from here," she told him.

Lanning shook his head, disgusted at their situation. He cursed and kicked over a sealed bucket of paint, denting it with the point of his boot.

The door gave way to the dead, tearing loose from its hinges, to come flinging inward. The dead spilled through the now open doorway. Lanning jerked up his M4, freshly reloaded, and met the bastard things with a barrage of bullets that shredded the bodies of the first of them to enter the room. Caroline opened fire with her AR-15 too. For a brief second, the tide of hungry dead was stemmed but only for a second. The ranks of the dead seemed endless. They came on relentlessly, determined to taste the blood of the living souls trapped within the room.

Agent Lanning was one of the heads of Task force Augur yet despite his rank, he had no psychic talent. He had risen to his position by being a hard-headed, often brutal, and cunning bastard and those attributes showed clearly now. As his M4 clicked empty and the hand that reached into the pack that held extra magazines for his weapon, emerged from it empty as well, Lanning screamed. It wasn't a shriek of terror or the wailing of a man who knew he was about to die. Instead, it was a furious battle-cry as tossed his M4 aside and drew the machete that rested in a sheath upon his leg. The blade came free, gleaming in the dim, flicking light that bled into the room from the shield filling the sky outside its sole window. Caroline's AR-15 clicked empty as well. She, too, discarded her weapon but unlike Lanning, whirled about, running in an attempt to try to find another way out.

Lanning launched himself forward at the dead. His machete sliced away the grabbing hand of a dead man dressed in tattered coveralls. It swung back around to thunk into the forehead of a mostly rotted woman wearing a White Snake T shirt. Lanning yanked the blade free of her skull as her body toppled onto the floor near him. The machete's blade was slicked with black gore as he drove the weapon's razor edge into the side of another dead man's skull. Bone crunched, giving way to sharp metal. The body of the dead man twitched as Lanning kick away a dead woman that leaped at him. The sole of his boot met her face midflight leap, smashing her nose and sending teeth flying from her mouth. Lanning grunted as one of the dead got hold of him from behind and sunk its teeth into the meat of his shoulder. He thrusted the blade of the machete into the top of the monster's skull and felt putrid black matter spraying over him. Lanning pulled loose from the now truly dead thing that had held him and its corpse thudded onto the floor.

The dead had cornered Caroline at the rear of the room, blocking her path to its window. Not that she could have jumped out of it anyway. The window was high above the park outside. It might not have been a fatal fall but it sure would have messed her up bad anyway when she hit the ground. The height was just too great. Her AR-15 gone, Caroline was unarmed. She had no other weapon to fight the dead gathering around her with. Caroline still had no choice but to make a desperate, last futile stand against the dead. She punched a dead woman's that snapped at her with yellow teeth. Her fist smashed into the joint of the woman's jaw, breaking it. The dead woman's lower jaw hung loosely beneath her top row of teeth, dangling there, useless. Caroline lashed out again, knocking the dead woman from her feet. But there were so many more of the monsters. Cold hands took hold of her arms. Others clutched at her legs as deaders that had been messed up but not stop by the bullets fired into the ranks crawled to her and began to climb up her body, nails cutting painfully into her skin. Caroline struggled with all the strength she had, fighting to break free of the dead that swarmed her. They tugged her down. She hit the floor amid them. Nails shredded her skin. Teeth bit away chunks of her body. Her wailing voice rose in pitch from the pain then abruptly fell silent as her world went dark. The dead man that bit into the main artery of her neck continued to gnaw upon her there as Caroline's body spasmed a final time and then went limp in the hands of the dead that held her down.

Lanning saw Caroline disappear beneath a swarm of the dead. Her screams echoed in his ears. His own plight was a dire one. Outnumbered and with nowhere to run, all he could do was keep fighting. A dead woman came at him, her withered lips twisted in a horrid snarl. Lanning's machete lashed out, smashing into her mouth. She stumbled backwards as he swung again. His second swing buried the weapon's blade in the side of her skull. Lanning jerked the weapon free. He grunted as a dead man plowed into him from behind. Lanning's body lurched forward as more of the dead took advantage of him being off balance. One of the thing's grabbed the arm holding his machete, biting into it. Lanning screamed as he saw his own blood splattering up into the monster's face as its teeth pierced his flesh. He ripped his arm free of the dead thing holding it, leaving a chunk of meat inside its mouth. Despite the pain, Lanning managed to keep his grip on his machete. His knuckles were white, and he gritted his teeth against the pain. The balled-up fist of his left hand slammed into the face of a dead man, breaking several of the man's teeth from its impact. Lanning figured he was dead. He had seen plenty of evidence that the bit of the deaders worked just like it did in the all the horror films about zombies. It passed the thing's infection onto him. Even if he found a means of escaping the dead pouring into the room with him, his hope of survival was gone, as dead as the creatures around him.

A grenade dangled from the belt of his combat armor. Lanning snatched it loose, popping the grenade's pin. Several of the dead things sprang at him together. He didn't try to evade their grasping hands. Lanning endured the pain of their nails digging into him as they took him to the floor of the room. He glanced from one set of glowing green eyes to another, almost smiling, as he let the grenade drop free of his grasp on it. The grenade bounced onto the floor, the impact setting it off. The ensuring explosion killed him instantly at such point-blank range. The walls of the room shook from the blast, blowing apart the dead that had been holding him down.

"I've lost contact with Lanning and the others," Gary told Wagner.

Wagner glanced over at Harrison. The powerful TK's frown matched his own.

"We have to assume…" Harrison started but Wagner finished his sentence before he could.

"That the dead have broken through and are inside the castle now," Wagner nodded. Lanning was the toughest S.O.B. That Wagner had ever known. If Lanning, Shandra, and the others hadn't been able to hold the dead at bay, what hope did they have especially given that they were likely to soon be fighting a battle on two fronts. In addition to protecting the castle's lower entrance, they would need to keep an eye out for the dead coming at them through the castle itself now as well.

"What the frag are we going to do?" Gary asked the two of them.

The four S.W.A.T. Officers were watching them as well, all looking to them for an answer.

"All we've got to do is hold out long enough for Director Stevenson to get help to us," Wagner said.

"Sure thing," Harrison sighed. "Let's do that."

"I don't think there's any other choice as to what we can do," Wagner shrugged.

"We got incoming!" one of the S.W.A.T. Officers yelled.

Wagner and Harrison looked in the direction of the entranceway they were protecting. Dozens of dead men and women were racing towards it. The S.W.A.T. Officer who had first seen the monsters was already firing into them with his AR-15 as the others moved into position to create the best kill zone they could. It was a pretty effective one too. Their rounds ripped into the ranks of the dead, mowing the things down. Even so, it was clear that they weren't going to be able to keep the monsters from getting through and into the castle. There was just too many of the dead. For each one that fell, several more came running from the park around the castle to join the battle.

"Come on Wagner," Harrison said. "It's time for us to earn our paychecks."

The TK stepped forward, his eyes hard and cold, as he appeared to focus his concentration. About a half dozen of the dead that had pushed through the fire the S.W.A.T. Guys were laying down rushed at him. Harrison's telekinesis lifted one of them from the ground and tore the thing limb from limb splattering the black putridness of its blood through the air. With a wave of his hand, Harrison crushed two more of the dead, pulping them where they ran. Wagner moved up to join him. Bolts of energy blasted out of his eyes, slicing through a dead man and spilling his entrails onto the ground. Wagner's gaze swept sideways, hitting another of the dead. They cut the creature's body entirely into two along its middle. Its two halves dropped away from each other to land twitching in pools of black gore.

"We got company!" Gary shouted from behind them. Wagner glanced over his shoulder to see a group of dead coming down the stairs out of the castle's interior into the hallway where they were.

Gary's automatic pistol spat bursts of fire at the things. His first shot mangled the flesh of a deader's face, sending the creature reeling backwards, his second knocked one of the thing's off balance sending it toppling down the stairs. The thing landed hard, snapping its neck from the angle at which it struck the floor.

All Wagner could hear was the snarls and shrieks of the dead. There were so many of the monsters that their voices drowned out the dying sounds of gunfire. The deaders storming the castle from the outside had reached the firing line that S.W.A.T. Guys had set up and were among them now. One of the S.W.A.T. Officers squealed as deader tore away her nose with its teeth. Another of them was taken down as close to a dozen of the dead dog piled him. The remaining two S.W.A.T. Officers were in full retreat, attempting to fall back. One of them scrambled past where Wagner stood still raining hell upon the dead at the entranceway to the castle with his eye beams. Wagner couldn't look at the man without killing him so kept his attention focused on the dead. His eye beams sputtered and then ceased. Wagner had used them up in their entirety this time. There would be no recharging his system to get them powered up again. Wagner knew he could try to but that wasn't his plan. Reaching out with his mind and his psychic talent, Wagner locked onto to Harrison's telekinesis, imprinting Harrison's talent upon himself. It was what Lanning had ordered him to do. Wagner let loose of the other powers he carried within his system and let Harrison's become his everything. Doing so allowed Wagner to magnify Harrison's already incredible level of telekinesis when he brought the power bear upon the dead. A shockwave of telekinetic force flowed out of him into the dead storming the castle from outside of it. It rolled over the monsters, grinding them to pulp and clearing the field beyond the entranceway as far as Wagner could see. Well over a hundred of the monsters perished, destroyed by the one single blow Wagner had dealt the things.

"Holy frag," Harrison muttered, losing his own concentration and turning to stare at Wagner beside him. Smirking, Wagner gave Harrison a sharp nod.

The moment between them was brought to an abrupt end by the scream of a woman behind them. She had been the last of the S.W.A.T. Officers. One of the dead had closed on her, wrestling her AR-15 from her grasp, and somehow managed to spear her with it. The barrel of the rifle protruded from the woman's back as the snarling deader twisted the weapon about inside of her body. The other S.W.A.T. Officer that had moved to help Gary below the stairs lay dead on the floor his ripped apart guts being shared among several of the dead. Their lips smacked as they feasted upon them.

Gary came staggering toward them covered in black pus and his own blood. His eyes were glowing a bright shade of green. It was impossible for Wagner or Harrison to be able to tell if Gary was still alive or dead. Either way, his body belonged to the evil of the Sha'Daa now. Gary still clutched his automatic pistol and brought it up at Harrison, squeezing the weapon's trigger. Harrison turned the rounds the gun spat aside with a wave of his right hand. Having loaded up Harrison's power, Wagner could feel it as the powerful TK used it. He felt the energy building inside Harrison before a blast of telekinetic energy leaped out of the man to smash into Gary. Their once teammate was lifted from the floor and flung into the wall to the right of the stairwell that led up into the castle. Wagner heard Gary's bone crack and shattered from the impact. Gary's limp form slid down the wall to sprawl out on the floor in a puddle of both red and black. He wasn't taking any chances on Gary getting up again however, so Wagner used his own telekinesis to relieve Gary's body of its head, tearing it from his neck.

"Where the hell is Stevenson?" Harrison raged, lashing out at the dead still coming down the stairs. The blast of telekinetic energy that smashed into the creatures broke their bones and caved in their skulls.

Major Flint rode in the lead APC. A second one followed it through Central Park towards the castle where Agent Lanning's squad had taken shelter many hours before. All communication with the squad in the castle had been lost. Not even Task force Augur's telepaths could reach them, nor its locators get a lock on their positions. The squad in the castle was truly cut off and alone. Major Flint's mission was to reach the squad and get them out of the place and to the relative safety of the containment lines set up around the park. The men on the lines were still locked in the fight of their lives despite the barrier that Director Stevenson had been able to trade the mysterious salesman who reputedly had showed up at every recorded Sha'Daa event throughout time. The strange energy field was doing its job keeping the undead monsters the Sha'Daa had summoned into being from getting out of the park but that left those on the containment lines trapped inside with the things. The firing lines had given up large portions of the park's perimeter and regrouped to better concentrate their remaining firepower. As many units on the line had shifted their positions, Major Flint had acquired two APCs for the task Director Stevenson had stuck him with. Aboard each of them was five, heavily armed soldiers and one psi-talented member of Task Force Augur with combat-oriented powers.

Hughie rode in Major Flint's APC with him. The man was what one would call a Flitter. His Psi-talent was super speed. Hughie could move so fast that he seemed to blur to the human eye and had the reflexes to match. His weapons of choice were a set of matching katanas. Some might have laughed at the man's weapons but not Major Flint. He had seen a video clip of what Hughie could do with the swords he carried. Let loose, the man was a whirlwind of death moving at speeds approaching Mach 2. Joseph was the other Psi assigned to Major Flint's small group. He was a Chlorokinetic. That might be a big word to some but what meant was simple. Joseph could control and manipulate plants to have them do his bidding...and there were a fragging lot of plants in Central Park.

The top .50 calibers of both APCs roared, sweeping their arcs of fire over the army of the dead that chased after them and came at them from their sides. Only a handful of the dead were stupid enough even in their various states of rot to think they could stop the heavy armored vehicles head on and those that were ended up splattered against their fronts or crushed beneath their wheels. The APC Major Flint rode in bounced as it drove over the body of one such deader. He liked the term zombies better but deaders was the official name from the creatures they were engaged with.

The ride to the castle wouldn't have been a long one if it weren't for the sheer numbers of the deaders that the two APCs had to fight their way through. Major Flint prayed that those of Task Force Augur holed up within the castle's walls would live long enough for his people to reach them.

Then suddenly, everything went to hell in a handbasket. A deader with eyes that glowed a much darker and intense green than of those around it stepped out into the path of Major Flint's APC. The creature held it's palms out, open, facing downward at the ground. He wasn't a psychic but Major Flint knew that whatever the thing was doing was about to mess them up big time. Blasts of vibrations flew from the deader's hands into the ground, rippling through it to impact the APC he rode in. The ground itself was thrust upwards in jagged hunks. The APC was thrown onto its side, skidding along, carried on by its own momentum. The people inside of the heavy vehicle with him screamed as they were tossed and thrown about, smashing into its walls and roof. When the APC finally lurched to a halt, Major Flint found himself laying, looking up at its side door. He was shaken up and badly bruised but most of the others in the vehicle weren't that lucky. Major Flint looked about to see one soldier lying dead, impaled by his own rifle. The weapon's barrel jutted through his neck. Its red dripping tip protruding from the bottom rear of the man's skull. A woman who wore the rank of private on her sleeve was wailing like a banshee. Both of her legs had folded up under her body, backwards, clearly broken. Major Flint couldn't believe the woman wasn't unconscious from the shock of the pain. Tears streamed over the curves of her cheeks as the woman tried to move herself off her twisted and blood smeared legs. Major Flint saw the white of bone sticking out of them through her uniform and her flesh at numerous spots along their lengths. Odds were even if the woman soldier survived the next few minutes, she would never be able to walk again.

Hurling himself up, Major Flint watched as Hughie, completely uninjured, saved by his superhuman reflexes and sense of balance, got the APC's door above them open. Hughie scampered through it. Major Flint followed after him but not before grabbing up a M82 Barrett and readying the powerful rifle.

The thing that had rolled their APC was engaged with Joseph. It had taken out the second APC just like it had their own. Joseph stood on top of the overturned vehicle side. Large vines and other plants grew all around it. They waved about in the air like snakes, some of them lashing out at the lich. That was what the deader with the Geo powers had to be. The vines that Joseph controlled whipped around the lich's arms and yanked them from the sockets of its shoulders. Others wrapped around the lich's body, holding it, as more wound about its neck. Before the vines could finish their work, Hughie was there. One of his katanas flashed through the air, severing the lich's head.

The few soldiers that had survived the damage done to the APCs well enough to remain in the fight took up defensive positions around the one that Joseph stood on. Their weapons chattered and roared, pouring a furious barrage of fully automatic fire into the ranks of the dead coming in their direction. Hughie went to work thinning out the number horde of deaders. He danced among the flying bullets, amid the dead, taking heads and severing limbs.

Another lich came soaring in from out of the sky and landed in front of the overturned APC Joseph stood on. The lich's eyes glowed a bright green as its hands swung up to target the Chlorokinetic. Black energy, darker than the night, streaked from them into Joseph. He screamed as their blackness engulf him. All that was left of Joseph was his bones which clattered onto the armor of the APC where he had been standing.

Hughie came at the lich from behind. The thing whirled about to meet him, but he was too fast. Hughie's blades chopped off its left hand at the wrist and sliced through its right leg just above the knee. The lich toppled into the grass. Hughie came running back around for another pass at the lich and this time the blade of his right katana opened up its skull right down its middle. The lich's head popped like an overripe melon in an explosion of black gore.

No more lichs appeared to attack them but Major Flint knew they were far from out of the fire yet. The number of dead around them had to be in the hundreds if not the thousands. They were surrounded with nowhere to run except into the arms of the hungry dead.

"Form up on me!" Major Flint yelled, rallying his troops, as he climbed atop the APC that Joseph had died upon. There were three soldiers left and they joined him there. Hughie kept up his attack on the deaders, darting among them, sending dozens back to hell with each second that ticked by. That was fine with Major Flint. He hadn't expected the Psi to join them anyway. Hughie 's onslaught was the only reason they hadn't been overrun already.

Hughie sped through a group of the dead leaving an explosion of carnage in his wake. His swords had sliced the monsters behind him to bits. As he swerved about to change his course, a deader leaped at him from out of a tree. Hughie hadn't been expecting an attack from the direction the thing came at him in. He tried to twist around and alter his course back the way he came. At the speed he was moving at, the attempt was just too much. Hughie got tripped up and stumbled. His body smashed into the ground with the force of a tank shell. The bones of his right shoulder shattered and crunched from the impact. His body bounced into the air and when it came back down, Hughie landed hard on his back, knocking the breath from his lungs. As he sucked air back into his lungs and tried to get to his feet, dozens upon dozens of the dead fell upon him, their hands clawing at his injured body. Hughie barely had time to start screaming before the dead tore him apart.

Major Flint fired a shot with his M82 that pulped the upper torso of a deader racing towards the overturned APC he stood on. The soldiers around him were doing all they could to drive back the dead that were trying to climb up the sides of the APC and get at them. It wasn't enough. A soldier screamed as a cold, dead hand caught one of his ankles and yanked him down from atop the APC. The man disappeared into the crowd of deaders gathered around the vehicle. A deader bounded onto the APC right in front of Major Flint. The thing was too close to him to get off a shot at it with his M82 Barrett. Major Flint turned the heavy rifle in his hands, shoving it outward at the deader in attempt to knock the thing off the APC. The deader caught the rifle though and pushed back against it with more strength than Major Flint expected. He was the one who got pushed over, not the deader. Major Flint lost his grip on the rifle as he toppled over. The deader flung the rifle away as it threw itself onto him. Major Flint went for the pistol holstered on his hip. The weapon came free and he brought it up to press its barrel against the side of the deader's skull. Major Flint used the flat of his other arm, wedged up beneath the deader's chin, to keep the thing's snapping teeth away from his flesh. He squeezed the pistol's trigger and blew out the deader's brains with a single, point blank shot. Its body went limp as he rolled the monster off of him.

Scrambling to his feet, Major Flint looked around. The men and women of his team were dead. He was the only living, breathing human left on the battlefield. The dead surrounded the APC, climbing onto its side where he stood. Major Flint shot the closest of the monsters. The round he fired entered its left eye and exited the rear of its skull. The deader fell away from the side of the APC into those behind it. Major Flint's pistol cracked in rapid succession as he blasted at another deader in front of him and then spun to fire at three more coming up onto the other side of the APC. His booted foot lashed out colliding with the forehead of a deader trying to grab his legs.

"Frag it," Major Flint raged. He stopped shooting at the dead and dropped into the APC through its open side door. The interior of the APC was dark other than a few scattered console lights and he landed badly. His left ankle snapped beneath the weight of his body. Major Flint grunted at the pain, catching himself by slamming a hand against a wall. He could hear the dead above him. Without anyone on top of the overturned APC to challenge them, God only knew how many of the monsters were already up there. Major Flint limped towards one of the vehicle's storage compartments built into its side walls. He opened it. The bulk of the compartment's contents fell out over him. A medkit grazed the side of his head drawing blood. Curing like a sailor, he found what he was after though.

The first of the dead dropped into the APC with him as Major Flint clutched the grenade bandolier he had taken from the storage compartment. His pistol cracked three times as put two rounds into the deader's skull, sending it stumbling backwards to crash into the rear of the APC and slid down the wall there with brain matter leaking from the holes the shots had blown in its forehead. The third round ricocheted inside the APC, sparking against its the metal of its walls until it hit him. The round entered his thigh. Major Flint cried out, dropping to one knee as more of the deaders entered the APC through its open side door. He pulled the pin from one of the grenades on the bandolier flashing the dead coming towards him a wicked grin.

"See you in hell you bastards!" Major Flint shouted and then slammed the bandolier of grenades, hard, onto the wall of the APC beneath him. Fire and shrapnel filled the APC interior. A moment later, the entire vehicle blew taking dozens of the deaders outside with it.

Harrison and Wagner ran for their lives. They had abandoned their position defending the castle's lower entrance. There was no point it. Everyone else inside of the place was likely dead. Harrison lashed out with his telekinesis crushing the bones of several of the deaders trying to close on them while Wagner used his to keep the path ahead of them clear of the monsters. Their plan was to make it to the containment lines set up around the park. If they could make it there, they could join up with the rest of Task force Augur and the large military unit supporting it. It had become their only hope of staying alive. Trying to hold out at the castle was no longer an option. The place belonged to the dead now.

Something with huge, wide-spread, bat like wings came swooping out of the sky ahead of them. Not too far away something exploded. Plumes of orange and red fire leaped upwards from whatever it was that blew. The creature that landed in their path paid no attention to the distant explosions. Its glowing green eyes were focused on them. The dead all stopped in their tracks, freezing in place where they were.

"Well…this can't be good," Harrison said. Wagner stared at the thing in front of them. It stood almost ten feet tall with a wingspan longer than that. The claws of its hands gleamed in the odd light cast by the shield that filled the air above the park.

"Humans. . ." the thing said in a voice that reminded Wagner of the shrieking screams of tortured souls. "Your time has come. This world belongs to us."

Wagner's gut told him that the thing was a demon released into the world by the gates of the Sha'Daa. Its form was utterly nightmarish, a mess of rotting flesh and glittering, lizard like scales.

"Wagner!" Harrison yelled, snapping him out of his shock at the sight of the thing.

Harrison was already throwing out a blast of telekinetic force at the winged abomination. Harrison's attack sliced the thing's legs out from under it. Wagner followed up seizing the demon's chest with the power of his mind and squeezing it. The demon's torso splattered sending black goo flying everywhere. Some of it splashed over Harrison even as the telekinetic did his best to leap away from it.

The dead continued to remain where they were, motionless, just standing there like statues.

"Harrison," Wagner called out, taking a step towards him. "You okay man?"

The telekinetic turned to face him. Everything that was human was gone from Harrison's expression. His veins bulged from his skin, black and swollen. Harrison's eyes crackled with green energy as Wagner stared into them.

Wagner tried to *will* a telekinetic barrier into place to block the attack he knew Harrison was about to throw at him. He couldn't get it formed in time. A wave of telekinetic energy from Harrison smacked into Wagner, picking him up from the ground, and flinging him several yards through the air. Wagner stopped his body from landing in the grass. His body hovered mere inches above it. Spinning about in the air, Wagner righted himself. The thing that had been Harrison glared up at him. Wagner heaved a fist through the air, hurling a blast of force back at Harrison. It hammered into the thing that telekinetic had become, caving in its ribs. Harrison slumped to his knees but quickly looked up at Wagner again, snarling.

Knowing that he had to finish Harrison as fast as he could, Wagner lashed out thrusting both hands outward at him. It took all the power he had left but it did the job. A gale force of telekinetic energy washed over Harrison, first tearing away the flesh from his bones and then scattering the bones themselves into the wind. His power spent, Wagner was unable to keep himself aloft. He tumbled into the grass of the park as the dead launched into motion again. They came at Wagner from all sides. He punched one in the nose, kicked at another, and then was pulled from his feet by the sheer number of the monsters overwhelming him. Wagner thrashed about, fighting to his last breath, as the dead ate him alive.

Director Stevenson frowned as the reports came in. One of his aides, Patrick, a telepath with limited clairvoyance informed him that Major Flint and the force dispatched to reach the castle had met a horrid end before ever reaching it. That news was followed by confirmation that Lanning's group at the castle were dead anyway. All of them lost to the dead and the demons spilling out of the gates created by the Sha'Daa. On the upside, the shield that the Salesman had traded him was still holding. Not a single creature spawned of the Sha'Daa had escaped Central Park that he knew of…and that was what mattered.

"Your orders sir?" Captain Higgins, who was now the acting C.O. of the military support assigned to aid Task force Augur asked.

"We hold the line," Director Stevenson growled. "No matter what happens son, we hold the line."

From somewhere deep inside the park, a wave of green energy burst outward from its center. Director Stevenson saw it coming but there wasn't a damned thing he could do it. The wave of energy washed him and those around him, blinding them all, and then there was nothing but cold and an eternal darkness. The last thing Director Stevenson heard was the sound of a great and powerful demon laughing.

# Strange Bedfellows

by Michael H. Hanson

*"The ghosts that we see, are us or our friends in another dimension."*
— *Anthony T. Hincks*

THE GOLD AND AMBER CREATURE THAT was once known as Sergeant Burt Buchowski of the United States Marine Corps literally tore its way through several dozen zombies that were charging towards the nearest East Harlem exit off Central Park. He knew that every single one of these monstrosities had to be stopped. They were a rampaging human-shaped virus that was driven to spread their sickness exponentially, as each person they killed came back to undead life as a fellow mindless zombie, thus their army was growing in droves throughout the park.

In recent weeks the press had dubbed him The Golden Avenger, a rarely spotted vigilante who preyed on muggers and rapists, and so that became his new identity, a bizarre being born of unforgivable and secret military experiments using tailored insect DNA on desperate soldiers dying from a wide variety of battlefield-related toxins and diseases. Escaping his captors just over a month ago (the final stage of their testing involved complete vivisection of his new body), the Avenger realized he was several times faster and stronger than the average human being with a gold-amber epidermis impenetrable by all but the highest jacketed caliber of ammunition. When he was not killing and feasting on only those who hunted him relentlessly, he spent his waking hours as a Protector within Central Park. And then all hell had broken loose this morning.

Avenger had dug his way out of his temporary warren in The Ramble not long before sunrise to begin his rounds, traveling back and forth across Central Park, doing his best to remain hidden behind shrubbery and trees, and even underwater for long periods of time.

Without notice, while he was silently skirting the park zoo, an intense flash of green light flooded downward from overhead and his triple eyelids automatically and without thought dropped down to protect his multi-faceted sight. A moment later normal sunlight replaced the earlier verdant incandescence. Avenger shrugged off the weird event and went back on his stalk for innocents harassed or worse by those he would target for his own brand of justice.

After moving toward the Summer Stage through trees for about four blocks paralleling Fifth avenue, Avenger stopped not far from the wide walkway known as The Mall and which led to the Bethesda Terrace. What he suddenly beheld stopped him in his tracks. He wiped his right palm across his eyes (it was only the backside of his hands that were covered with barbs that could punch through brick and concrete and score ten-point steel) to clear his vision, but it didn't work.

"What the hell…," Avenger growled under his breath, as it appeared to him that he had just entered a special effects movie. Suddenly forgetting about any attempt to hide himself from public sight, he moved toward The Mall. Walking back and forth on this walkway was a small host of people, but to Avenger's eyes, they fell into three distinctly different groups.

The first were just ordinary folks as real and solid looking as himself and it was among these pedestrians that attention fell upon him as about a dozen pulled out their cell phones to take shots of him while yelling "hello" and "keep kicking ass, Avenger!"

The second group of civilians looked like flickering richly colored holograms, translucent, and not quite solid. He could tell that the normal folks did not see these oddities as they regularly passed right through them as if they were not there at all.

And then came the third group, strangest of all, that looked like pure, clear transparent shells of people, no color to clothes or skin or hair, appearing as barely visible glassine wraiths. The normal people did not see them either and walked through them like they were mere apparitions. Avenger also noticed that the colored holograms and the clear transparent folks did not notice each other either, passing through one another without the slightest indication of awareness. It was as if three sets of people were out of sync with each other, but somehow sharing the same space.

Looking about himself Avenger realized that the trees and distant buildings all appeared weird, and he realized that he was experiencing some form of triple vision, as every stationary solid object seemed to have some kind of extra shadow or reflective double surface not quite in sync with it, giving them all an indistinct wavering appearance like anthropomorphic objects bouncing to jazzy music in old Warner Brothers cartoon shorts.

A loud scream suddenly distracted him as a woman and her child ran past him.

"They're coming from the ground," she yelled as he turned around, and then he saw them. Dozens, no, hundreds of spots on the surrounding soil pushed upwards as people, or corpses of people wearing decayed strips of clothes were crawling from the Earth and staggering toward shocked crowds. The first of the Zombies to dig their way out, a woman dressed in what looked like a sixties Go-Go Dancer shirt, mini-skirt, and knee-high boots, grabbed a shocked male groundskeeper and tore open his throat with her ravenous teeth. This snapped the surrounding crowds out of their shock and into full-blown panic and they fled in every direction amidst pure chaos.

Avenger, twice as fast as any Olympic gold medal sprinter, shot across the grass and directly at the Zombie that had just committed murder. With several rapid thrusts of his articulated fists, and the triple rows of blade-like spurs that covered the sides of his forearms and elbows, he carved the undead dancer into a pile of seven unmoving pieces of meat.

This action caught the attention of many of the surrounding zombies who instantly quit chasing the civilians and made a beeline for Avenger.

Fine by me, he thought, just makes it that much easier to get my mitts on you freaking abominations from hell.

What at first appeared to be a one-sided battle slowly turned into a merciless massacre as Avenger tore a relentless swath through the ever-growing number of undead that continued to surround and attack him. When five or more of them jumped him at the same time and knocked him to the ground, they instantly found that their clawing hands and jagged rotting teeth were no match for his stone hard amber skin that covered him from bald head to clawed toes. The great strength behind all four of his limbs, which were each covered in deadly diamond-hard and razor-sharp barbs, quickly tore the vile attackers apart, and he was back on his feet, faster, and much nimbler, than any of these disgusting abominations. The minutes flew by and the rancid smelling piles of body parts grew.

A few hours later, just as he finished eviscerating the last zombie in sight, a green flash of light, as bright as the one that had surprised him in the early morning, appeared and disappeared. Something felt very wrong and Avenger instantly realized that the piles of zombie body parts all around him had disappeared.

This just gets fucking weirder and weirder, he thought. Loud splashing sounds caught his attention and he sprinted toward the large manmade lake known as The Harlem Meer. Though no normal parkgoers were in sight as he ran, dozens of the colored hologram-like apparitions and glassine wraiths sprinted back and forth across the surrounding landscape in seeming panic, as if they were being chased by unseen terrors. As they were currently nothing more than unneeded distractions, Avenger did his best to ignore them from this point on, focusing on his efforts on the reality that he could affect.

In moments he reached the inner shore of The Meer and the shock of what he saw made his jaw drop, revealing the double set of contracted amber insect mandibles that hid within his mouth and were as deadly and powerful as every other part of his radically altered anatomy.

Walking into the water, park side, and beginning to swim across the lake toward the surrounding city, were decayed-looking eight-foot-tall wingless birds. Like all the human zombies Avenger had slaughtered earlier, these creature's eyes glowed green. Whatever the origin of these oddities, they were definitely something that had not walked on the Earth's surface for at least two million years. He instantly knew they were up to no good and sprinted down the beach slope and leaped upon the backs of the few stragglers that had not yet made it into the water. He made quick work of them and dove into the lake swimming rapidly and quickly catching up with the pack.

The giant feathered raptors soon heard his loud splashing and turned as one to converge on Avenger in the center of the lake from all sides. Soon the water boiled and frothed in the ensuing chaos of giant avian skull and beak sparring with Avenger's gauntleted appendages.

ØØØ

Walking back up the beach on the park side of the lake, a tired and limping Avenger dropped to the ground to gain some measure of recuperation. Scars, perhaps more accurately described as cracks in the jewel hard surface of his skin, ran along his skull, chest, and right hip. The raptors had beaks nearly as sharp as his own arm spurs and backed by their dense skulls had almost proven equal to his own unnatural weaponry. He'd never been harmed in this way before and had no idea how long it might take to heal, assuming such damage to his person could heal at all.

Hearing screams in the distance, Avenger stood back up and slowly jogged in the darkness in the general direction of The Ramble. Without notice another bright explosion of green light splashed across the surrounding landscape and just as quickly disappeared. No change had occurred to the surrounding land, but Avenger realized he could no longer hear screams from ahead. Perhaps he was too late to save any victims.

A few minutes later he entered the thirty-six-acre woodland retreat and climbed to the top of the tallest tree he could find to survey the territory. His night vision was unusually good and movement quickly caught his eye.

"Oh, you've got to be shitting me," he mumbled.

A couple of hundred feet away, what appeared to be a small herd of zombified dinosaur velociraptors were circling about fifty humans that had thrown together a makeshift circular wall of benches, trashcans, and whatever branches they could scrounge up. He knew they were velociraptors because he had been a huge fan of those ancient Jurassic Park movies when he was a little boy.

What is up with this crazy park? he thought. Pondering everything he had experienced over the course of a full day, a twisted sort of logic began to form in his mind. That first flash of green light followed by the triple image of people and objects, then that zombie woman dressed like someone from the sixties. Then another flash of light and he was facing giant zombified wingless birds that probably had not existed since shortly before the first hominids started dropping from the trees. A third flash of green light and now he was seeing zombie dinosaurs. Avenger knew that he wasn't simply moving backwards in time as most of the land's recognizable contours and manmade structures of the Park were clearly visible and exactly where they should be. Different eras of dead life were being resurrected, perhaps randomly or perhaps not. If only he could figure out the answer to this puzzle than maybe he could do more than simple battles and rescues, and finally put an end to this nightmare.

Screams filled the night as the velociraptors started attacking the hastily built barricade. He dropped from the trees and sprinted forward. How he would fare against these deadly ancient hunters was a question he had no answer for. Innocents were being threatened and there was no other palatable option in the ten-chambered heart of this former Medal of Honor recipient. They outnumbered him a dozen to one, and at first glance when they came into view it looked like they were seven feet tall, nearly as fast as him, with jagged rows of teeth and sharp foreclaws more than ready for battle.

When he had closed within ten yards of the nearest zombie dinosaur the entire pack all took notice of him and raised their heads as one to howl out a loud chorus of ear-piercing alien shrieks.

I guess it's Go Time, he thought.

Avenger and the nearest raptor leaped at each other simultaneously.

"Oorah!" the former Marine Sergeant Burt Buchowski yelled before his glistening golden form impacted with a vicious, resurrected creature that had not existed on planet Earth in seventy-one million years.

# Fire Within, Fire Below

## by Gustavo Bondoni

*"The moon is dark, and the gods dance in the night; there is terror in the sky, for upon the moon has sunk an eclipse foretold in no books of men or of earth's gods."*

— *H.P. Lovecraft*

**K**AREN HELD THE SOLDIER'S GAZE, unflinching.

"If you want to stop me, you're going to have to shoot me. Are you willing to do that?"

She nervously fidgeted with an orange plastic bracelet, the one they'd put on her wrist at the hospital when her second daughter had been born, premature and with heart trouble. It was the only sign that she was scared. She'd been wearing it when the little girl died in the neonatal ward. She remembered seeing it as striking the window to the ICU when the doctor told her the news, remembered seeing it on her wrist while her fist struck the glass. Weak blows. Ineffectual.

She hadn't taken it off in the six months since and had taken to fidgeting it when nervous. It was a part of her, now.

The troops shuffled their feet, letting their leader do the talking. He was an enormous man with dark chocolate skin who looked to be around forty. He had three chevrons on his arm. Karen had no idea what that might mean, for all she knew, the guy might be a five-star general. "No, ma'am. We won't shoot you. Don't have to. Any one of us could immobilize you in a second."

"I need to get into the Park. My daughter is in there."

"There's some weird stuff happening in the Park, ma'am."

She looked around the man. Central Park South was deserted, and she could see soldiers in the distance, at Columbus Circle. But apart from the troops barring her way very little could be seen in the way of weirdness. The trees in front of her looked the same as they always did: a wall of green rising from the sidewalk, pierced by the Drive at Sixth Avenue. The only thing missing was the usual horde of tourists. On a hot midsummer's day, they should have been everywhere.

"It looks the same as it always does. And I already told you, I'm going in."

"No, you're not. I don't want to have to arrest you. Cable ties are very uncomfortable and we weren't issued with handcuffs, so that's we've got. Do yourself a favor and just stop."

Karen fought to control herself, to keep from crying. "Are you even listening to me? My three-year-old is in there, just a five-minute walk from right here. Her summer play group was at the carousel and the den mother just texted me to go get her. I'm not abandoning my kid, and I don't believe you're going to tie me up like some terrorist for that."

"I'd certainly rather not, but it's my stripes if you go in there. I have my orders."

"Screw your orders."

"Ma'am…"

He never got to finish his warning. A flash of light, deep inside the park, made him close his eyes. Karen, who had her back to it, saw the man's uniform, the buildings behind him, the entire world suddenly turn green.

"Son of a…" the soldiers rubbed their eyes and blinked.

But Karen didn't stop to help. Even just reflected off the walls of the city's skyscrapers, that green light was the most evil thing she'd ever seen. It twisted her in gut and hurt her exposed skin.

And Brittany was in the Park with whatever caused it.

She ran for the nearest entrance, not even stopping to wonder how long the soldiers might be incapacitated.

Karen barely even gave a second thought to the unexpected resistance she encountered when she left the sidewalk and her feet hit the path. Normally having the air bend and stretch as if trying to stop her would have scared the hell out of her. Any other time she would have run back the way she'd come as fast as she could.

But the invisible barrier gave way and she stumbled into the Park.

What drove her was too close to her heart for her brain to interfere.

Sergeant Williams swatted the M4 down, pointing the muzzle towards the street.

"Hold your fire, soldier," he said.

"But she's getting away, Sarge," Corporal Santillán replied. She was five feet tall and thin as a rail, but what she lacked in physical size she more than compensated for in feistiness.

"That woman isn't the enemy," Corporal.

"I know that, sir. I was going to shoot her in the leg to keep her safe. There's some bad juju in that park."

Williams controlled his smile. Only Santillán would shoot a civilian to keep her safe. "There hasn't been anything reported in this sector, soldier."

"Did you not see the green light?" She didn't look happy.

"I saw it."

"That looked close enough for me."

"I know. Ngo, call in the incident."

"Sure thing, sarge."

Williams waited for his comms to bring back the reply. "Can't raise anyone, sir. All I'm getting is static."

*Of course.* It was the Army way, after all. Things would always work until the very moment you needed them. Actually, things never worked, but they *particularly* didn't work when you needed them.

He looked to his right, to see whether the soldiers at Columbus Circle were doing anything.

There were no troops at Columbus Circle. There were no buildings there either. All he could see in the distance was a pale mist, tinged with green.

He thought of the desperate woman walking into the Park, alone, he thought of the summer play group of three-year-olds. He squeezed the stock of his own rifle.

"Screw this," he said. "Soldiers, we're moving out."

"Which way?" Santillán said.

Williams nodded toward the park. "What do you think?"

"I think we'll all get kicked out of the army. I thought you said our orders were to stay where we were, come hell or high water."

"Well, the situation's changed and we can't reach the Lieutenant. So, we have to act on our own initiative."

"Yeah, that worried mother was kinda cute, wasn't she? Just your type, too: blonde and innocent-looking."

Williams ignored the jibe. "She is a citizen in danger who informed us of other citizens in danger. Kids in danger. We're moving out."

"Hey, no need to get pissed. I was already moving. I want to see what's in there and kick some ass."

"Yeah, I know."

He left one private and Ngo, his comms guy, not actually part of his squad, but assigned specially for this mission, with the Humvee and motioned for the other seven soldiers under his command to follow him. Every instinct was telling him to have his troops assume some kind of cover formation…but it would have felt ridiculous. They were literally crossing the street to take a walk in the park.

They strode across Central Park South, each alert for anything out of the ordinary, but each also wondering what all the fuss was about. They trusted the powers that be to know what the hell they were doing…but each of them had also been assigned to useless duties before. Williams knew exactly what they were thinking.

Corporal Santillán was on point. She stopped suddenly and looked back, confused. "There's something here," she said, pushing her hand against the air in front of her.

"I don't see anything."

"Come and feel for yourself."

Williams did as he was told. She might have lost her mind, but until he made certain of it, he would take the Corporal seriously. She wasn't the kind to screw around.

One second, he was walking along with no idea that anything might be amiss, and the next, he stopped. The sensation was akin to running into a spider's web, invisible strands slowing his progress, barely felt. But these strands were strong enough to slow him significantly. He stopped.

"That lady pushed through," Santillan said. "I saw her stop right here and then she kept going. I figure we can get through as well."

"Yeah, but do we want to?"

Williams sensed that the quick jaunt in and out of the Park, the one he could easily hide from superiors who had other things to worry about, was spiraling out of control. This suddenly impenetrable wall of air, he knew, was the boundary beyond which he could not even pretend to have been following his orders.

His stripes, and an eighteen-year career, were pretty much forfeit if he took another step.

"Oh, come on, Sarge. You're not gonna go chicken on me now, will you? You saved her from getting shot in the butt. Fine. But that means we need to go in there and protect her from whatever is happening on the other side of this Jell-O curtain."

"Damn you, Corporal."

Santillán gave him a wide grin but said nothing. She knew when she'd won.

Williams returned the grin. "Ladies first," he said.

The corporal didn't argue. Using the barrel of her M4 like a pin in a balloon, she pressed ahead. Williams was sure he could actually see the barrier, a film ahead of them, just slightly greenish in the surrounding air, stretched out by the gun and, then, with a stumble, Santillán was through. She turned around and pressed against the barrier to return, but it seemed to resist her efforts, so she shrugged and turned in towards the park.

Williams followed, and did exactly the same thing. On the inside, the barrier, whatever the hell it might be, felt like a brick wall. No one was getting out that way.

He motioned his men to follow him and wondered how you got decent counsel during a court martial.

"I have got such a bad feeling about this," he said to Santillán.

"I thought sergeants weren't allowed to have feelings," she responded. "Don't they beat that out of you at sergeant school?"

"You're in a good mood."

"We're finally doing something. Weren't you tired of sitting on your ass waiting for the world to end? Admit it."

"Whatever. Let's get ourselves organized."

Two concrete paths snaked up a hill. According to his maps of the area— the best was actually a subway map with a big MTA logo on it—the walkways snaked to either side of a playground while the one on the right eventually passed near the carousel. If there were kids inside, they would be in one of those two places.

If they were still alive, that is.

"Take the path on the right," he ordered.

Carlos Báez gritted his teeth. His stomach fluttered, but he knew he'd run out of choices: there was no next paycheck coming, and if he wanted to eat that night, he needed to man up and take what he needed. Fortunately, Central Park was considered one of the safest places in the city. There had been something like four muggings in total in the past year.

The woman approaching along the secluded lane certainly didn't seem particularly alert.

But then, why would she? She was maybe thirty yards from Columbus Circle, an office worker taking off early—it was just about four o'clock—or an executive returning from a late lunch.

Yeah, that was probably it. The woman looked about thirty, with straight black hair—shoulder-length—and an expensive-looking black and white suit. Her heels didn't seem suitable for long-distance hikes through the Park, but he'd seen enough New York fashion silliness to know that she might actually be heading for Harlem. You couldn't take common sense for granted in the city.

She was still about twenty yards away, close enough that she would spot him as soon as she turned her head. Just in case, he placed the sweating hand that held the switchblade behind his right buttock, hiding it from view.

Strangely, though, the woman didn't appear to be looking towards him, or watching where she was going. She had her head turned to look straight back, towards the street, fifteen feet above. And then she looked downwards, towards something right behind her, hidden from Carlos by a turn in the path.

She broke into a run. Now she was looking in Carlos' direction, but ignoring him. After a couple of steps, she kicked off the shoes and just abandoned them where they fell, sprinting in his direction in the uncomfortable work clothes.

He didn't stop to wonder how or why he'd gotten so lucky. He timed his movements perfectly and stepped right into her path. She slammed into him at full speed.

Carlos expected her to apologize or to insult him for not looking where he was going. Instead, she froze for an instant, long enough for him to slice the leather strap holding her purse on her shoulder.

She didn't even seem to notice what he'd done. She just shook her head and ran off in the same direction she'd been going, deeper into the Park.

Carlos couldn't understand it. He looked to see what she was running from, but there was nothing there but something that looked like wisps of smoke in the wind. One passed and caressed his face, then another. It was weird, but it certainly didn't seem like something that would terrify anyone used to New York weirdness into unheeding flight. Hell, it was probably just steam from some manhole cover.

Then, a few feet away, the smoke got thicker. He watched incredulously as it coalesced into a dark shape. His knees locked in place and he realized how much braver the woman he'd just robbed was than he could ever be; she had managed to run. He was frozen to the spot.

The form facing him, eye to eye, was a wolf or a dog of some sort. But if it was really there, and not just a product of his imagination, it was the biggest he'd ever seen. It was, perhaps, two feet tall at the head, but bulky. Carlos estimated that it had to weigh more than he did, and it was well-muscled to boot. He had no doubt that it could kill him without help.

But it had plenty of help. Behind the leader, a pack of them appeared.

Each had dark grey fur which seemed unhealthy somehow, enormous tufts sticking out as if about to fall away. And they smelled like something that had been dead for days.

The leader looked him straight in the eye and Carlos realized that what he'd thought was a reflection, was nothing of the sort. The animal's eyes glowed with a light of their own…an evil green light. A light that was a twin to the violent flash in the sky just minutes before.

The beast stared at him and Carlos felt himself being weighed, measured…

And accepted. A single nod from the beast, followed by a grown that was more of a moan, a sickly gurgle, and they were off in a body.

He watched them streak up the path and overtake the woman, still visible nearly fifty yards away. A piercing scream was cut short, and she disappeared beneath the pack. They seemed to be feeding, like vultures on a carcass in a nature documentary.

That brought Carlos back to his senses. It was one thing to cut a leather strap and try to steal a purse and quite another to be arrested in the vicinity of a badly mutilated corpse.

Especially if the corpse's purse had your fingerprints all over it.

There was a path up to street level just a few steps away. He sprinted over and headed for Central Park West right at the corner of the Park. He was surprised to see it was deserted at that time of day. Normally, this area would be carpeted with tourists. Better this way. The fewer witnesses, the less he'd worry.

Carlos redoubled his pace. On the street, he could lose himself in the bustle of the city.

He slammed into a wall and fell, nose bleeding, back into the Park.

"That's not the way out," a voice said. "Not for you, anyway."

A tall, rail-thin guy in a black overcoat and fedora stood just beside the stairs. He smiled and flashed a gold tooth that was more unsettling than anything else he'd seen so far. It seemed to reflect everything back at him.

He raised a hand in self-defense and realized he was still clutching the blade, still open. "Don't mess with me, man. I've got a knife and I'm not afraid to use it."

The tall guy pushed himself off the wall and took a step toward Carlos, but he did so slowly, non-threateningly. "You're afraid, all right. Completely petrified. But you're afraid of all the wrong things."

"Oh, yeah?"

The smile widened and the gold tooth shone even more. "Yeah."

"So what should I be afraid of? Those wolf things?"

"Dire wolves? It would be a good start. But I'd be more worried about the fact that they didn't kill you."

Carlos chuckled and lowered the knife a bit. This guy might be weird, but he didn't seem threatening. "Of all the things that happened to me today, that was the only thing that went right."

"When Hell's beings recognize you as one of their own, I wouldn't say that's a good thing."

"Better than being dead."

The guy looked into Carlos' eyes. "Being alive is more immediately useful, perhaps. You might even have enough time to end this on the right side."

"I don't know what you're talking about, man."

"No. I don't imagine you do. But I have something you need all the same. Even if you don't know you need it."

He was suddenly wary. "What?"

"This." The man in black held up a metal band.

Carlos eyed it critically. It was yellowish, but certainly didn't look like gold. "Doesn't look like much."

"I didn't say it was what you wanted. I said it's what you need."

"A metal ring?"

"A brass ring."

"And how much do you want for it?" Carlos sat back to hear the outrageous opening price. Living poor in New York had made him a prime connoisseur of the art of the hustle.

"I don't take money. I make trades. Give me that purse, and I'll give you the ring."

Carlos realized he was still holding the leather pocketbook with its severed strap. Every cell in his body resisted the request: this was his first scalp, proof to himself that he had the balls to actually rob another human being…even if the conditions had been a little unconventional.

Then his mind kicked in. This thing was the most damning kind of evidence. You really didn't want to be caught holding the possessions of a murder victim… and unless those big dogs had simply wanted to play, that woman was bound for a slab at the morgue on Twenty-Eighth Street.

If there was enough left of her to take over there.

He handed the tall guy the purse. The other man flipped the ring high into the air.

Carlos watched it twirl, end over end, reaching the top of its parabola and start coming down. He reached out and grabbed it, then turned to face the man who'd traded for it, a satisfied grin on his face.

The tall guy was nowhere to be seen.

Karen stopped to look around and to try her phone. No service; no surprise.

There was something really off about the Park today.

It wasn't so much that there was no one on the path with her. Even on sunny summer days, some walkways were more heavily used than others, and this particular one, the one that led from the Seventh Avenue entrance up the hill towards the playground, normally held only light traffic. Instead of a gentle walk around the steep hill, this particular path went straight up, like a Roman road, cresting the hill and skirting a jagged outcropping of the granite that ran beneath the Park.

It wasn't even the silence. Though unnatural for summer, she'd been in the Park in winter often enough that the quiet didn't unduly disturb her.

It took Karen a few moments to put her finger on it, but when she did, she shuddered. The air was the wrong color.

It wasn't just a trick of the light, either. Or maybe it was, but it was everywhere. The air was tinted—almost imperceptibly—green, as if the light that had exploded earlier had never quite gone away. The effect wasn't visible unless she looked at the trees and the grass: they were much less green than they should have been. The contrast had disappeared.

The entrance to the playground nestled in a hollow below. The enclosure was entered through tunnel between two blocks of restrooms: one side held women's room and girl's room, the other, men and boys. A roof united the blocks and formed a short tunnel.

There were figures in the playground, but most of them were streaming out the exit. Brightly dressed children and sedately attired adults seemed to be leaving in droves. She saw one little girl in blue speed away on a scooter.

Karen began to run that way.

"Just a second," a voice said. The words were soft, but the voice powerful enough to stop a frantic mother in her tracks. She looked over to see a tall man in black wearing a hat from the seventies staring intently at her. "There's nothing in nature as dangerous as a mother lion, but even mother lions sometimes need help," he said.

*Oh, great. A Lunatic.* "Look, man, I'm kind of in a hurry here."

He nodded. "Yes. We all are. These are the strangest of days. Sha'Daa, you know." Karen didn't. She had no idea what he was talking about. "But sometimes, it's worth stopping. Have you thought about what you're going to do when you get down there?"

"I'm going to grab Brittany and run like hell."

"Hell has other ideas, I'm afraid." A smile that looked more like a grimace displayed a golden tooth that shone greenly.

Though her whole body screamed at her to *go*, Karen found herself mesmerized by the guy. "And what do you know about that?" She looked him up and down. "You some kind of preacher?"

"No. I deal in more worldly goods. You could say I'm a salesman. Johnny's the name."

"Well, Johnny. Great to meet you. I'm out of here."

"Not without this, you aren't. Without this, you'll still be here four hours from now…except you won't be breathing. And neither will little Brittany."

"What in the world is that?" It was a metallic thing, smaller than her fist, elongated on one side.

"It's what you need. A whistle. A very special whistle."

"Why would I need that?"

"It's the only way to make yourself heard around here."

"Whatever. How much is it?"

"I'll take that plastic bracelet."

Karen felt her stomach turn over. "No. Keep it," she said. "I've already wasted too much time here as it is."

She ran down the hill into the crowd of young and mature people. Suddenly the Park wasn't deserted anymore. It seemed to be filled to capacity… and every single one of the people inside was coming out of the entrance to the playground.

Karen craned her head, trying to spot any sign of Brittany. What had she been wearing? A white t-shirt and green sweatpants. Where was she?

There! A white shirt scurried between two large women and Karen raced after it. But it wasn't Brittany. Another little girl with brown tresses cried for her mother.

"Come here," Karen said, her heart breaking for the child while the rest of her cried out to ignore the strange kid and focus on finding her own daughter, the only one she had left.

But she couldn't. The little girl would get trampled. She pushed through the crowd and deposited the crying munchkin on a clear stretch of grass. Then she turned back to the multitude.

"No. Don't go, please."

She hesitated, torn, and a hand came into view in front of her. It was holding the silver whistle. "Really, you need to take this. You don't have a lot of time…they're nearly here."

"Who is?"

"Listen." An inhuman, impossible howl filled the air, torn from a ragged throat. "You need this. Give me the bracelet."

"It's the only thing I have of her. They wouldn't let me hold her after she died."

"I know. But you still have the other one. Let's make the trade."

"Screw you," Karen snarled. She slid her finger under the orange band and pulled with all her might. The plastic stretched and finally snapped. She handed it over and snatched at the whistle. "This had better work."

But the guy was gone, leaving her with a gaping wound in her heart and a silver trinket she didn't know when to use.

"Well, no time like the present."

She blew into the whistle and felt…something go out. Whatever it was, though, it wasn't sound. The thing didn't make any noise.

"Dammit. I should have known," she said.

She was about to throw the silver bauble away in disgust when movement caught her eye. The milling crowd was thinning out, all of it turning north as soon as it left the playground like lemmings off a cliff.

All but one.

A tiny white speck was moving against the tide, head cocked as if listening for something.

"Over here!" Karen cried.

But Brittany couldn't hear her.

Karen blew the whistle again. Nothing happened except that Brittany's head came up.

Their eyes met and Brittany ran forward. Seconds later, she was in her mother's arms.

"Thank god," Karen said, and buried her face in her daughter's hair.

Brittany looked up eyes wide. "Mommy, you need to blow it again. Blow more."

"What?"

"Now, mommy!"

Karen looked up to see…something…approaching. Lots of somethings, in fact. Grey, lithe forms. Animals.

"Blow!"

Karen obeyed automatically. She lifted the whistle to her mouth and blew as hard as she could.

"Don't stop. Please don't stop."

The front rank was almost upon them, and she could see individual animals. "You've got to be kidding me," she said between puffs. She held the two little girls close. Even if they'd wanted to run, it was too late. The creatures were too close.

They were huge wolves. Saber-toothed tigers. Mammoths. Friggin' mammoths. Even some enormous kind of jumbo-sized armadillo. A whole bunch of other critters.

Every single one of them had glowing green eyes.

She took another breath to blow again and gagged. The stench was over-powering, but it wasn't the smell of wild animals—it was the stench of rotting meat. And every animal in the crowd was grey, with pieces of fur sloughing off in great clumps.

They looked like zombies from a Romero film. One of the bad Romero films.

And even without the evil glow of the green eyes, everyone knew that when zombies roamed the land, the state of living was temporary. She hugged the children close and, just to do something, kept blowing into the whistle. The end was a second away. Soon, the nearest of the saber-tooth tigers would lunge, and it would be over. She hoped it was quick, at least for the girls. They didn't deserve to suffer.

But the strike she expected didn't come. The malodorous tide coming over them parted like the Red Sea and passed to either side.

Karen kept blowing into the whistle. Her lungs felt like they were going to burst. Her throat burned. Her lips were cramping up. Every time she took a breath, she was certain that the putrid air entering her lungs dripped with every bacteria that had ever lived…but she kept blowing because whenever she stopped to breathe, she was sure the animals on either side looked in their direction, that they came closer.

Eventually, the thundering herd passed, leaving behind churned grass, the funk of forty thousand years and piles of discarded fur, skin and viscera. Flies began to congregate.

Karen released the sobbing girls. Brittany didn't want to let go, but the other girl looked up at her. "I want to find my mom," she said.

She looked to be about four. Maybe a small five. "What's your name, honey?"

"I'm Jessie," she said. "My mom is called Grace. Will you help me find her?"

"Of course, Jessie. We'll find her. Where did you see her last?"

"In the playground. Everyone started walking suddenly, and I got pushed by a bunch of big kids and when I got up, my mother was gone."

"Which way were they going?"

Jessie pointed.

She pointed where the people had gone.

It was also the same direction the zombie herd had disappeared in.

"What the hell?" Santillán shouted. A quick, three-shot burst to the head took down what looked like a lion that had jumped out of a clump of bushes and torn a private's arm off.

"Bad mothers," Williams replied. "Just look at the eyes."

"I think I could have told you that without any extra clues, ya know?"

"Yeah, I guess you could. Anyone trained as a medic?"

"Nope."

"Figures. Pick him up and—"

Williams never finished. With a deafening roar and a putrescent breeze, something the size of an APC charged out of the trees.

They dived to the side to avoid getting trampled but the…enormous furry elephant?.. was followed by armored turtles or something.

"Shoot them!" Hicks shouted. He opened fire.

The armored things—Williams thought they looked kinda like some fossilized armadillos he'd seen in a natural history museum, glyptodons or something like that—went down easily. A single shot to the head was enough to dispatch them.

The mammoth was another story. As Hicks peppered its flanks, the behemoth turned in his direction, rotting ivory tusks slimy in the greenish air. The huge head lowered and the animal charged.

To his credit, Hicks didn't flinch. He poured half a magazine into the thing's skull, and he would have stood his ground to empty the magazine if he hadn't taken a ten-foot-long tusk to the gut.

His scream was the loudest, most painful yell Williams had ever heard. It echoed in the Park and went on and on and on as the mammoth tossed its head and made a soufflé of Hicks' entrails.

"You bastard!" Santillán shouted. She opened up.

But her fire made no difference. The ugly, rotting thing was already mortally wounded. Hicks had taken it out even as he, himself, died. The mammoth collapsed on top of him.

A roar in the woods brought them out of their shock. More animals were coming, hundreds of them.

"Run!" Williams shouted to his surviving soldiers. "Up that rock over there. We can hold out all day." *Or*, he thought, *until we run out of bullets*.

They made it up and Williams counted heads. Five soldiers remained of the eight who'd entered the Park. He'd seen two of them die and hoped his final man had simply run in a different direction. He wasn't optimistic on that score.

Most of the animals walked on, ignoring the soldiers. Only a few made a desultory attempt to climb the granite outcrop. They slid back down without a shot being fired.

"It's all fun and games until the terror birds show up," a voice said.

They turned to see a guy in a trench coat and a fedora, looking like he'd just emerged from the pages of an old detective comic.

"Where did you come from?"

"Oh, here and there. My name is Johnny. I'm what you'd call a salesman."

"Yeah. We need you like a fish needs a bicycle."

Johnny grinned. Gold glinted. "Funny. But you might need me more than you think. I have what you need."

"I have everything I need right here," Williams said, showing the guy his M4.

"Firepower isn't much use unless you know where to direct it, is it?"

"We're going to stay right here and blow up anything that looks like it might be coming up the hill."

"Sounds like a fine plan, except for one thing…you're supposed to be protecting the citizenry, not saving your own butts. This isn't helping that blond woman, is it?"

Williams caught the man's gaze and looked away.

Johnny broke the silence. "Okay, you wanna trade?"

"What do you have for us?"

"This." He pulled out a folded rectangle of paper about six inches across. Williams began unfolding and soon had a map about a yard square.

"What is this?"

"It's a map."

"Yeah, I can see that. But what is it of?"  He studied it. The diagram depicted what appeared to be a complex of some kind. One of the buildings had a huge, eight-pointed star in the center, and the rest were united by tortuous corridors. "Looks like the plans to some kind of industrial installation. And what are all these weird symbols?  Half of this isn't even in English. The rest looks like an old War Department document from World War II."

"I'm impressed. You know your military history."

"Yeah. I also know that I've never been anywhere near this place, and I doubt I'll have time to get there today. I have a feeling I might be a bit busy with the zombie wildlife."

"You'll know the place when you see it."

Williams knew he should send the freak to hell, but something about the intensity of Johnny's gaze made him stop. There was something so sincere about him.

"What do you want for it?" Williams asked, struggling to fold the map back the way it had been.

"Those insignias on your shoulders," Johnny replied.

Williams glared at him. "You've got to be kidding. I *earned* those. Besides, they aren't just velcroed on."

"If you'll just let me…" Johnny placed his hand on Williams' left shoulder and it came away with his sergeant's insignia. A second later he did the other arm. Williams didn't even feel the thread give way.

"Three stripes for each arm makes six in total. It's a fair trade."

He walked down the hill, apparently unconcerned that the area was infested with undead wildlife and was soon out of sight. Williams nearly called him back to tell him that the deal was off, but he didn't. He knew that he'd forfeited the insignia of the U.S. Army when he'd knowingly disobeyed his orders and entered the Park.

But what was he supposed to do? Let a mother desperately searching for her child go into a theater that the Pentagon had told them would be dangerous even for seasoned troops, and to go in alone?

No. The army he could answer to, but his conscience was another matter entirely.

He turned to his troops. "Well, you heard the man; we're not doing anyone much good up here. How about we get a move on?"

Santillán peered around. "Yeah, there doesn't seem to be much enemy activity down there."

"Enemy?" Williams said with a grin. "Those didn't look like combatants to me, Corporal."

"Anything with eyes like that is the enemy, Sarge."

They climbed back down the hillock. The rock was worn by the feet of countless tourists. He normally hated the hordes of people who flocked to any attraction no matter how banal but today he would have loved to see them.

They confirmed that the two soldiers they'd been forced to leave behind were, indeed, dead, and that the last guy wasn't around before heading east, where the playground was supposed to be.

"Over there," Santillán pointed.

Looks empty to me.

"Not quite. Look at that stone fort."

"What I'd give to have your eyes, Corporal. All I see are some colored blobs. What have you got?"

"I make it a couple of kids and an adult." She turned to look at him. "The adult seems to be your blond chick, and all three of them seem to be moving around. Unless they're zombies, they look like they're OK,"

"Well, whoever they are, we need to get down there. They're civilians in danger."

"Right on."

It took them a couple of minutes to reach the playground. They had to scale some tricky rocks and then walk down a concrete fort which some genius had decided would make a good water game. A current ran down the stone like a miniature river which cascaded down several stone levels.

"Modern moms must be more tolerant than my old lady," Williams said. "If I'd gotten wet every day at the playground in Springfield, she would have had the mayor lynched. Or she would have lynched him herself."

They climbed down carefully and walked across. The three figures watched them cautiously.

Williams saluted. "Ma'am, what you did was reckless and unnecessary."

The woman didn't flinch. "It was exactly the right thing to do. This is Brittany." She hugged her daughter. "And this is Jessie. We need to find her mom."

"We're doing nothing of the sort. We're going to find a defensible position and hunker down until we get backup. I've already lost three men because of you."

"We might as well stay here," Santillán said. "This little stone dome looks like a good spot to fight. Or we could use the concrete fort, but that would mean getting our feet wet."

"I'm going to find her mom. She went that way."

"That's the way the animals were going, Ma'am."

"Then I guess I'll be going without you."

Williams shook his head. "I admit you're brave, but this is just silly. You'll get yourself torn to pieces. If you won't stop for your own sake, at least think of the kids."

"There's a kid here who needs her mom."

"Um…guys?" one of the soldiers broke in.

"What?"

"We've got incoming."

Williams looked. He rubbed his eyes and looked again. "What the hell is that?"

The soldier, a young private from Alabama, said: "I guess that must be what the man referred to when he said we should look out for the terror birds."

It was an accurate description. Zigzagging towards them up the path were a multitude of giant ostrich-like creatures. They moved slowly on wicked clawed feet and stared madly around in every direction. Feathers fell like rain, leaving them mangy and mottled. Their exposed skin was dotted with festering sores.

"I thought they would fly."

"Things that big don't need to fly," the soldier said. "What in the world are they?"

Williams glanced at the woman. "Any ideas?"

"No. But I would say they've been dead for a long time."

"Yeah, we kinda realized that. Don't get a lot of living zombies around."

"Not that kind of dead. More like extinct. I saw a saber tooth tiger earlier. And a mammoth. We're getting hit with stuff that's been dead for…. I don't know…a billion years or whatever."

"That makes no sense," Williams replied.

"Tell them."

The terror birds marched on, apparently unconcerned about whether they made sense or not. The front ranks reached the fence at the southern end of the playground and simply hopped over with little difficulty. Some of them had to be at least ten feet tall.

The enormous slide and swing sets crumbled like matchwood under the combined weight of the onslaught. The next fence, between the playground for larger children and the rubber-floored area for smaller tykes was only about three feet high. It collapsed immediately.

"We don't have enough ammo to take them all out," Williams shouted. "Can we get inside the stone dome?"

Williams looked over the dome. It was a great position to keep unarmed opponents at bay. The structure was a hemisphere twenty feet in diameter at the base, solidly built of concrete and lined with stones. Kids could climb up and down without too much danger of hurting themselves in a fall onto the rubberized floor. The back side had a couple of slides that allowed kids to drop into a sandlot.

The most interesting feature was that tunnels pierced the dome: one, vertical opened up to a ladder at the top while a second, horizontal, allowed, in normal circumstances, kids to crawl in.

Now, Williams decided, a rifleman in each could easily tear the birds a new one.

"You and you stay with me," he motioned to a couple of soldiers. "Santillán, I need you to take Hermes and make a run for it with the woman. We'll try to hold the birds here."

She hesitated, about to argue.

"That's an order, corporal. Now go." Santillan herded the woman towards the exit ear the bathrooms. Then they turned north.

Williams put one soldier in each of the two ground-level holes and stationed himself at the top of the ladder. For a heart-stopping second, he thought the birds were going to go after Santillán's group. In a near-panic, he squeezed off a shot which, more through luck than marksmanship blew the orange-sized head of one of the birds clear off its neck. The beast collapsed.

The sound got their attention, and the birds turned en masse, displaying the incredible coordinated movements of a flock in flight—even though they were neither a flock nor flying. The birds charged.

"Oh, good. Now they're pissed," one of the soldiers said.

Williams had to smile. They might get pecked to pieces by rotten beaks or clawed to smithereens, but you could always count on the pessimistic understatement of what passed for humor among the enlisted men. He always though he'd rather die defending his country—or whatever it was he was doing now—than give that up.

Now he was going to get his opportunity.

The early birds got the slugs. They shot quickly, using their rifles' three-burst functionality and dropping a bird per burst, or maybe more.

But there were too many of them to stop before they reached the dome, and quite soon, the first one rushed up the side of the dome towards the opening where Williams waited.

He took great pleasure in blowing it to pieces, but the joy was short-lived another replaced it almost immediately. Three more came after that.

Soon, he was forced to retreat into the hole, or risk getting clawed to shreds. He found the other two men waiting for him, stooped inside the too-small tunnel at the base of the ladder.

"We got swamped, sarge," one reported.

Williams looked past him and smiled. The carcass of one of the giant birds blocked the entrance almost completely. Nothing was going to get in that way unless a bunch of birds that couldn't have been too smart to begin with—and were now zombies—managed to figure out about blocked holes.

The other side had been dealt with the same way.

The stench brought tears to their eyes.

"This can't be good for us," Williams said.

"You want to go out there and tell them to go away?"

"Nah, I'm good."

An undead bird fell on the other soldier with a wet plop. It flopped around a bit before the remaining man put a bullet in it.

"Great, now I'm deaf," the fallen soldier griped once the echoes had died away.

"But you're alive."

"Yeah. For now," Williams said. "But we're not going to be able to seal the hole up there."

Several beady-eyed heads looked quizzically down on them. Evil green glow filled the tiny enclosure.

"How about going down?" the soldier covered in gloop from the bird asked, pointing to a manhole cover at the base of the ladder.

Williams sighed. "I don't even want to think of the kind of undead critters we're going to run into underground." Memories of alligators in the New York Sewer system filled his mind.

But it was the only way out. He bent to see if they could shift the thing.

Carlos watched the parade.

Grey, dead creatures herded a long line of people uptown towards Sixty-Sixth Street. They moved slowly but steadily along the paths and, where possible, through the grass, trampling the weak green fences the Park Authority used to denote where people should and shouldn't go.

Carlos knew no one paid any attention to the fences. Well, no one who mattered did, anyway. Maybe some stockbrokers from the Street or some newbie just in from the Midwest. But not real New Yorkers.

The animals, at least in that regard, were about as real as New Yorkers got.

Every once in a while, someone, usually a young guy, tried to break away. Maybe they spotted a gap in the animals, maybe they were more afraid of what would happen when they arrived than they were of facing the creatures. Whatever the case, he never got far.

The latest was a muscular black guy in his twenties wearing a dark blue t-shirt and long shorts. Carlos watched in admiration as he vaulted over a couple of lions into a large patch empty of animals and then leaped the fence between the path and the ball fields.

He made it halfway across the diamond before a brace of tigers with enormous teeth ran him down and butchered him.

"Damn. Good show, but not quite enough," Carlos muttered to himself.

It was disturbing to watch, especially when the animals ate someone who didn't try to run—a woman or a child. But worse still was the animals' attitude towards Carlos himself.

First came the smell, the unmistakable stench of an open grave. Then an animal appeared, anything from huge rats to mammoths. Green-eyed scrutiny followed and then the animal equivalent of a shrug before the creature wandered off again. It wasn't quite acceptance, but more a sense of… indifference.

On one hand, he was terrified of the moment the indifference turned to aggression but, on the other, he wanted it. Being ignored by these creatures left him feeling unclean.

He followed the rotting migration as it drove the humans in its path, a travesty of the natural order. In the distance, he could see the carousel. He remembered going there as a treat when he was a snot-nosed kid. Nowadays, he knew the Park was just a few minutes by subway from the bustle of the Lower West Side, where he could get work sometimes, but back then he'd believed that Central Park, with its well-tended green lanes and shiny concessions, some of them actually housed in *buildings*, was on the other side of the world. Perhaps it was, in the same way that Manhattan was pretty much the other side of the world from Brooklyn's Fourth Avenue. Even the walk to the subway at Union Street was an exercise in gentrification from his house.

It was a treat for Sundays in Autumn, when the charms of Coney Island's Boardwalk paled due to the wind off the Atlantic. Wind was never a problem in Central Park, and you could eat ice cream until October. The best days were the ones where his parents had enough saved up to go to the Zoo.

But those were infrequent. More often, they would walk past the entrance and his father would take one look at the prices and curse the tourists. He thought he was doing it under his breath, but Carlos could hear every word.

They would go to the Carousel, then. Two rides each. That was what his dad could afford, so that was what they got. Carlos remembered being happy about it, too.

The happiness, however, was always tinged with a little sadness. Standing in front of the merry-go-round was a green pillar just a little bit taller than he was. It told the story of a little girl.

The little girl's favorite place in the entire Park had been this carousel, but then she died. She was still a little girl when she died, so her parents had paid to repair the ride so other girls and boys could enjoy it. He'd cried the first time he heard the story—he'd been too young to read, then—and every time he got off the ride, he touched the pillar and hoped the little girl was happy that he'd had a good time, wherever she was.

Of course, his father had descended further and further into drink, and the money for the rides—even the money for the subway—had dried up. He'd been seven years old the last time he'd been there.

Now, fists clenched, he watched a column of evil desecrate the temple of his childhood, his last happy memories. He was angry, the kind of angry that got people who crossed him beat up. The kind that had landed him in a holding cell more than once after a night's drinking. The kind that, once, had…

He preferred not to think about that. No body, no crime.

So he watched to keep himself from remembering and as he watched, the anger turned into amazement. He'd seen hundreds of people pressed onto the rotating platform, many more than the tiny enclosure could hold…and yet none of them came out and the animals returned empty.

It made no sense, and yet it was happening not fifty yards from where he stood.

The animals herded the last of the tractable people onto the ride and were left with one final victim. She struggled and was torn apart. Thus, relieved of their burden, the animals went purposefully off. He knew, without knowing how he knew, that they'd gone in search of new victims, that the Park was being scoured of humanity, and that those who weren't killed offhand to sate the undead hunger of the herd were being driven here.

Then he spotted something he wasn't expecting. Two soldiers in green camo escorted a woman and two kids towards the carousel.

Carlos immediately ran towards them. Though he normally avoided any contact with authority, now seemed like a good time to make friends with the humans with guns.

The soldiers trained their rifles on him, but when he held up his hands to show they were empty, the rifles lowered, and the troops smiled. "I didn't think we'd find anyone alive in here," one of them said. She was a tiny thing with beautiful dark eyes. "How did you evade the animals? Looks like they got everyone else."

"I…" the truth was a raw wound. He avoided it. "I really don't know. I ran into some trees and they just went past. Up near Columbus Circle. Then I tried to get the hell out of the Park, but it was like trying to walk through a wall."

"Yeah. We were near there. No way to run that way."

"So, what now?"

The woman grinned. "We're looking for Jessie's mom."

"What?"

"We think the animals got her."

"You should be trying to find a way out!"

"That doesn't seem to be in the cards right now, so this is as good an activity as any. I'm Santillán, by the way. Corporal Santillán."

"I'm Carlos," he replied.

"Pleased to meet you."

"Did you see a huge pack of zombie tigers go by? Any idea where they went?"

"Yeah. But you won't believe me if I tell you."

"Right now, I'd believe it if you told me they turned into a pack of fairies and flew away."

He described what he'd seen, and the three adults looked skeptically at the carousel. "It's empty now," the woman in civilian clothes said.

"Look, I know what I saw."

The little soldier spoke. "Let's check it out. Maybe there's a second level or something."

"It's just a merry-go-round. I can see the back from here," the taller woman said.

"I said we're going to check it out."

"Whatever."

They walked down the hill, Santillán on point, the mom and kids a few yards behind and the other soldier bringing up the rear. Carlos pulled up beside the soldier in front and spoke quietly.

"Thanks for believing me," he said.

"Don't get that a lot, huh?

"No," he replied dully.

"Didn't think so."

"Why do you say that?"

"It was the way you looked at the uniform. I can see a problem with authority a hundred miles off."

"You can?"

She laughed, a weird sound in the desolate Park. "Sure. I was just like you. On the street, getting into fights."

"Weren't you a bit small to get into fights?" Her face told him he'd goofed. "I mean…"

"I know what you mean. But I didn't fight fair. In the twenty-first century, no one expects a girl to pull a straight razor. Hell, a lot of them didn't know what it was even after I'd cut them a couple times."

He whistled. "And you ended up in the army?"

"It was that or in jail, and I look terrible in orange."

"What about your trouble with authority?"

"If you ask Sarge, he'd probably say I still have it. But I don't think so. The army has a way of beating it out of you. But even more than that, it has a way of teaching you that respect can come from other places. Most times that works better than sending recruits around the camp on their hands and knees in a snowstorm." She smiled, lost in the memory. "Although I will admit they're both pretty effective."

"Anyway, thanks for standing up to me. That blond bitch back there looks like the kind that always gets her way. She probably drives an SUV to her house in the Hamptons every day from work, just so she doesn't have to take a train."

"Cut her some slack. She nearly lost her kid today."

"Yeah, I guess."

"Besides, I knew you were telling the truth."

"Huh, how?"

"Look at the tracks. The grass is torn up pretty badly all the way to the carousel, and beyond it, too. So, I know the heavy animals definitely did what you said. I can't really see if the people went into the carousel or not, but I've seen stuff today I didn't think I'd believe, so one more wouldn't change much.

"And if it turns out you were lying all we need to do is to keep following the animal tracks."

"But you *do* believe me, right?" For some reason, that was the only thing that mattered to him right then.

She studied his gaze for a few seconds. "Yeah, I do."

He nodded, satisfied.

They reached the pillar, and Carlos was happy to realize it hadn't been trampled or destroyed. He laid a hand on it, the way he always did.

Then he stepped back in alarm. It had begun to glow a sickly green…the same green as the eyes of the zombies.

"Welcome one, welcome all," a voice said. They turned to see that the ticket booth, yellow with bars in front of the window, was occupied.

"You," Santillán said.

"Hello," Johnny replied.

"I thought you were on our side," Karen said. She'd reconciled herself to the loss of the bracelet. It was absolutely clear to her that had she not possessed the whistle, both she and Brittany would now be nothing more than gobbets of flesh being digested by an undead abomination.

Johnny looked them over, taking each member of the group in, pausing twice as long on the dark guy who'd joined them last as on any of the others. "I'm not supposed to take sides," he said with a wink. "Not openly, at least. But I'm allowed to sell tickets to a ride to anyone who wants them."

Karen spoke: "And I suppose you don't want money for this either?"

"That's right. Like for like. A trade must be made." He held up six yellow tickets, old fashioned ones made of thick paper.

"And what do you want for them?"

"This is a special ride. How about those earrings?"

Karen almost protested but shrugged instead. "Sure. You can have these. My husband bought them for me. Before he left me because he couldn't take my grief when our daughter died."

Johnny just nodded and handed the ticket over.

"What about Brittany?"

"If she wants to ride, she has to make her own trade."

Again, Karen's protest never got out. Brittany pushed her aside and, standing on the tips of her toes to reach the counter-top held out two lollipops which she must have had in her pocket. "A ticket for me and one for Jessie, please," she said.

Johnny solemnly pushed the tickets across and nodded.

The rest made their exchanges.

"So now, what?"

"Now, you ride."

"What the hell?" the man beside Williams said.

The manhole cover had been a bear to move, but the combined brawn of three infantrymen had eventually shifted it, after two more of the enormous birds had dropped in and been dispatched. It had revealed a dark, deep hole to nowhere.

They climbed down a long series of iron rungs, and the air, summer hot in the playground above, turned cool and clammy. The narrow tube soon opened into a larger space. They felt more than saw the change…the tiny amount of light filtering through the cover above was barely enough to see by, but the way the air swirled around them was a giveaway after the close confines of the concrete tube. The wall beside the rungs, likewise, lost its pronounced curvature.

"I think we've reached the bottom," one of the soldiers said. His voice echoed as if they were in a cavern.

Williams stepped down beside him. "Anyone bring a flashlight?"

"Yeah, Sarge. Give me a sec."

Light, a pencil-thin beam—or what looked like a pencil-thin beam as it lost itself in the more-than-normal darkness but was actually the powerful beam of a Five Hundred lumen Surefire P2X—illuminated an empty, dust-covered corridor. Clearly artificial, it had a flat floor and arched roof and wound its way under the Park.

A nervous few minutes later they reached a large room. The echoing of their footsteps simply stopped when they entered, as if the room was so large that the sound never reached the other end to bounce back.

That was plainly ridiculous, though. They could see the roof and a pair of the walls. The room was big—conference hall big—but not monumental.

The center, covered in the dust as everything else in the tunnels, stood a walled-off section.

"Let's see what that is," Williams said.

They approached slowly, as if the concrete structure were about to sprout legs and jump at them, but nothing happened. They walked around and observed it.

The first thing they realized was that if this was indeed a room within a room, it had no doors. No way in or out. Heat radiated from it.

More puzzling was the way the dust seemed to accumulate at the base of the walls. The air currents didn't seem strong enough to move dirt around that way, and besides, wind action would likely have piled the dust higher on one side of the room than the other. This dust, however, was evenly piled all around the central structure.

The mound started about ten feet away from the wall, sloping gently upward until, at the center, the detritus was waist high. Williams dropped to one knee and put his hand in the dust. It was greasy and slightly warm. It smelled like ash, with the undercurrent of barbecue. He touched the wall and pulled his hand away quickly; it was hot to the touch.

"Can you shine the beam on the wall?" he asked the soldier. "High up there. Wait, go back a little. There, see that?"

"Looks like a bunch of black lines."

"Those are vents. That's where this stuff," he kicked the dust at his feet, "is coming from."

"Oh. And what is it?"

"Damned if I know. Some kind of ash."

They restarted their circumnavigation, trying to spot an opening they could actually use, but none presented itself.

The room took a long time to walk around. It was also looked weird. Weird enough that Williams thought it must be a trick of the flashlight against the wall at first. But, as they rounded the central structure, he realized that it wasn't the light, but the room itself. It wasn't square, or even round. Sharp corners reached out from a central core.

Williams held up a hand. "Wait, let's go around one more time." He dug a deep furrow in the greasy dirt with his boot and they walked around again. The soldiers looked at him as though he as losing his mind as he counted the corners. At eight, he stopped and searched for the furrow. It was right where he expected it. "Guys, I know where we are."

He unfolded the map the creepy dude in the hat had given them and knelt as far from the pile of dirt as they could. "All right," he said, pointing at the star in one of the chambers on his map. "This is us."

"If that star is the room in the middle of this one," one of his men said, "then this complex is the size of Texas."

"That's right soldier—heads up!" A pair of evil green dots, knee-high in the darkness, were the only warning they had.

There wasn't enough time to run for it or to reach for a gun. Williams and one of the soldiers dove to one side, but the final man wasn't quick enough. Before he could duck, before he could even react, he was gone—dragged through the darkness by something low to the ground, but massive.

By the time Williams got to his feet, the last soldier had his M4 up and was vainly trying to locate their assailant in the darkened enclosure.

No, Williams said to himself. Not the last soldier. He looked at the man's face. He had a name. Oliver.

Williams knew what he'd been doing. Once they were inside the Park, with no way out and more enemies than they could reasonably expect to overcome, he'd stopped thinking of his troops by name. He'd blocked off the memories of the things they'd done together. He refused to remember that Jamal—dead of a missing arm—had loved to play blackjack against himself on any bus ride. That Shawn, the man who'd just disappeared without even a scream to mark his passing had actually been a Mormon missionary in Africa before he enlisted, and that he'd always refused to answer the accusation that he'd only enlisted to get out of ever having to go on a mission again.

But he wouldn't do that to Oliver. For all he knew, the kid was the last of his squad, the last of the men and women who were his brothers in arms, and he would celebrate the man's life and be proud to die by his side.

For he had no doubts about that in the least. They would die, and they would die horribly. It was just a question of when.

"What now, Sarge?"

"Let me think a second…Oliver." He picked up the map and looked at the rooms and words and numbers. One chamber, up at the very top of the map—he assumed that was north, although there was no rosette or even the simplest of arrows to confirm it—looked more important than the rest. Several passages led into it and the text was heavier there, with red lettering in some alien script indicating…well, he assumed it indicated what the place was good for. He jabbed it with his finger. "This is where we need to go."

"Why?" Oliver asked.

It was a good question. The man was going to his death, so he deserved a good answer. "Because I don't have any better ideas."

Oliver nodded. "Did you see what got Shawn?"

"Barely. I think it was a croc of some kind."

The private smiled. "You mean the old rumor about the New York City sewer system is true?"

"I don't think so. I think this is something else entirely."

Then they tried to get their bearings. The complex had a lot of rooms and if they got lost, they could be in there for days.

And Williams knew they wouldn't even last a few hours.

Carlos selected a yellow horse and watched the rest of them mount up. The little girls seemed to have forgotten that they were locked in a life-and-death struggle against stuff none of them would even have imagined the day before. They raced between the animals and chose the ones they liked most. They even laughed a little.

The mother, Karen, followed a few yards behind them. Even in the midst of the situation they were in, she appeared to be more concerned with never letting the kids out of her sight than anything else. He'd heard the term 'helicopter parent', always hovering over any children, but had never really paid it any heed. This was a perfect, perhaps ridiculous, illustration of it, though.

On one hand, it must be irritating as hell for the kids…but on the other, he envied them. There could be no doubt in their minds that someone actually cared.

The soldiers mounted a couple of horses behind the kids. Even they had reverted to type as soon as their feet touched the boards of the merry-go-round: they were seeing it from a tactical vantage point and, for whatever reason, they'd decided that being in the rear was the way to go.

As she held the pole that would, unless this was some kind of cosmic joke, move her horse, Santillán caught Carlos' eye. She raised her eyebrows as if to say: "Well, what can you do?"

"All aboard!" Johnny's voice boomed from the entrance.

"Hey!" Carlos shouted. "That's not what you're supposed to…"

The carousel started with a sudden jerk, and the music began to play. Tinny notes fell from hidden speakers as wooden animals gathered speed.

Carlos waited a couple of seconds to go around and get a look at the park outside. Most of the trip around took place within the carousel's green building, but about a quarter of the circle was open to the outside. Even after all these years, he knew in his bones exactly how long a single revolution would take. He should see the exterior…now.

But there was no exterior. There were no windows, just the endless continuation of the back wall around the front.

Carlos knew he should be bewildered, overcome by the sense of strangeness, but he was numb to all of that. Instead, the cadence of the horse, the rhythm of the music and the gentle outward push of the centrifugal force lulled him. They took him back to the last time he'd been there. The real last time, not the last time he liked to remember.

It had been a bitter, grey day in January. He was twelve and the carousel was a fading memory from childhood, but his mother had herded him—and his ten-year-old brother—onto the subway. They emerged on 7th avenue and walked the three blocks to Central Park.

Carlos remembered standing there, stunned. It was like having one of his cartoons come to life: the Park was a legendary place, lost like Avalon among the mists of his memory.

That day, his mom had nixed the idea of two rides, which he'd asked for automatically, unthinking. It had just come up from the depths of his being. His mom had said no. They could only have one ride each. She wiped away a tear as she counted out the singles. He'd thought it was the wind making her cry.

When the ride ended, his mother had sat them down on the bench near the carousel. Only a few stragglers braved the blustery afternoon, so they had privacy.

"Kids, I have to tell you something," she said. Carlos remembered thinking that the wind must have been particularly strong as the waterworks were on full display. So innocent. So *stupid*. She paused, then continued in a rush. "Your father and I…I mean…We're getting divorced."

The rest of that day was gone. He could remember nothing but the anger that tore into him and never let him go. He supposed his mother had probably tried to tell them that it would be all right, that she would still love them. That nothing was going to change.

But if that was what she said, she lied to them.

Things did change, starting with Carlos himself. He let his anger go, and transformed himself from a shy, unremarkable student into volatile problem child, and eventually, less than two years later into a gang-banging dropout.

By then, however, no one cared. His mother worked herself to the bone so she could give them less than they needed. She was never around to worry about him. Less became even less as time went on. A crappy two-bedroom was too expensive. Eviction followed, and they moved further and further from the marginally respectable parts of the Borough.

Leaving Brooklyn, of course, was unthinkable, but the gentrified areas near the river soon became a distant fantasy, kind of like what the Park and its carousel used to be.

He'd been in fights, he'd leaned on store owners, he'd gotten low-paying jobs through connections and 'liberated' merchandise for his friends. He'd gotten into one particular bar fight and been bailed out by associates who hadn't even batted an eye when the other guy stopped breathing, just told him that they'd take care of it for him.

Since that night, he'd always wondered when the other shoe would drop, but it hadn't. Not yet. For his own part, though, he didn't seem to be able to keep even the most menial of jobs, spiraling downwards to the hustles that even immigrants just in from South Sudan didn't want.

Finally, he'd lost even that, and he'd been reduced to mugging women in the Park.

Full circle, as it were. He was back in the place where the wheels had fallen off his life. Before that, he'd been poor, but happy. He'd had a mother who loved him and a father who completed the family…even if he was more to be feared—especially when he drank—than respected. It wasn't a life of luxury, but he'd felt safe.

As the carousel circled, all that anger—anger he'd thought he was long over—came back. The memories of the place, the helplessness, the sense of betrayal made him grip the pole in his hands as if he wanted to squeeze the life out of it and, through it, cut off some wellspring of critical nutrients to the horse. He wanted everything around him to wither: the horse, the rest of the animals, the carousel itself, the Park, New York. Hell, the whole world could rot from the inside and take him with it. He wouldn't care. At least he could watch all the assholes out there, the smug, safe, normal people, get what was coming to them.

An animal growl emerged from his throat. Carlos glared at the five other people riding the merry-go-round with him. All solid, respectable citizens.

Then something caught his eye. The center of the ride, a pastel cyan cylinder, suddenly disappeared. It fell away into an abyssal opening in the center of the ride.

Carlos turned his eyes away. Something burned in the hole, burned brightly enough that it hurt to look.

But he only managed to look away for a second. Pain or no pain, he was mesmerized by the sight of the hole getting bigger. Board by board, the rotating platform disappeared and the hole in the middle grew. He saw one piece of wood spiral down into…what the hell was that, anyway? It looked like the Earth's core had suddenly taken up residence right there, in a chamber just below the carousel in central park.

Or maybe not. Fire swirled and blazed, occasionally sending an orange or yellow tongue almost all the way up to them, giving the impression of lique-fied rock. But it was just flames…the flames of Hell itself.

Something grey skittered up the wall across from him and then disap-peared. Some kind of large animal, too far away to see what it was, except to give a vaguely feline impression. Another climbed laboriously up after, and this was easy to identify: a zombie mammoth.

So, this was where they were all coming from.

Soon, though, he would have other things to think about. The hole in the middle had almost reached the pole holding up his horse. He'd watched a number of other animals topple into the flames below, and his was likely next. The soldiers and Karen had already left their own steeds and headed for the furthest edges of the circular platform.

Even though he'd already studied the endless wall around them and seen that there was no way out, Carlos followed. If he was going to burn to a crisp, he didn't want to be the first to go.

The platform kept disappearing until only a single row of rotating boards remained. He sweated in the heat.

Suddenly, for no reason that he could discern, he remembered the ring the Salesman had given him. A big brass piece, and now he remembered where he'd seen it's like before: as a small child, his father had once taken him to another merry-go-round, on Staten Island. This one had been seriously old-school, and the man who ran it had held out a pole with a brass ring on the end. Any kid that could snag it would get a free ride.

Carlos had failed miserably, and his dad had been pissed.

But the ring was an exact double of the one he now held in his hand. And something was telling him that the ring had the power to save them all. He just needed to figure out how to use it.

But did he want to?

Two soldiers. A couple of obviously well-to do members of some upper-middle-class family. Another brat, probably just as rich.

Himself, of course. But if he lived, what did he really have to go back to? Maybe it was time to see what happened when the veil was lifted, whether the next great adventure was better than the one he was embarked on.

It couldn't be worse, could it?

If he'd been a brave man, he would long since have dived into the fiery storm below and damn the torpedoes.

But he wasn't. He would die, but only if the others, hated or not, came with him.

Movement drew his attention. A man—hairy, dirty, unkempt and dressed in rags...and with glowing green eyes, but a man all the same—climbed the edge of the wall beside him and fixed him with the evil glowing gaze.

Carlos wanted to take a step back, to get the hell out of there, but he was frozen in place.

The zombie reached out a hand and this time, Carlos did step back.

Then he realized what was happening. He wasn't being attacked; he was being offered sanctuary. All he had to do was to grab the creature's hand and he would be pulled to safety.

The zombies saw him as a kindred spirit. Evil helping evil. That was why the animals hadn't torn him to pieces: they could smell the stains on his soul.

He could live and still condemn the others to the fiery depths.

Carlos turned to look at them one last time, smug that they were the ones who had to worry, now while he had a security blanket. Hah.

Karen hugged Brittany close. The soldiers looked around for another way out, testing the walls as they rotated past. Santillán looked his way but, seeing that he didn't have a solution to the immediate problem, turned back to the task at hand.

Only Jessie, the other little girl, seemed to understand what was about to happen. She stared down into the fire.

Carlos suddenly knew that her mother was down there, burned to ashes, killed with all the rest of the humans herded here to power the infernal engine. The little girl would never see her mother again, even if she didn't die today.

The platform was now barely as wide as their feet. Soon, the little girl would topple after her mother. She wasn't even trying to step back anymore. The fire, apparently, had a hypnotic effect.

The zombie made an impatient grunting noise and gestured with his hand. The significance was clear: now or never.

Suddenly, he realized he couldn't let the girl die. She'd suffered enough, too much to abandon her to burning agony.

He released the ring.

It fell only about six feet, and then hovered. Carlos watched, mesmerized, as the brass band flattened out and then, impossibly, began to expand. It was soon wide enough to touch the outside wall of the carousel at every point of its circumference, then started to expand inward, creating a platform below them.

Santillán reacted first. She stepped off the precarious ledge and checked whether the new surface created by the ring could hold her weight. She tested it with one foot but soon dropped the other onto the metal, not because she wanted to but because the original wooden platform was no longer wide enough to hold her. One by one, everyone else dropped to the brass.

Carlos watched it grow inward until it met itself in the middle, all the while matching the carousel's speed. As soon as it closed off the fires below, the heat died out and the carousel music started up again. The brass floor began to generate thin parallel lines and to lose its metallic sheen until it looked just like the old floor of wooden boards it had replaced.

Then lumps appeared in its surface and they all had to dodge as poles sprouted to the roof. The poles bulged in the center into fantastic shapes that, moments later, resolved themselves into animals.

The transformation was complete when the outer wall recovered the windows Carlos remembered from his childhood, and the original carousel was fully restored around them.

They slowed to a halt and the music stopped.

Everyone rushed towards the exit and only stopped once they were out of the rotating chamber that had come so close to killing them all.

The Park was deserted. No people, no insects, not even any zombie animals disturbed the peace. New York's skyline, normally visible from there, was hidden behind a green haze in the distance.

A single windblown candy wrapper tumbled along the asphalt until it caught on the low branches of a bush.

Johnny waited in the path. He looked up as they approached, and Carlos felt himself being exposed all the way down to his deepest being.

"That," Johnny said, "was much too close."

Williams fired. One slug to the head was enough to take down the saber-toothed tiger in their way. But it was also a reminder that they were running low on ammo. If they encountered another herd, the fight wouldn't last long.

Oliver walked beside him, flashlight at the ready. Fortunately, the tunnel leading from the big room was not wide enough for anything to sneak around them in the dark. If the animals wanted to attack, they could do so from in front or from behind, but they couldn't outflank them.

"It's hard to tell scale on this thing," Williams said, "but I think we'll get there in another hundred feet or so."

"To the room you showed me? Already?"

"No. That one is a little further ahead. I want to stop somewhere else first."

Oliver just nodded and didn't ask further questions. He was, in that way, the perfect soldier. Williams felt a little guilty for keeping him in the dark, but there was a good reason: you didn't get a man's hopes up unnecessarily.

What Oliver couldn't do was disguise his nerves, and the way he expressed it was to keep up a continuous commentary on everything.

"Can you believe this is down here and no one knew about it?"

"I'm not sure no one knows. There are probably generals and shit who've known about this place forever. Hell, they might be trying to tunnel in even now. We might run into a platoon of Rangers around the next corner."

"I hope they don't shoot us."

Williams knew they wouldn't get shot by their own men. He knew it because, deep down, he was utterly certain that there was no one down there but Oliver and himself, and that no one else would get down there in time to make any difference.

It was a pity. This place would have been a godsend to any forces attempting to stage a counterattack against whatever it was that had overrun the Park. The complex was staggering in scale and, if the map were to be believed, had several hidden exits which would allow defenders to strike from cover in various points nearby. Unless his interpretation was completely off, the northernmost chamber they were approaching was up near 86th street.

"We'll be fine."

The next room they entered was a small chamber about fifteen feet square. One wall was covered with cabinets which, when Williams popped them open, held a rat's nest of wiring. For a second, hope welled, but it was soon quashed. The dust covering the old cloth-sheathed cabling was a sign that trying to turn anything on was more likely to cause a lot of sparks and, most likely, a fire, than achieve anything productive.

He shrugged and played around with the wires anyway, jiggling this one and that until he managed to create a shower of sparks.

Both soldiers took a hurried pair of steps back, but nothing exploded or combusted.

"At least we know there's juice in there," Williams said.

"Yeah. Maybe we should leave it alone."

"You're probably right, but I would feel a lot better if we could turn on the lights." They'd seen plenty of fixtures, complete with old-fashioned incandescent bulbs, dotting the roof of the tunnels.

"Well, if you set fire to the tunnels, that should also light our way. Of course, the oxygen down here won't last very long if everything's on fire…but at least we'll be able to see the monsters."

"I don't think they're monsters," Williams said, fiddling with the wires again, in a place far from where the sparks had come up. "They seem more like regular animals…well, big mean ones, I guess, that turned into zombies."

"That sounds like the perfect definition of a monster, if you ask me," Oliver replied.

"Look. This one is loose. Be ready to dive for cover. You don't happen to have a set of insulated pliers in your pack, do you?"

"That's not the kind of stuff I like to drag around on deployment," Oliver replied.

"Yeah, I guess you're right. Well, here goes. If I start jerking around, tackle me." He nudged the wire.

Every single connector in the switchbox erupted in a shower of sparks and they dove for cover, shielding their eyes against the sudden illumination.

As soon as it started, however, the fireworks ended.

Blinking against the afterimage, Williams frowned. "It was worth a shot, I guess."

"Wait. It worked. Well, somewhat. Look."

Williams peered into the darkness. Whatever Oliver was referring to, there certainly weren't any bulbs lighting the way. But…he blinked again to drive away the final effects of the sparks and to assure himself that it wasn't just a trick of his eyes.

It wasn't. There really was illumination out there. Not bright. Red lights.

Whatever he'd done had triggered the emergency lighting. Such as it was.

"All right. We'll make it work. Better not put away that flashlight just yet, though. I want to be sure we can see those critters in the red light before we think of saving the batteries."

They started back along the corridor. "Where now?" Oliver said.

"This way." Williams still didn't want to get the other man's hopes up.

"Behind you!"

The lion-like creature almost got Williams before he could bring the M4 to bear. It barked twice and the creature fell.

"Thanks," Williams said.

"Nice shooting," Oliver replied. He kicked the dead, foul-smelling creature with the tip of his boot. "I don't get it, though. Most of the things we've been seeing are extinct animals. Saber tooth tigers. Mammoths. Hell, they've even got giant armadillos in the parade. But this one looks like a regular lion. A bit bigger, maybe, but just a lion."

"I hope you don't mind, but I'll just stick to shooting them. You can analyze them all you want."

"I wish my phone was working," Oliver said. "I really can't stand not knowing what that thing is and how it fits with the rest of them."

They headed down the corridor again. "You think the rest of them fit together?"

"Sure," Oliver replied. "Smilodon and Mammoth, obvious ice-age creatures. From around here, too. Same with the terror birds. But lions? I suppose there must have been extinct versions of the common lion around here. Probably came over the Bering Land Bridge like so much other stuff."

"I have no idea what you're talking about," Williams said. "I just know that those things have been dead a while."

"A lot more than just a while, Sarge. We're talking tens of thousands of years. More in some cases."

Williams grunted. "No wonder they smell. Now concentrate on the task at hand. They might have been dead forever, but I've seen what they can do. We need to stay alert."

No sooner had he finished saying it than something low and long slinked away into the darkness.

"Saber-toothed alligator?" Williams asked.

"There's no such..." Oliver realized he was being teased. "I wasn't able to get a good look in the dark."

They entered a slightly larger room. This one was full of storage bins and even had a small shed in the center.

"What's this?" Oliver asked.

Williams headed straight for the shed. He opened the door and waited for his eyes to get used to the even dimmer light within.

"This is something we can use. Stock up."

Ten shotguns stood in a rack. It was locked, of course, but a couple of careful shots into a wooden support member—who used wooden racks to lock up firearms?—made short work of the security. He pulled a couple of them down and inspected the first. It had been recently greased; someone knew the tunnels were down here and, unlike the electrics, the weaponry had been kept in order.

He shone the flashlight on the barrel. Ten gauge. Nice.

The ammo, likewise, was not only new, but loaded for bear. Boxes of zero-zero-zero-zero buckshot lined shelf after shelf.

It made Williams think that whoever had set this place up was either determined to do a lot of damage to any human enemies they might have to defend against...or they had an inkling of what might actually happen.

He wished they'd been able to man the installation, though. A good supporting cast of human defenders would have come in extremely handy right about then.

They discarded a bunch of modern equipment that was serving no purpose and  filled their satchels with shells. Each grabbed a shotgun and moved off.

"Hope these old things don't jam," Oliver said.

"Who says they're old?"

"That's a Nineteen-Twelve model Winchester. Probably from the forties."

"So you're an expert on shotguns and on prehistoric animals?"

"They go together. I hunt."

"With a time machine?"

Oliver showed no amusement. "Most hunters know a lot about animals. I just know a little more."

They continued their walk. Williams' objective lay to the north in the shape of the big room on the map with all the text around it. He was pretty certain that something very significant lay inside, and that it was the most important chamber in the entire complex.

The corridor opened up and became rectangular, wide and flat enough for two Humvees—or, more likely Jeeps, considering the place's age—to drive down, side by side. Tall enough for a tank, too.

But it was also in rough shape. Water marks, dimly visible in the red light showed where flooding had reached waist high, probably during that hurricane a he remembered studying in school as a kid.

Puddles scattered along the corridor reflected the light in eerie ways, as if a darkened underground tunnel full of zombie carnivores wasn't bad enough.

When Oliver spoke unexpectedly, Williams jumped.

"Rats."

"What?"

"Where are the rats? We're in New York City. Underground. The last time I was here, I took a subway. There was a whole platform roped off because it had been invaded by rats. I could see them. It looked like a living carpet."

Williams shuddered. "Maybe the army is better at keeping its installations free of vermin than the subway guys."

Oliver looked around at the peeling paint and potholed floor. "You really think so?"

Williams grunted. "Probably not, but I'm not worried about rats. Hell, even if the zombies ate them, that's probably a good thing, right? Maybe, once this is over, we can use those rotting monsters for pest control. I call dibs on the patent."

Oliver smiled weakly. "You can have it. Vermin control isn't the sexy career I'll want if we get out of this alive."

"You mean you don't want to be a private all your life?"

"No. Not even a sergeant."

"Watch it, kiddo. I don't want to have to wash your mouth out with soap."

They trudged in silence for a couple of minutes. Could the big room really be so far away? Or had they gotten mixed up in the spaghetti of interconnected corridors? For all he knew they might be going around in circles.

His compass was no use; it had been spinning around since they entered the park.

"Sarge," Oliver said. "You might want to look behind us, casual like."

Williams did. At first, he saw nothing in the dark redness but then, an almost imaginary motion flickered in the distance. "I see them," he said. "On my mark, we run for it and try to find a place to hole up. Something we can defend until we run out of ammo."

"Too late, sarge."

Williams looked forward. A herd of big cats, both saber-toothed and regularly toothed, blocked their way.

Karen fumed.

"What the hell was that?" she said. "You nearly got us killed."

"I merely sold you tickets," Johnny replied.

"You're a part of this."

The impassive face showed no emotion but somehow Karen felt that the weight of the world was on the man's shoulders when he responded: "You have no idea how true that is. I'm probably more of a part of this than anyone else. And I've been preparing for the Sha'Daa my entire life. It's possible that others might be confused by what I end up doing."

"Well, I don't want anything from you. Not even if you have a tank or something else with impenetrable armor that those creatures can't get through."

"I understand how you feel," the Salesman replied. "But I also think some of your companions have a different opinion."

Karen sat on one of the benches that were arrayed in a semicircle around the entrance to the carousel with Brittany on her lap.

Santillán replaced her at the Salesman's side, close enough that Karen could hear what she said.

"I want something for Carlos."

Johnny smiled. "Did you have anything specific in mind?"

"Something that will stop him from being scared," Santillán replied. "I saw what he did in there."

"What did he do?"

"It's not what he did, but what he nearly didn't do that worries me. He almost went over to the other side, didn't he?"

"But he didn't. He passed his test."

"But that fear is still inside him. If he breaks…"

"Look at him," Johnny said, nodding to Carlos. Santillán looked in the appropriate direction and Karen followed her lead.

The guy knelt on the ground. He was rearranging Jessie's hair and speaking to her softly, obviously comforting her after the ordeal they'd just survived. The little girl was actually smiling.

"I don't think you need to worry about him cracking," Johnny said, turning his attention back to Santillán. "But maybe you're worried about your own reactions."

The words sounded ridiculous to Karen. If there was one person who wouldn't crack, it was the corporal. She was the kind of soldier who'd chew her way through an armored division if she had to.

Instead of denying it and kicking the guy's ass, however, Santillán looked down. "I don't get any of this. I was trained to kill other people and break things, and I'm damned good at it. But in there...I couldn't get us out. If the kid over there hadn't dropped that ring, I'd be as dead as the rest of them." She put her head back up. "Just as dead as the poor bastards who got herded in there before us. They are dead, aren't they? The people in the playground? The little girl's mother?"

Johnny nodded. "But you're not. And a lot of that is due to the fact that you can shoot straight."

"Fat lot of good it did me in there."

"Then take this." The Salesman held out a necklace, a simple thing: leather things holding a large metal medallion. "I'll trade it for the little gold cross you're wearing now. The one your grandmother gave you."

Santillán hesitated only a second. Then she pulled a thin gold chain from within her uniform. The trade was made solemnly.

Then, Johnny walked over to where Carlos was still talking to the little girl. He also made an exchange there, but Karen couldn't see what was given or what was asked.

"Why is the air green, mommy?" Brittany said.

"I don't know, dearie," Karen replied.

"It's pretty. We should make a picnic."

Karen looked up at the sky. Her phone showed nothing but a blank green screen when she looked at it, and she'd long since given up wearing a watch. The sun had moved across the sky, but in summer it was so hard to tell how late it was. Maybe six? Could it actually be her dinner time already?

She shuddered. Nightfall in a city like New York was nothing to worry about. The streets were always well-lit and full of friendly faces, at least in the places she frequented. But getting trapped in the Park at night with the green-eyed zombies...was another story entirely.

Still, she thought she'd heard that this was the longest day of the year, or close to it at any rate. They still had some hours.

"What happened to the monsters, mommy?"

"I hope we won't see them again."

"Heads up, people!" Santillán had positioned herself between the group and the carousel.

A crowd began to trickle out of the entrance towards them. *Zombie cavemen*, Karen thought, before her mind automatically kicked in to see if that was an ethnic slur. Then she laughed at herself. They had to be beyond the boundaries of political correctness, right?

Besides, those *were* zombie cavemen. Lots of them, and rotting, pungent examples of the breed, too.

A couple of barks from the soldiers' rifles made them change their mind about attacking the group, and they shambled in a different direction.

"They're not going to stop coming out of there," Johnny said, loud enough for all of them to hear.

"How many are inside?" Santillán asked.

"All of them."

"What does that even mean?"

"The forces of evil have access to every single person who lived in this area during the time that the animals you saw lasted. We're talking about a few million years to choose from, although you won't run into anyone too modern. Some of them were hunters, so I'd recommend that you move out."

"Us? You're not coming?"

"I have a busy day planned."

With that, the guy walked onto a path half-hidden among some bushes. When Carlos ran up to follow, the guy was gone.

So was the path.

"We go north," Santillán said.

"Why?" Karen asked, silently overriding the voice in her head that insisted it wasn't north but uptown. She couldn't seem to accept the grim reality of the situation. Was she going crazy?

"Because we've already been south, and we can't get out that way. So north is our only real option." The soldier turned to Carlos, still trying to figure out where the guy in the trench coat had disappeared to. "What's up north?"

He looked uptown. "The Sheep Meadow."

"Not great. I've seen it: nothing but grass. We'd be sitting ducks. What's north of that?"

"Cherry Hill."

"A hill? Sounds good. At least we'll have the high ground if those things find us."

"It's not much of a hill. It's full of trees. There's a fountain, there, too. And we'll have to cross the street right over there." He pointed beyond the carousel.

"I don't think much traffic is going to be rolling through today. We had instructions to seal off the Park, and I know there were units assigned to the streets. No one is going to make it past those guys."

They set off single file. Karen walked close to the middle, Brittany in her arms. No three-year-old could have kept up the pace that the soldiers wanted. Carlos had Jessie on his shoulders.

Crossing the Sheep Meadow was the hardest thing she'd ever done. Santillán, after mulling whether the cover on the paths was preferable to the advantage they'd gain from being able to see anything that wanted to attack them a long way away, opted for visibility, so they cut straight across the grass.

Abandoned beach blankets dotted the landscape. A hat lay here, a ball there. Water bottles seemed to sprout from the ground. Each was a reminder of a normal day brutally interrupted. Where were those people now? Her bet was that they'd been incinerated in the chamber under the carousel.

At one point, though, they came across a stroller, one of those that you can remove the seat and clip it into a car seat base. The stroller was empty, and it was clear that the baby that had occupied it was truly tiny. Probably a child making its first outing in the world.

She instinctively reached for her bracelet. It wasn't there.

But the memories were. Standing beside the neonatal ward as her husband held her. Feeling her legs give out beneath her. Wanting to die. Wanting to wake up so the nightmare would end. The wailing sobs.

Leaving the hospital without a newborn in tow.

"You all right, ma'am?"

The soldier behind her, a guy who looked like a photo on a recruiting poster—pale, buzz-topped and, somehow, too young and thin for the camouflage uniform he wore—put a hand on her back to steady her.

"Yes, I'm fine." Curt, much shorter with him than she should have been.

"It's just that you looked like you were about to fall."

"I put my foot in a hole. I'm all right."

Karen continued trudging ahead after he moved back

Santillán was pretty disappointed when they reached Cherry Hill. "Let's rest here for a couple of minutes," she said. "There are some much steeper places around, we just have to look for a good one. This place is indefensible."

Karen put Brittany down and sat heavily beside her. "Ma'am, I can carry the girl if you want."

She looked at the gun he was toting. "I don't think so."

"It would let us all go much faster."

She knew they'd stopped because of her. She didn't think anyone would be impolite enough to openly talk about it, though. "I'm never letting go of her," she replied, grabbing her daughter's hand again.

"It doesn't matter," a voice said.

Santillán faced a gap in the trees. Faces appeared between the trunks. Men and women with blank expressions slowly crept towards them, green eyes blazing like harbingers of pure evil. Many of them were naked, others were dressed in what looked like animal furs.

The corporal stepped towards them, leveling her rifle, probably thinking that if she was about to go, she would do so in a blaze of glory.

She never got the chance. One of the primitives saw her move and, taking two steps forward straightened and released a hefty wooden spear.

It hit Santillán right in the sternum and dropped her to the ground.

Then, the zombie cavemen charged.

Williams only hesitated for a second. He'd already known they were going to die, so why not do it with gusto? "Oliver, there's something I always wanted to say, but I never thought I'd get the chance."

"What's that?" Was there a tremor in the kid's voice? If there was, he'd come by it the hard way.

"Charge!"

Williams lowered his M4 and ran straight towards the zombies. An inarticulate yell behind him told him that Oliver had followed suit. Controlled bursts at head height of the animals opened a path in the front ranks. He grinned with satisfaction as a four-foot-tall armadillo's head exploded.

Then he targeted the lion beside it, but he was too late. Chalk that one up to Oliver.

By now, the damage they'd done was a few rows deep. Their mad dash had reached the front rank of the creatures.

Williams hurdled the fallen armadillo and kicked aside some kind of medium-sized zombie deer, then focused on clearing the way ahead. To his amazement, he realized that, after the solid phalanx at the front, the animals thinned out behind.

He grinned. They were actually going to make it.

Something slammed into his side and sent him reeling. He looked up to see two twelve-inch teeth, the upper incisors of the saber-toothed tiger that had upended him. The tunnel's red emergency lighting combined with the green illumination from the creature's eyes to turn the sight into something out of a drunken nightmare.

Williams had been trained to react, to defend himself and to fight back. Not just in the army, but ever since early childhood in a house with too many older brothers. His squad had been ambushed in the Middle East just before the U.S. pulled out and he hadn't even flinched. He thought that nothing could scare him anymore.

But this was a creature from out of humanity's past. The reaction to it was hardwired in a part of the brain that was so primitive that it wasn't even human. Modern man had never lost the fear of this animal because modern man had never encountered it, never tamed it or put it in zoos. This was a killer from the ancestral night, and Williams froze like a recruit facing live fire for the first time.

He lay there, knowing that he, like so many hominids before him was going to die. Nature was going to win this round, and there was no reason to complain. Earth had its own balance sheet, and this one would be credited on the animals' side of the ledger.

The tiger reared back, opened its mouth wide and plunged forward.

Its massive head exploded in a spray of foul-reeking gunk. Williams had never smelled anything sweeter.

Oliver rushed to his side and offered him a hand. Williams took it and was pulled to his feet. "You're stronger than you look, soldier," he said as they sprinted towards the back end of the corridor.

"I have this hard-ass sergeant who pushes us like our squad has to single-handedly win the next war," Oliver replied, easily keeping pace. "He's stuck in the last century. He'd probably keelhaul us once a week if he was a squid."

Williams chuckled and looked back.

Behind them, the animals milled in disarray as the ones that had been following them crashed into the phalanx that had failed to hold them in place. The trap intended to close onto them from both sides was now busy fighting each other. Apparently, even being made a zombie wasn't enough to make the wolf lie with the lamb—or, in this case, the tiger with the mammoth.

But he wasn't going to bet on them taking too long to sort things out. Once they did, they would come after them hard.

The corridor ended and opened into a room. Williams stopped and looked back.

"Help me with this," he said.

They slid a concrete-reinforced rolling door across the opening and bolted it shut on the other side.

"I don't care if they do have mammoths. No animal is going to get through that thing unless they learn to use a bazooka."

"Sarge, you're bleeding."

Williams looked down to see the left front of his uniform black with blood. Only then did the pain in his shoulder register.

"Damn. I'd better have a look. Keep an eye out for alligators or what-ever." He cut away the fabric with the knife he always had with him. It was an Ontario Mk 3 Navy knife, the kind that SEALs carried. And it was much better than anything the army had ever issued him.

The gash was deep, but not very long. Had he been on base, he wouldn't really have worried about it: a couple of stitches and a few days of light duty would have put him right.

But he wasn't on base, and he knew the rules. If the zombies bit you, then you were a goner. Infected. He didn't' know if real life zombies worked that way…but he couldn't bet against it.

He'd already assumed he would die. Well, know he knew he would have to hurry if he wanted to get anything useful done before he did.

"I'll be fine," he announced. "We need to get moving."

"Still north?"

"That's what the map says."

Oliver nodded and they moved into the next corridor.

"How are you for ammo?"

"For the M-Four?"

"Yeah."

"I'm out. I took that last tiger with the shotgun."

"Damn. I'm down to my last clip."

They advanced quickly and each step made Williams' shoulder throb.

"How much further?" Oliver asked.

"Just a bit. One more room and one more corridor."

The room was a small one that held an assortment of orange vests of the kind used by construction workers. No hard hats, though, which seemed a bit strange. They moved into the final corridor. This one was barely wide enough to hold two men abreast.

"Well, if we have to make a last stand, this is as good a place as any. We can hold here forever." *Or until I turn into a zombie and eat your brains,* Williams thought.

Oliver said nothing, he just kept walking, shotgun held across his chest like the sheriff in a gangster film. They reached a door from which light poured into the tunnel.

"This should be it," Williams said.

"Oh my God."

The chamber was enormous. It held a bright, lightbulb-shaped orb on a pedestal in the center. The structure was connected to power lines running every which way: cables as thick as William's thigh, in some cases. An illuminated desk that looked like something out of Star Trek curled around the base of the pillar, complete with black chairs. The structure was too far away to see whether the desk was festooned with raised and illuminated buttons and switches, but he knew it had to be. There was no other option.

Even in the glow of the fantastic edifice, the corners of the room were lost in shadow.

A walkway constructed of wooden planks wound its way from the door to the central structure. Williams looked down to see what they were walking over and saw nothing below them except for deep channels, roughly parallel and separated by high concrete walls. Each channel ended at a grated tunnel in the base of the wall.

"It looks like a big water treatment plant," Oliver said.

Williams was tempted to ask him if he was an expert on that, too. "So, where's the water?"

"I don't know, but I suspect that tower is part of the system that controls it."

The channels beneath them were populated by zombies. More specifically, by zombie gators or crocodiles or whatever. They didn't look like anything modern that Williams had ever seen in a nature show, so maybe Oliver was right about all the animals being extinct versions of stuff.

Williams shot a couple of them, just on general principles and because they'd killed one of his men. Immediately another would take its place. He made a mental note not to fall off the walkway.

They reached the central island, and Williams was delighted to see that the desk was, indeed, covered with sixty's style illuminated buttons, lit up like the Christmas trees of his youth. Clearly, the power to it was working, even if the room lights weren't.

But the components that immediately called attention to themselves were several steel wheels of the kind you would expect to find on submarine hatches. Big, chunky, solid things intended to rotate heavy metal parts.

Williams nodded at them. "I guess that's the answer to my water question."

"I suppose. I've never seen anything like this. Who combines electronics and physical controls this way?"

"Based on the ergonomics of this place, I'd say the government."

Oliver looked around. "Like...the New York office of..." he hesitated, "weird underground complexes?"

"I was thinking more the Department of Defense. This looks like one of those secret installations the conspiracy theorists are always going on and on about. A Men in Black kind of thing, probably built to resist a Nazi invasion during WWII, and then kept in shape because it was too secret to cancel. Except those are always hidden out in Montana or something." He shook his head in admiration. "You'd think hiding it under a tourist trap like Central park would be insane, but it seems to have worked. Had you ever heard of this place before?"

"No." Williams could see Oliver wasn't convinced.

"What?"

"It's just that we found it too easily. Under a manhole cover in a playground. Don't you think a group of teenagers would have found a crowbar a long time ago and had a look around? I mean, growing up in Kentucky, it was the kind of thing we were always getting up to. There was this one place by the Ohio River with a big grate across it that we couldn't get open. One of the guys' dads had a blowtorch and we lugged it all the way down there—and that was a heavy tank—to cut a hole through the bars. You know what we found inside?"

"No idea."

"A bunch of old paint cans and rags. Worthless junk, but I still took one home with me as a trophy. There's no way this place would have remained hidden since the war. And that means people found it and ignored it because they already knew it was there."

"Maybe you're right. But that still doesn't tell us what all of this does."

Oliver scanned the desk thoughtfully and ran his hands over the rows of buttons. "I think it probably floods the tunnels. Water comes in through there," the private pointed towards the barely visible far wall, "and runs through those channels into each of the rooms and corridors."

"That's a pretty good guess," another voice said.

The muzzles of two guns whirled to face the newcomer. The tall man in the fedora approached slowly, open hands indicating he wasn't a threat, and convincing no one.

"What are you doing here?"

"Making a trade, hopefully."

"You've already taken my stripes," Williams said.

"I'm not here to trade with you." Johnny turned to Oliver. "Would you like to know what's really going on down here? Why this place was built, and what it hides?"

"I don't know. Why can't you just tell the Sergeant?"

"Because he wouldn't be able to take the truth. It would undermine everything he thinks he knows about good and evil."

"So why me?"

"Because you already know how evil can hide in good. Paint cans aren't the only thing that can be hidden on a lonely riverbank, are they?"

Oliver looked away. In the light from the huge bulb above them, he could see the private's knuckles whiten around the barrel of the shotgun. He tensed, but Oliver didn't seem to have violence on his mind...at least not against Williams. The creepy Salesman would have to look out for himself. The private leaned back against the railing.

"Jumping won't do you any good," the Salesman told him. "You still have amends to make."

"I've been making amends since the next day. I enrolled to make amends. No matter what I do, I can't undo the past."

"But you can help to ensure that there's a future. Do you want to make the trade?"

"I…don't know. What do you want from me?"

"I want that little toy horse. The one that talks to you at night. The one that she was carrying that day. It's a very special horse, and it needs to go back to the toy store where her parents got it."

"I don't have it with me. It's in the barracks."

"If you accept the trade, I can pick it up. I have to go to Chicago to deliver it anyway, so it won't be too far out of my way."

Oliver remained silent for a long, long time. Out of the corner of his eye, Williams saw green pairs of eyes appear at the far end of the chamber and creep slowly towards them along one of the walkways but didn't dare speak. He realized he was holding his breath—something told him that he mustn't interrupt, that if this deal went sour, something awful would happen.

"All right. I'll do it."

"Good. A deal has been made. A trade has been accepted."

The Salesman walked around the desk and was lost to sight behind the pillar. But Williams was paying him no attention; his eyes were fixed on Oliver.

The private's mouth hung open and a thin line of drool fell. He seemed to notice and snapped it shut, but the vacant expression was replaced by a look of utter horror. "It can't be," Oliver said. "I…"

"What?"

"No, no. I'd never do that to you, Sarge. The guy in black was right about that. It would kill you."

"What did he tell you?"

"I…he didn't tell me anything. He put it in my head. Awful things."

"Tell me soldier. That's an order."

"You ain't got no stripes anymore, Sarge. You can't order me around."

Williams took a step forward, but Oliver held his ground. "You can do what you like, I won't try to stop you. But you'd be wrong to do it. There are more important things to do right now."

"Yeah, like what?"

"Keep the zombies away from me. I need to put out a fire."

"What fire?"

"Just keep them off me. A couple of minutes, that's all. Then we can let them kill us."

"Screw that."

He raised the M4 and used the last few bursts to stop a mammoth approaching along a walkway. How the thing had gotten through the tunnel, and if it really expected to reach them without bringing the bridge down was beyond him, but its bulk was the perfect cork to block access for the zombies behind.

His celebration was short-lived. Something that looked like a lion simply jumped up and clawed its way over the dead elephant. It roared in triumph, but the sound came across as a wet gurgle. It didn't matter in the least, a thing that size, with glowing eyes didn't need a tremendous roar to turn people's guts to water. Its mere presence was enough.

He discarded the now-useless M4 and pulled his shotgun out of the pouch. He popped a shell in it and waited until the lion was ten feet away before filling its head with buckshot. It collapsed to the ground, oozing grey liquid.

As he turned to another walkway, along which an enormous horned cow was charging towards him, he noticed Oliver spinning the wheels on the desks. He would spin one all the way around like a man possessed, then, not stopping for breath, rush off to the next and repeat the operation.

Williams, for his part, sidestepped the cow like a matador and, when it tried to change direction, its legs got caught in one of the walkway's support posts. With a bone-cracking wrench, it slammed to one side and tore off the bannister before plunging into the canals below.

"Good way to save ammo," Williams muttered. Then he blasted one of the saber-tooth cats. He wondered if there had ever even been that many of them in the wild. It seemed like, with all the ones they'd killed on this jaunt, that the species should have been extinct. Or made extinct again, at any rate.

Three animals were coming for them along three different walkways.

But they stopped, and so did Williams. A deep roar filled the complex, and the entire world began to shake.

"Earthquake!" Williams shouted when he regained the ability to speak.

"No. That's just me. Get me thirty more seconds," Oliver replied.

Water rushed into the room along the canals. It came in torrents, cold and clear. He could feel the spray of its violent progress against his skin, feel the temperature in the chamber plummet.

Zombie alligators attempted desperately to climb up canal walls, but they were swept away with the first frothing rush.

"There! I'm done," Oliver shouted. "We need to get out of here."

"This way."

Williams ran onto the only walkway not blocked by zombie wildlife and ran as fast as the pain in his shoulder let him. They reached the door just yards ahead of the nearest charging animal and then Oliver calmly turned and shot two retaining pins out of the walkway. One first, then the other, with the animals just inches away. The bridge fell into the water below.

"How did you know to do that?"

"I know everything there is to know about this place," Oliver said. Then he shuddered.

"So how do we get out?"

"I'm not sure we have enough time."

"What do you mean?"

"Just run."

They did, crossing chamber after chamber, tunnel after tunnel. Some were wide, some narrow. In one place, he had to duck to avoid bashing his head against the wall. Williams began to sweat much more than usual. "Is it me, or is it hot in here?"

"It's not you." The words were delivered with certainty.

"You know what's happening, don't you?"

"I know we need to hurry."

Wisps of smoke or dust could be emanated from every door. Williams sniffed. He couldn't smell any smoke. The smell was clean, warm and clean.

He suddenly realized that it was steam. They must be near a steam pipe that had ruptured and was releasing its contents into the complex. Did New York even have steam pipes anymore?

"Are you sure we want to go that way?" he asked. "Looks like a steam pipe or something burst up there."

"It's not a pipe," Oliver replied grimly. "We need to run."

It was getting uncomfortably hot. The air had gone past tropical rain-forest to sauna levels of heat and humidity, and it didn't look like it was going to let up before it cooked them alive.

"Right over there," Oliver said.

Steel rungs at the end of the chamber they just entered led up a wall and into a circular hole in the roof. The private sprinted towards it.

"Wait!" Williams shouted.

Oliver didn't hear him. A living carpet poured into the room from all sides, cheeping and squeaking like a failing bearing on a truck.

Rats. Thousands of them.

A sound of thunder exploded within the room as Oliver fired the shotgun. A space in front of him cleared as the buckshot went through them, turning rats into ground beef. But he never got a chance to reload. The rats closed in and climbed up his body. The screaming Oliver kicked them off, but for each one he dislodged ten took its place.

The agony increased in volume. Oliver's arms flailed. He fell to the floor.

The steam was starting to make it hard to see, but it appeared to Williams that these were just normal rats, alive and sleek and furry. They had normal eyes when they started. Each one would jump in and bite a chunk out of the prone soldier and then, once done, would retreat with a gobbet of flesh in its mouth and green, evil eyes.

Apparently, New York's rats had chosen sides.

The heat became nearly unbearable, but he couldn't tear his eyes away from the furry mound covering Oliver. At one point, the rats fell away from the soldier's face. Williams nearly turned away, expecting to see nothing but a mass of gore. But Oliver, though bloodied, was still recognizable.

He was smiling. "It's wonderful," he gasped. "I can feel the taint leaving me. They're drinking it up." Then his muscles went slack and the head collapsed back into the writhing pile.

Williams's skin burned. He held his breath, trying to keep his lungs from scalding. But there was only one way out: through the rats. He brought up the shotgun, lined it up to clear a path to the ladder and fired. The floor in front of him cleared of rats and he sprinted.

It was a desperate gamble. He expected to end exactly the same way Oliver had, but the rats were sluggish, weak. Only one reached him, and his boot creamed it underfoot. He didn't even have to slow down to do it.

Williams nearly shouted for joy until he realized that the rats were dying of scalded lungs and that, quite soon, he would be joining them.

He climbed up the ladder, mouth clamped tightly shut against the urge to breathe.

A thirty-second eternity later, he reached the manhole cover above and understood why no one had opened the first one they'd found. A tiny version of the sluicegate wheels on its underside locked it from below.

He turned the wheel and pushed with all his might. His injured shoulder nearly made him scream with the pain. He managed to hold the sound in, conserving the tiny amount of breath that remained. He didn't want to breathe scalding steam.

Blackness was closing around his vision as the cover moved, and he was nearly unconscious when he pushed it aside.

He collapsed onto soft mulch under the leaves of a nearby bush.

"No!" Carlos screamed. He ran to Santillán and picked up her gun. He'd seen plenty of guns lately, but nothing like this. And he'd never fired one in his life. The people he knew who'd owned guns were all in jail. He hoped she had the safety off, if a rifle like this one even had a safety.

He aimed at the caveman who'd thrown the spear and pressed the trigger. The guy's ugly mug disappeared in a spray of grey sludge, but that was pretty much all that happened, as the unexpected recoil from the rifle pulled it upwards.

"Holding a gun like that is a good way to kill yourself," a voice below him said. "So is taking a gun from a US Army Corporal. You're lucky I like you." Santillan smiled up at him. "Now give it back."

Carlos hurriedly handed her the rifle and helped her to her feet. A few controlled shots from the shoulder removed the nearest of the zombies from the equation.

"We should probably get out of here." With her free hand, Santillán pushed him back and followed, gun never wavering from the zombies behind. "I hope these aren't the kind of zombies that can run, like the ones in that movie."

Carlos thought about how the animals had moved. Purposefully, reasonably quickly, but without the grace that animals are supposed to have. "I don't think they are. But I think they're a hell of a lot stronger than when they were alive."

"They can't hurt us if they can't catch us."

Mist was beginning to rise all around them. It seemed completely out of place in a sunny field in the middle of summer, even taking the eerie green tint into account.

They herded the rest of the group into a semblance of order, Carlos put Jessie on his shoulders and the other soldier made a final doomed effort to get the stubborn woman to surrender her own child.

She refused, not caring that her actions would slow everyone down.

The zombies came behind. When they got too close, a burst from the final soldier, the guy who Carlos hadn't been introduced too, would cut down one or two and cause the rest to mill about in confusion. That bought them distance, which they would then lose back to their undead stalkers as they waited for Karen to make it up the latest hill.

Following Carlos' direction, they headed uptown, across the Bow Bridge—the surface of the lake was lost beneath a dense fog that made it seem like the lake itself had disappeared, boiled into steam—and into the maze that was The Ramble. If the zombies' brains were as rotten as their bodies, then they could never manage to navigate that maze of passages.

Carlos, on the other hand, could find his way around in the dark. He'd been practicing to do exactly that. People went in there at night. Couples had sex. It was a stupid thing to do because the cops would drag you out if they caught you, but people did it anyway because no one thought they would get caught.

He'd decided it was the perfect place to mug people. Catch them with their pants down and they won't give you much trouble. And it was unlikely that they'd report it to the police. Perfect.

Summer was the ideal time to try it, and he was planning on doing it that night. He'd learned all the routes through the winding lanes, both the concrete footpaths and the secondary dirt trails that never appeared on any map, and that might lead from a cul-de-sac to a small meadow in a valley.

No, the creatures would never be able to find their way around.

Unless, of course, they could smell living people in the Park. Then, all bets were off.

He strode up to the front of the group. Santillán was peering into the dense fog ahead, trying to see what was waiting.

"They're behind us," Carlos said.

"I'm not worried about the cavemen. I'm worried about all the animals. There's a herd out here somewhere, and we have no idea where they went." She sighed. "But I can't see a thing in this gunk. Which way?"

"Take the right-hand branch. We can cut straight through."

She moved forward onto the indicated path and then, a couple of steps in, turned and smiled. "Thanks for coming for me."

"I thought you were a goner. It hit me pretty hard."

The smile widened. "Yeah. I saw that. I liked that."

"You did? I was waiting for you to kick my ass for doing it."

"I like that you cared. No one else even moved. Not even Gomer over there. Sure, he would have risked his life to save me if we we'd been out in a desert somewhere fighting Arabs or whatever, but if I was already dead…he didn't give a damn. You did. You should have seen yourself: trying to avenge my death like Rambo."

Carlos felt himself turning red. He stuttered something, and he laughed.

"Hey, don't get mad," Santillán said. "A girl can really fall for that kind of thing."

If anything, that made it worse, and they trudged along in silence until they started climbing a hill. Finally, he screwed up his courage to ask the question he'd been holding in. "How did you manage to survive? I thought you were a goner. Please don't tell me you're a zombie now."

She laughed and put her hand into the neck hole of her uniform and pulled out some kind of deformed lump of metal. "This thing saved me."

"What is it?"

"It's junk now, but it was a pretty thick medallion when I put it in there. When that Salesman guy gave it to me, I thought it was some kind of magic thing, but I apparently just needed a big hunk of iron in my shirt. Let me tell you something: if that dude with the golden tooth offers you anything, take it, no matter what it is, and no matter what his price."

"Yeah. I think I got that message already. He sold me a…"

The other soldier jogged up. "We need to wait for Karen," he reported.

"Dammit. You're going to carry that kid for her if I have to shoot her," the corporal fumed. She stalked down to where the woman was struggling up the hill. Karen couldn't have been more than ten yards behind them, but she was completely lost in the fog.

"You doing okay up there, Jessie?" Carlos asked the girl on his shoulders. The weight was starting to hurt, but he refused to slow down. He could take it for the child's sake. They'd already tried piggyback, and Jessie hadn't been able to hold on.

A scream cut through the pea-souper around them. Karen. Carlos ran as fast as he could down the hill towards it.

The zombies were only feet from Santillán. She took careful aim and dropped the closest.

"Run, now."

"I can't…" Karen began, but a yell and the sound of gunfire behind them cut her off.

Then the other soldier, the one they'd left behind on the path, screamed.

"They're ahead of us and behind us. What do we do?"

Santillán growled her answer. "Into the forest."

The trees appeared to be on the zombies' side as they scratched them and tore into their clothes, giving each inch grudgingly.

Last into the undergrowth was Santillán. She replaced the clip in her rifle and lay down covering fire. Then she came in behind them.

Finally, the trees thinned out and Santillán grabbed Karen's arm and dragged her up a hill at high speed. They actually came up out of the mist and could see for some distance…the park was all concealed under a blanket of thick white cotton.

The corporal turned to Karen. "How the hell did you even manage to survive, anyway? You're going to get us all killed, not just your daughter."

"I'm going to save Brittany if all of the rest of you have to die for me to do it. You just want to take her from me. Just like her father. He said I couldn't take care of her until I got over the death…" She wasn't able to go on.

"Mommy, tell them about the whistle."

Santillán gripped her arm. "Yes. Tell me. Quickly."

Karen said nothing, her eyes vacant, and ineffectually attempted to remove her arm from the corporal's grip. The kid came to her mother's rescue. "When mommy blows into it, the monsters can't see us."

"That's stupid."

"It's true. I saw it."

"Can you show me the whistle?"

Karen fumbled inside her pocket and retrieved a shiny metallic whistle, a bit larger than the typical gym teacher's standard.

Santillán snatched it and glanced Carlos' way. He shrugged and she rolled her eyes. Then, without hesitating, she put it in her mouth and blew. It was obvious by the way her cheeks puffed out that she was giving it a good effort, but no sound emerged.

"I don't think this works," a slightly purple Santillán said.

"It works," Brittany replied. "I could hear it."

"So could I," a voice above Carlos' head pitched in. In the excitement, he'd almost forgotten that he was carrying the other little girl. "It's like singing."

Brittany nodded back. "Yes. Singing."

"I couldn't hear a thing," Carlos said.

"The monsters won't find us. Please."

So, they advanced through the ever-thicker fog, taking turns keeping the whistle going. Either it was working, or they had the most incredible luck because, despite getting lost in the strange curlicues of The Ramble and coming close enough to touch zombie animals several times, the alarm was never raised.

Eventually, they came to a place where a wooden bridge crossed a shallow stream beside a ravine.

"Stop," Carlos said. "I know exactly where we are. That way is north," he pointed across the bridge. "If we go the other way, we'll eventually hit Seventy-Second Street again, with the sheep meadow on the other side. Which way do you think we should go?"

Santillán said: "I think we should keep moving north. Maybe we can get out that way." She turned to the other woman, but she was lost in her own thoughts, exhaustion etched on her features. But no one offered to carry Brittany. There was no one else who could do it, even if Karen released her grip on the girl.

They trudged along a misty bank. The lake still invisible under the white mist. At first he'd thought it had to be some magical substance coming up from Hell to take them all with them, but the more they walked through it, the more it stuck to his skin and soaked his clothes, the more he was convinced that it was just regular water vapor. Perhaps some strangeness kept it close to the ground, or perhaps there was just a whole lot of it. It swirled around in the wind, disappearing into the sky only to be replaced by more and more.

They bypassed the Great Lawn along a footpath to the West Side. Carlos though the grass, the trees, everything, looked to be ravaged, as if a tornado had hit…but with everything covered in dense fog, he couldn't tell. He'd get a tantalizing glimpse of uprooted trees or torn up turf and then the wind would change, and the middle distance would disappear behind the ever-present white veil.

Carlos still kept looking into the steam, trying for a glimpse of…

He didn't want to admit it to himself, but he was pretty sure the world outside the Park had long since ceased to exist. He just wanted to catch sight of some skyscraper still standing to know that zombies hadn't eaten the city.

That obsessive staring paid dividends.

"Wait," he said. "Stop. There's a bunch of dead guys coming this way."

"Where?"

"Up ahead."

They found a secondary path—mulched as opposed to paved—and melted into the trees.

"I'm pretty sure we lost them," Santillán said.

"Yeah."

Unfortunately, the path acted as a funnel and the mist within was like walking through cotton candy. Santillán stumbled on something.

"Stop. I found another body."

They'd been encountering dead bodies all over the place. Not enough to account for everyone who must have been in the Park when it got cut off, but enough that they'd developed a method. Santillán would check for a pulse while Carlos distracted the kids. They thought Karen was so tired that she wasn't even aware of what was going on around her.

"This one's alive." Then a pause. "Oh, God. Get over here!"

Carlos let go of one of Jessie's legs, grabbed onto Karen's arms so they wouldn't get separated in the mist and dragged her over to where Santillán's voice was coming from.

They found the corporal struggling to help an enormous black man to his feet. A man in uniform.

"Carlos," Santillán said. "Meet Sergeant Williams, the toughest bastard to ever wear the uniform."

The way she looked at the man, pride mixed with respect gave Carlos a twinge of jealousy. The big guy looked like he'd gone a few rounds with Muhammed Ali, but he hadn't been knocked out. A black stain covered the front of his uniform, and there seemed to be blisters on patches of his skin. His eyes were bloodshot, and he stood with difficulty.

"Sarge, this is Carlos." And now the look was directed at him. "He's one of the good guys…even if he doesn't know it yet."

The big man's eyes turned to him, weighing, measuring, unconvinced. Finally, he spoke in a rasping voice. "It takes a lot to impress the Corporal, kid. I'd shake your hand, except you seem to have them occupied."

Carlos quickly let go of Karen and completed the ritual.

"If you don't mind my asking, why do you keep blowing into that whistle? It's not like there's any sound coming out."

Santillán interceded. "The Salesman guy, the guy with the hat. He sold it to Karen. We think it keeps the zombies away."

"It would have been a big help down in the tunnels."

"What tunnels?"

Williams turned unsteadily around and pointed to an open manhole cover, camouflaged with six inches of dirt and shrubbery. "Those tunnels."

"What in the world were you doing down there?"

The sergeant clenched his teeth and took his time answering. "It was the damnedest thing," he said, finally. "I think we were putting out a fire."

Williams needed serious medical attention. The wound on his shoulder was still seeping, and he was pretty sure he had some nice burns on the skin exposed to the steam. First degree for sure, probably worse in places.

But he was alive, and so was Santillán. Of course, that didn't surprise him: Hell hadn't created the zombie that could do that woman in. After all the rest of them were long dead, she would continue to kick zombie asses until she ran out of ammo, then use her knife until the blade broke and then kick, punch and bite the crap out of them until they decided to go annoy someone else.

Still, that she'd been the only other member of their squad to survive hurt. It hurt badly, and he wanted to hurt someone back.

"Do you know where the zombies went?"

"We think they went uptown," the guy called Carlos said, around the whistle. Santillán pulled it out of his mouth.

"What's that mean in English, city boy?"

"North," Santillán replied.

"And which way are you guys heading?"

"North."

He smiled. He should have known that the best corporal he'd ever served with would do her job. "Good. Mind if I join you? I brought this."

He held up the shotgun and Santillán raised an eyebrow. "Not exactly regulation."

"Why don't you let me worry about that," he replied.

"Yes, Sarge."

They headed north and soon found the way blocked by the back of a brick building. "That's the 86th Street Transverse," Carlos said.

A gap in the wall opened onto a narrow sidewalk. The street was embedded in the middle of the Park, crossing from east to west. Only a few dozen yards were visible in the mist, but what they could see was packed with abandoned cars. A few bodies lay in the street, but other than that, it was eerily empty, like the rest of the Park.

"They must have reached the place where they couldn't get back out and just stopped where they could." Williams shook his head. "They should probably have stayed in their cars with the windows up."

"I don't think it would have done them much good," Carlos said. He nodded towards a grey Toyota. A window had been smashed open and a trail of gore ran down the driver's door.

The park suddenly seemed too small, smaller than the tunnels below. It was as if the whole world consisted of what they could see in the mist and that the occasional glimpses of more distant places were just mirages, products of a decaying mind.

The mist was real. The mist held more evil than even the tunnels, and it was all coated in white, just waiting for them to walk into range so it could pounce.

A tendril of white steam brushed him, blown by a soft breeze, and Williams shuddered.

"What's across this street?" he asked.

To his surprise, the woman carrying the child, the one they'd followed in here in the first place, and who hadn't spoken a word since they met again, spoke. "It's the Reservoir. I jog here when I can."

"That's the big lake, right?"

"Yes." The woman seemed almost too tired to stand, but she held the kid in her arms with no sign that she would put her down to rest.

He thought back to the MTA map of the Park. Who had he given that to? It didn't matter, whoever had it was dead now. The Reservoir was almost as wide as the Park, and it was huge. But there was some space on the southern west side where there was some space between the water and the West Side. He remembered the crocodile-zombie things in the tunnels, and he had an idea that a big lake would be the perfect place for them to lounge around waiting for someone to stumble over them.

They turned left—westwards—and ran straight into a small pack of enormous wolves herding a group of young men. Working like sheepdogs, they nipped at the heels of anyone who strayed. Unlike sheepdogs, when they nipped, they drew blood.

As the group drew into sight, the green eyes turned their way and a couple of large males—or what would have been males when they were alive—separated themselves from the pack.

Santillán raised her M4. Then she did something strange. She took her left hand off the barrel and put the whistle in her mouth. Blowing, she began to walk towards the two zombies.

Instead of responding to the challenge, however, the two wolves simply padded back to their pack, as if they'd never seen the group.

The corporal walked straight up to the nearest of the undead abominations and stood next to it, puffed cheeks indicating that she was blowing hard on the whistle.

When she lowered her rifle, Williams almost screamed at her. But nothing happened. She took another deep breath and in that instant all the wolves turned to look at her, but as soon as she began blowing again, they turned away. Santillán calmly pulled out her knife and drove it into the nearest wolves' skull with an audible grunt.

The zombie fell to her feet.

She moved on to the next.

Williams watched, mesmerized as she took out the entire pack, ten or eleven zombie wolves, hundreds of pounds of muscle and fang, dropped by a tiny soldier who was barely taller than the biggest members of the pack.

In the end, the last couple of zombies realized something was wrong and they stirred, but they didn't have the sense to run, and Santillán killed every last one of them.

"Hey!" the corporal shouted at the youngsters in the group. She walked up to the nearest, a guy a good two feet taller than she was, and rapped on his head. "Anyone home?"

The guy reacted. He blinked a couple of times and suddenly seemed to realize where he was. "Oh, God. The army's here. We're saved. Thank you!"

"You're not out of the woods yet, kiddo," Santillán replied. "But you can help us get there. You game?"

"Whatever you say. Those things were gonna kill us, weren't they?"

"You betcha."

By this time, Williams had reached her. "What the hell was that, corporal?"

"It saves ammo," she replied and walked off to see if she could get the rest of the kids on their side.

A few moments later, he realized his mouth was hanging open. He closed it and sighed.

Carlos handed Jessie off to one of the kids. At any other time, this group would have been full of swagger, owning the streets. Now, they huddled together, trying to stay as close to Sarge as they could. The one who took the girl onto his shoulders was much bigger than Carlos, yet he looked at the three-year-old like she could save them.

There were six boys in the group, dressed in the Harlem uniform of sweats and basketball shirts. Every one of them wore a baseball cap.

Sarge turned to them. The big soldier looked like he would keel over at any moment, but when he glared daggers, there was no doubt who was in charge. "Are any of you armed?" he asked.

The youths might have been scared, but some responses were ingrained. They milled around and mumbled, none of them catching the eye of Authority.

"Did you hear me? You," Sarge put his finger on the nearest kid. "I'm not here to bust your balls. I need to know what kind of weaponry we have against the things out there. Now talk."

"I have a knife," one of the kids said, showing a switchblade. "It's just a small one, though."

"Good. You see what Santillán did there? Think you can do that? You look like a strong guy."

The kid puffed up. "If they stand still like that? Yeah, I can do that."

"Good man. Anyone else?"

They weren't armed. Clearly these kids were just kids. Not everyone in Harlem ran with a gang, unfortunately.

"All right, let's move."

Santillán walked beside him. "What are we doing, Sarge?"

"You just gave me an idea. Our job is to protect the public from whatever the hell is happening in here."

They walked onto a path alongside the Reservoir, invisible in the mist. A sudden gust of wind moved the white steam aside.

Carlos froze.

"Did you see that?" he hissed, working to keep his voice under control. "The Reservoir is gone." Everyone turned to him. "I mean it's still there, but there's no water in it."

They all looked. An obliging gust blew a deep, wedge-shaped hole into the mist and the truth of Carlos' words became clear. Stunned silence reigned as they viewed the deep hole where the lake should have been.

"Where'd it go?" Karen said.

The big sergeant gave a start. "I think I know. And I think I also know where all the steam came from. We were putting out a fire...well, this is where we got the water. Must have been one hell of a blaze, though."

Carlos exchanged a look with Santillán. "I think we know where the fire was, Sarge," she said. "And yeah, it was a big one."

They quickly told him the story of the conflagration below the carousel, making sure that Jessie couldn't hear any speculation regarding what might have happened to the people caught in the south of the Park.

"A fire that size, plus all the water in the Reservoir...no wonder we're covered in steam."

Even as he said it, however, a cool breeze began to blow, and the mist stirred itself. Tendril by tendril, wisp by wisp, it floated into the air and disappeared.

It revealed a ravaged wasteland. The Park around them, just yards away from the footpath they'd been following, looked like it had been bombed from orbit. Gaps in the trees showed where trunks had been torn out of the ground. Craters pitted grassy areas. Smoke could be seen rising in the distance.

But Carlos paid attention to none of that. He was much more concerned with something he could see outside the green confines of Central Park. Through the green air, he could see a building, a single sky-scraping finger. Lights were on inside. A helicopter buzzed around the roof.

It meant everything to him. It meant the world was still there. All they had to do was to fight their way out of this mess.

A shot echoed to his left. He turned to see the Sergeant firing at a huge column of animals coming towards them. A mammoth, green eyes blazing even in the bright sunlight, bore down on Santillán. She blew into the whistle and the beast appeared to lose its bearings.

"Over here," kids called. "There's another path down this way."

"No," the sergeant's voice boomed. "Look."

The column of animals wasn't alone. Caught inside, hunted looks on their faces were dozens, hundreds of people. All walks of life were represented. Office workers and housewives, tourists and toddlers. They were being herded by the animals, helplessly putting one step ahead of the other, walking to whatever doom the zombies had decreed for them.

Many never made it. As Carlos watched, a restless-looking saber-tooth pulled down a young woman near the edge of the mass of people and gorged on her. Other animals joined in, tearing the body to gobbets. Bears and buffaloes and wolves all together without friction, in a crusade against the living. Plant eaters and meat eaters united.

"No!" Santillán screamed. She opened fire and managed to take down a number of the animals in the group.

"Hold your fire, soldier. Save you bullets for the ones we can actually help."

The sergeant handed Carlos a knife. "Do what you can," he said.

The messy work began then. Shielded by the constant sound of the whistle, they matched the animal convoy's progress southwards, and they killed as many as they could. Santillán and the sergeant accounted for most of them, dozens each—one bullet per animal—but Carlos and the kid from Harlem bagged themselves a few as well.

The first one was the hardest. He approached a wolf, one of the smaller ones, certain that it would hear him or spot him at the last moment and tear his throat out. When the smell of rotting flesh hit him, he nearly ran away, nearly peed in his pants. But he forced himself to move forward, conscious of Santillán's eyes on his back.

He struck the way Sarge had told him to: through the eye. No use breaking off the blade trying to pierce a skull. The wolf gurgled once and collapsed, and that was all there was to it.

He backed away slowly and saw Santillán looking. She nodded once, and he knew that, come what may, he would die before backing down.

It was slow going. The massed animals trudged through the Lawn and simply plowed aside the foliage and went straight across the Ramble like there was nothing there.

Likewise, they hardly noticed the humans chipping away at their numbers. Why would they? Carlos suspected the mammoths at the front of the pack trampled more of their own than the humans were culling.

By the sheep meadow, his feet dragged, and his clothes smelled of long-rotten death, but he refused to stop. Santillán had managed to get inside the outer interval of monsters to reach a group of people. She signaled to Carlos to go after one of the big lions and to the Sergeant to take a saber-tooth with his shotgun.

Then she fired over the top of the people near her at a wolf between the two other animals. As the wolf fell, and trusting Carlos and Sarge to do their jobs, she pushed as many of the people near her forward as she could. Some saw what was happening and enthusiastically helped. Others apathetically moved out of the way. Many allowed themselves to be pushed through the gap.

Though the operation was a comedy of errors, the end result was ten more people in the group, a motley assortment that included dazed office workers, a woman missing a shoe, two octogenarians and three kids.

They celebrated like madmen while the newcomers looked on in confusion and Santillán blew into the whistle.

"Let's go get some more," the Harlem kid with the knife exulted.

He turned back towards the animals, but never made it any further. A thick shaft of wood appeared to sprout from between his shoulder blades and he fell to the ground, blood bubbling from his mouth in in gushing spurts.

"What the fuck?" Williams shouted.

The answer came in the form of the cavalry charge from Hell. Eight zombie cavemen rode eight zombie mammoths into their midst, scattering soldiers one way, Carlos and the kids another, and trampling many of the people they'd just rescued. Their battle cry was a bubbling, defaced version of an elephant's trumpet. Behind came all the zombie cavemen you could ever want.

"Blow the whistle!" he yelled.

"I'm blowing as hard as I can!" Santillán replied.

But the cavemen kept coming. As the mammoths came around for another pass, Carlos found himself face to face with caveman with a sloping forehead. This guy must have been ugly even when he was alive. Unlike the dumb expression of the animals, however, intelligence lived in the evil green eyes.

The caveman had a spear and he thrust it at Carlos' face. He jerked to one side and the creaking zombie overbalanced, allowing Carlos to slash at his neck with the knife.

The thing's head flopped to one side and then fell onto the floor. The body stood for another second as if unsure whether it wanted to die or to keep going. Finally, it too collapsed into a putrid pile.

Carlos quickly tore the spear from the zombie's hand and tossed his knife to the guy with the dreads. He looked like he could handle himself in a fight.

All around them, shots were being fired, mammoths were stampeding and people were screaming.

A zombie advanced on Karen and Brittany. Carlos drove the point of his spear into its earhole. He'd half-expected his weapon to break in pieces, but the wood wasn't zombie fare. This had been carved out of good, if greenish, stock. They'd obviously made it after entering the Park.

He grabbed the sharpened stick this one was carrying and handed it to another of the kids.

A staccato burst of gunfire rang out and he turned to see Santillán surrounded by three mammoths. He sprinted in her direction but was still ten feet away when she calmly finished blowing the last of the riders from his mount.

She cocked her head at him. "You really thought you could save a trained American soldier armed with her service rifle using a spear? You are the cutest boy ever." Her smile as she said it strengthened his resolve to keep going.

"Let's get back to the kids," she said. "I'll keep us covered."

The attack from the caveman had faltered. Four or five of the mammoths still seemed to be active, and there were plenty of cavemen on foot, but, unlike the animals, the extinct humans didn't seem to relish the thought of fighting an enemy who fought back. They had faded to one side, allowing the defenders to regroup.

Most of them had made it through in good shape. One of the Harlem kids had a dislocated shoulder which even Sarge couldn't pull back in, but other than that—and the poor kid who'd taken the spear in the back—the original group was accounted for.

Santillán handed Karen the whistle. "Think you can take this on for a bit? My cheeks are killing me."

The mother nodded, but, as she was about to put it into her mouth, Brittany took it from her and, without saying a word, began to blow.

Carlos kept his eyes peeled for zombies. The lengthening shadows—he estimated it must have been after seven already—might hide anything.

The cavemen had retreated behind the long line of animals. It was disheartening to realize that the long, sweaty eternity of stabbing zombie after zombie really hadn't done much to thin the herd.

"What are they doing?" Williams said.

The cavemen cavalry had circled around behind the animals and the people they were driving like cattle and, with the weak zombie trumpeting that characterized them, charged straight into the rear of the column, trampling animals at the back and driving into the center of the formation.

The effect of the charge rippled through the parade of zombie mammals. First the rearmost bolted, and that triggered the ones ahead. Within moments, the entire group had forgotten the people they'd been driving. The entire pack stampeded.

Right towards where Carlos and the rest of the group were standing.

Karen watched the grey, mottled animals approach. There was something wrong with them, she knew, but it was a distant knowledge, blurry, like trying to read a sign underwater.

She also knew she was too drained to do anything useful. Probably dehydrated, too.

Well, at least there was something she could do about that.

An abandoned vending cart full of drinks lay on its side less than three feet from her. She rummaged around and pulled out a coke. It was a regular one, full of sugar and caffeine, but a tiny, unheeded voice in her mind screamed that there wasn't much time.

She drank deeply. Another voice was yelling. It wasn't in her head, though.

"Mommy!" It was Brittany. "Mommy, we have to run. Please."

The animals were closer, but it was impossible to feel alarmed. Her brain felt like it was wrapped in cotton. She took another long, deep drink.

"Mother!"

She started, wondering how Brittany dared take that tone with her. Then she saw her child's face, tears streaking through the dust.

Brittany was scared. Brittany was in *danger*.

Nothing was going to happen to Brittany. Not on her watch.

Karen ran to her left and through an open space in a trampled fence. *The Sheep Meadow*, again, she realized. That wouldn't help her. The thing to do was to get into a wooded area, to hide behind trunks big enough that not even the mammoths would want to ram them.

So, she raced along the fence as fast as she could, just barely ahead of the stampede. It was a strangely slow procession, but if they'd been moving quickly, she would have died then and there. Her legs ached as if she'd run a marathon, but that was only a drop in the ocean compared to the way her arms and shoulders burned from carrying Brittany around.

But what choice had she had? The people who'd offered to carry her before were all dead. If she'd given her daughter up, then Brittany would be dead, too. Like her sister, the little girl who hadn't even lived long enough to have a name. They were going to decide on the name in the final month… when she'd been born so premature, they hadn't even had the chance to do that.

Not even that.

Karen's tears ate away at the fuzziness, as if waking her from a bad dream. She heard the thunder behind her, smelled the rotting meat of animals intent on destroying her world. Adrenalin gave her strength for a final sprint.

After a long run, when she thought her strength would give out or that the mass behind her would catch up, she finally hit another gap in the fence, a gap that led onto a path among big trees. She ran as deep as she could and then hid behind the thickest tree she found.

A sharp crack—a rifle?—echoed through the woods. No. Not a rifle. It was the sound of a think branch breaking, maybe even the trunk of a small tree.

It was all around her, right behind her.

Brittany handed her the whistle.

Karen smiled, dropped the empty soda bottle, brought it to her lips with her free hand and blew.

The animals poured around her at full tilt. Not one turned to look.

Finally, they were past. Gone. Nothing remained in the little pocket of woods but the stench of their passing.

Karen put Brittany down. "Walk beside me for a bit," she said.

Brittany nodded, eyes big.

They headed back towards the Sheep Meadow. The shadows had grown so long that there was almost no direct sunlight in the open area, and what there was was far away. Karen shivered in the warm air, exhausted arms trembling.

"Let's sit here for a while."

The turf was torn and uneven, but it was soft. She sighed in pure ecstasy.

"Is it over, mommy?"

"It is for us. I don't think I can move anymore."

Footsteps approached and Karen lifted the whistle to her lips.

"Karen!"

They turned to look. A wild man with a spear was sprinting across the grass, closely followed by a gang of kids and a tiny soldier. She nearly bolted before she recognized Carlos in the lead.

"We thought you were dead for sure. You just stood in front of them. There was nothing we could do."

"I know."

He knelt down in front of Brittany. "Are you OK?"

Brittany nodded and Karen felt a rush of warmth for the man. She'd clearly misread him earlier, when she'd been convinced he was something sleazy. A mugger, a con man, a used-car salesman.

Now, covered in putrid slime, he shone like a knight in armor.

Jessie was sitting on the shoulders of one of the other boys. She clambered down and hugged Brittany like they were best friends. Kids were so good at cutting through everything and being real.

"We've got to move," Carlos said, earnestly.

"I'm not going anywhere."

"The cavemen are coming and that," he nodded to the whistle, "has no effect on them."

"I can't move," Karen sobbed.

"I'll help you." He put her arm around his shoulder and stood, supporting her weight.

She said: "I need to carry Brittany."

"No way." He gestured to one of the kids. The youth nodded grimly, bent and put Brittany on his back, piggyback.

"Can you hold on there?"

"Yes," her daughter replied.

"Good. Hold on tight. You'll be safe with me."

"I know," Brittany replied. "You're big and strong."

They walked south again, back the way they'd come.

"Where's the sergeant?" Karen asked the soldier, the dark-eyed woman who barely reached Karen's shoulder.

She swallowed. "He's holding the cavemen off in that maze with all the little paths."

"The Ramble."

"Yeah. He decided that no one was going to get over the bridge as long as he had any ammo."

They walked in silence for a few steps.

"But I haven't heard any shots now for five minutes. I don't think Sarge is going to make it. I never thought he could be gone."

Karen remembered the man who'd tried to stop her from entering the Park an eternity ago. Suddenly, finally, her terror had passed, and she was thinking clearly. "So, he died in a desperate last stand against zombie monsters and you're crying over him? Wouldn't that have been exactly how he wanted it? A guy like that isn't meant to die in bed. He's going to be a legend."

Santillán looked up, surprise in her features. "Yeah. You're right." Her plodding steps regained a sense of purpose, her head held high.

"Don't even think about it," Karen said.

"What?" The innocence in the corporal's voice almost made her laugh. Didn't these people know that trying to lie to the mother of a three-year-old was a futile exercise? She could tell from the slightest quaver when something was being hidden from her.

"You aren't the sergeant. You have to keep on living. If that means you don't get to be a legend, it's something you'll have to live with. You'll need to be satisfied with just being a hero."

"I don't know what you're talking about."

"Get us out of here safely, and you will."

They crossed West 65th street and the carousel came into sight. Dread gripped her when she saw the animals milling around the building, the only completely undamaged structure, she guessed, in all of Central Park. It would normally be closed at this time—she knew from bitter experience that the last ride was at 5:45—but light was coming from the interior.

Evil, green light.

"Hello." The guy in the fedora was back. He'd found an unmanned concession cart and appeared to be hocking drinks.

"I'm not thirsty," Karen called back. "And if I was, I'd just take what I need form an abandoned cart."

"I have some really special water. From the Ganges, in fact."

"Ugh. Isn't that the river where they bury all the dead people in India?"

"But no one ever gets sick if they drink it."

Carlos and Santillán walked over. "Just buy whatever he's selling," the soldier said. Then she turned to the Salesman. "I'll take it."

"No. This offer's only good for Karen." A gold tooth found a stray ray of sunlight and glinted.

Karen sighed. "I'm too tired of this. Just give it to me."

"There must be a trade," Johnny replied.

"What the hell. I have nothing left to trade. Just give it to me."

"I can't do that. But you need this water. It was blessed by a man high in the Himalayas. It cost me a lot to get this. I'll take your daughter's bow in exchange."

"No."

He sighed. "All right. But you guys really need this." He turned to Santillán. "What have you got for me? How about the letter your dad left you when he ran out on your mom?"

Santillán automatically reached for her breast pocket, but Karen stopped her. She took a deep breath. "I can't let you do that. Here, take the bow." She unhooked it from Brittany's hair, reflecting that whenever she wore a bow to a birthday party, it wouldn't last five minutes, even while the kids were sitting around eating cake. So, of course, it had survived the zombie apocalypse untouched. It was still clean.

In return, she received a canteen, cylindrical with a cork stopper and wrapped in cloth.

"Wow," Santillán said. "That is really old-school. You can imagine Lawrence of Arabia drinking from something like that."

"Was he in India?" Carlos asked.

"How the hell should I know?"

Karen thanked the salesman. "I suppose you're going to fade out of sight now, like you did before."

"No. I think I'm going to watch how this one plays out."

They turned to look back at the carousel. The light within was getting brighter, pulsating like a beating heart.

A ball of green-tinted fire emerged from the front entrance to the carousel.

Karen felt her stomach tighten. It was the same flame they'd seen underground. Diminished, weakened, not nearly as mesmerizing, but the same.

Something had doused its power, turned it into a shadow of what it once was... but it was still powerful. All it needed was a place to rest, to gather its forces.

She knew it wasn't of this world, but it could only gain power in this world. And it would, unless it was utterly destroyed.

Today, it had been defeated. It hadn't expected to have the reservoir dumped on it. But it wasn't dead, it could still destroy the world.

Perhaps not in Karen's time, but certainly in Brittany's. It would remain here, like a cancer, growing until it devoured the host.

That wasn't going to happen.

Karen marched down the hill, pausing only long enough to bark at the kid holding Brittany. "If this goes south, you run like hell, you hear me?"

The kid nodded.

Eyes focused on the ball of flame, one hand wrapped around the neck of the canteen, Karen barely noticed when Santillán and Carlos stepped to her side. She caught Santillán's eye and the soldier shrugged. "I still have a couple of clips left. Would be a pity to waste them."

"And you?"

Carlos turned red. "I'm here to take care of Santillán."

"Isn't he just too cute?" the corporal said with a huge grin.

The animals saw them coming and moved in their direction. At least some of them did. The rest appeared hypnotized by the glowing ball of flame.

"Crap, Brittany's got the whistle," Karen said.

"It's better that way. It will keep her safe. I've got this."

Santillán raised the rifle to her shoulder and fired. One shot, one animal on the ground. Another; another. Three for three.

And the path was clear. Karen sprinted forward, leaving her escorts behind. At one point, a lion-looking thing dove at her, but a shot in the head stopped it.

"Go!" Santillán shouted. "You're clear."

Karen knew she would die, that her legs wouldn't hold her any more after this sprint, but if it would save her daughter...

The light seemed to sense Karen's approach and tried to float into the air, but it was too late for that. She already had the cork out of the canteen, and she made a throwing motion that sprayed water forward and upward. Most of it splashed into the ball of fire with a sizzling roar and a huge puff of steam.

For a moment, it looked like the light would survive, like it hadn't been enough. But then the evil green flickered and went out. Something small and hard and black and dead fell to the floor.

Exhausted, Karen landed beside it. The animals could do what they wanted with her. She'd done her part.

Carlos saw Karen fall. He took a couple of steps in her direction, but the zombies closed ranks around her. With a sinking feeling, he imagined what would happen next—he'd seen it often enough over the past few hours. The blood would fly, the bones would be cracked for their marrow, and the undead things would leave another child without her mother.

And then he had other problems. The cavemen came back and charged into the clearing around the carousel.

Carlos looked up in surprise. Williams, he realized, had been a serious badass. Of the column that had been chasing them, he counted just one mounted rider, and the contingent on foot had been decimated to the point where he actually believed they could fight back.

Santillán fired one shot and the guy atop the mammoth lost his head. The corpse toppled onto the ground.

All right. He'd let her use her final few bullets on those guys. He was going after Karen, not for Karen's sake but for Brittany's. That kid, and Jessie, as well, had held it together much better than most of the adults.

He wasn't going to let that awesome little girl grow up with no mom.

Carlos steeled himself and charged, spear raised, fully expecting to get clawed and bitten but determined to get to Karen before they killed her.

And then, something strange happened. Well, stranger than all the weird shit that had already been happening, anyway.

The animals began to growl and screech and make assorted animal noises, cheapened by the fact that they were all dead and rotting. And then they attacked.

They didn't attack the humans, though. They attacked each other.

Saber-tooth tigers lunged at wolves. A pair of mammoths tried to trample a complete pride of lions as they, in turn, went for the jugular. Armored turtle-like creatures bashed everything in their path. The smallest animals, little rats and scavengers and whatever, were being ripped to shreds left and right.

One of the wolves turned to him and snarled, but it was a half-hearted thing after the real attacks of the past hour, more the sound of an animal warning him to back off than a precursor to disembowelment. Keeping the spear raised, Carlos went the other way.

That was when it hit him. The dead eyes glaring evilly from beneath the matted, rotting fur had turned black. Not green, black. The light was gone.

The things were still zombie, still smelled like death on a stick, but now the sense of evil had faded. Dangerous, sure. Unpleasant, absolutely. But just dumb animals who were, at present, intent on tearing each other apart just the way they might have if they'd invaded each other's territory while alive.

He spotted one of the cavemen, a gnarled little fellow, trying to take down a mammoth with what looked like a shotgun. The zombie human would press the barrel against it and push, making a noise like a strangled bang as he did so.

The mammoth took no notice. It was one of the ones in the fight against the lions.

Karen lay where she had fallen, untouched except for some kind of medium-sized lizard pulling at her sleeve. Carlos kicked it into the underbrush, a feeling of satisfaction suffusing through him as it arced through the air and disappeared. He hadn't realized just how good it felt to kick something as opposed to having to be terrified all the time.

He picked Karen up and carried her out of the melee. The animals barely noticed him.

The herds had thinned to the point of nearly disappearing. He couldn't see where they were going until, a few yards away, some kind of large bison, not hurt as far as Carlos could see, simply dropped onto its side and stopped moving. A second later, it scattered to dust.

But not every animal was keeling over. There was still a major furball happening right at the entrance to the carousel. Lions, tigers, wolves and the remaining mammoth were intent on clawing and biting and tusking each other into oblivion.

He watched the bison go down, watched the lions disappear one by one.

Finally, two combatants remained: a gigantic saber-toothed tiger, one that was somehow less of a zombie than the rest, and even had tawny-looking skin and, to Carlos' surprise, the caveman who'd picked up Williams' shotgun. Obviously tired of not being able to get the magic deathstick to work, he'd complemented it with a spear.

The tiger and man circled each other, neither seemingly aware that the fight they were reenacting was tens of thousands of years in the past, or that the battle they'd been revived for was already lost.

The intensity of the stare-down was as vivid as if they'd met each other at the entrance to the man's cave at the very dawn of human existence: one of the creatures looking for food, the other trying to defend its home and its family from the most fearsome monster he knew.

The man had more patience than the tiger. It struck first, launching itself from ten feet away, but with enough strength in the zombie legs to aim for the man's neck.

Even so, it wasn't enough. The spear rose up in a practiced motion and impaled the flying saber-tooth. The caveman stepped back, planting the butt of the spear on the ground and letting the packed dirt bear the brunt of the impact.

The tiger gave a final growl and died.

The caveman raised his arms—one hand still holding the shotgun—to the sky with a roar of triumph. Like every sound from a zombie throat, it was a shadow of what it should have been.

Another figure moved towards him. Santillán stood just a couple of feet away until the caveman noticed her. She held his gaze.

"Congratulations, motherfucker," she said.

A single shot from her rifle at point blank range removed the zombie's head from his shoulders. Santillán bent over to retrieve the shotgun and wrapped an arm reverently around its barrel.

Hundreds of people—live people, the ones that had been herded by the animals and had survived the stampede—pressed closer. A few were celebrated the end of their nightmare. They were hugging him, shaking his hand. Santillán, against her own protests, was placed on someone's shoulders and given a quick victory lap.

But many more had simply collapsed where they stood as soon as they realized they were safe. Some cried. One woman was calling out desperately for a boy named Tommy. It would take a long while for these people to feel normal again.

"Get them out. It's only over for you if you can get out of the Park in the next thirty minutes. The walls are down."

Carlos wasn't surprised to see the guy in the Fedora standing beside him. "It's a five-minute walk."

"Yeah, it is. So you'd better get started. Herding scared people is never easy." He turned as if to go, and then thought better of it. "You did well. Some people are harder to read than others…I'm glad you chose right."

"It was a close call. Closer than you think."

"It's always closer than you think." The guy walked off through air that was no longer green.

"Are you sure you're all right?"

The medical service people had swarmed them as soon as they hit Central Park South. Everyone who had so much as a bruise got dragged into an ambulance and treated for everything from dehydration to concussions. They'd even managed to carry out one guy who was bleeding badly.

"Yeah, I'm fine," Carlos said. "Take care of the rest of them."

Jessie sat beside him, crying. She'd looked desperately for her mother among the stragglers, but she wasn't there, and she was starting to suspect the truth.

"Do you know your dad's name?" Carlos said.

Sad eyes turned up to him without much interest. "He was called Eddie. Mom says he left us before I was born."

Anger, the old anger, flowed through him, but he got it under control. This wasn't about him, after all.

"I have something for you. Look." He pulled the book, the last thing Johnny had sold him, out of his pocket. A bookmark fell out and he glanced at it. It had been sold at some toy store in Chicago. Whirly-something. He put the bookmark in his pocket and opened the book.

"Once upon a time…"

It was about a girl who lost her mother and, magically got a new father. But it wasn't written for a young child, it was written for an adult. It was a warning, it was a test, and it was a promise of a different kind of life.

Something in the text made him keep reading, but at the end Carlos was disappointed. It wasn't the kind of story that could distract a little girl who'd just lost everything. What would come next for her? Foster homes? A life of living hell? Even Carlos had had his mother growing up. His life was better than wat awaited little Jessie.

"I'm sorry. I'll tell you a better story…there was this girl, no, this princess, who…"

"Don't worry, daddy. The story you told me was perfect. I love it when you read to me?"

"What, this? It's not even…"

Jessie hugged him. "Thanks, daddy. But I'm too sleepy for another story right now." She put her head against his thigh and closed her eyes.

"Oh, God. We need to get you some help." He looked around desperately. There were no paramedics in sight but, standing just out of arm's reach was Santillán. The soldier looked tired. "I need some help. Jessie…I think she snapped. She thinks I'm her father."

"Of course she does."

"But I'm not."

"Weren't you even listening to the book you just read? That sounded like a magic contract to me." Santillán sat on the other side of him.

"Come on. She needs help. She might have bumped her head or something. This isn't all right."

Santillán put a hand on Carlos' thigh and looked into his eyes. "Listen to me a second, she said. I'm not kidding. You're her father now."

"But that's…"

"Impossible? I would have though a zombie invasion was impossible, too. Where'd you get the book, anyway?"

"The guy in the hat…"

Suddenly, he realized what he was saying, what the implications must be. "Oh, my God."

"So, the real question isn't whether it's real or not. The question is how you feel about it."

"I…". He looked down at the little girl. Who was going to believe a munchkin like that was his? But then again, who was going to argue if she insisted? Was he any better than a foster home?

Too many questions. "So they let you go, huh?"

"They're too busy, I think. We might have gotten out of the Park, but this sort of stuff is apparently still going on all over the world."

"What, zombies?"

"That's the thing. It's not just zombies. Demons. Monsters. You name it, it's out there somewhere. Hell, they're even saying that the Park might not be safe either—something weird starting up again inside. They were talking about moving out in a few minutes, once they have everyone stabilized."

"So, you can go home?" He felt disappointed.

"What? No way. I'm in for the debriefing from hell when someone realizes that the rest of my squad is as dead as Elvis. I told them I needed to talk to you because I had a question I wanted to ask."

"What question?"

"It changed now. Now, I want to know whether you're going to pick up the burden you just set up on yourself."

"What?"

"That little girl. Will you be her dad, or won't you?" She held up a hand, and Carlos saw that the soldier was back. He wasn't dealing with the woman whose butt he'd tried to save so often over the course of the afternoon. "Just so you know, I think you can have anyone else read that book to her and take the load off your shoulders."

Carlos didn't hesitate. "No way," he replied. "I've screwed up a lot of things in my life. I think this is one I can actually get right." He had no idea how he'd manage that…but he'd get a job at McDonald's while he thought about it. He could go to school.

"Ah. Then I have another question." He looked into Santillán's eyes and the soldier was gone. "Can I help?"

He leaned in and kissed her. A long, sweet, exhausted kiss. "Not unless you tell me your first name," he said as they broke it off.

"Sofía," she replied.

He let it wash over him. "I like it."

She laughed. "Like you ever had a choice."

Then she kissed him again.

# Surfing The Quantum Swell

by Michael H. Hanson

*"There is at least one thing worse than fighting with allies—And that is to fight without them."*

—*Winston Churchill*

PROTEUS, TRULY EXHAUSTED FOR THE first time in his eons-long life, hovered a few feet above a field of hundreds of dead undead spread across The Sheep Meadow. As zombies, this fallen crowd (but a fraction of the resurrected that Proteus suspected were being birthed all across Central Park) had risen to spread their evil into the city itself, but with all his power he had ripped into their bodies, mostly unseen as his form was actually hundreds of thousands of tiny living particulates, rendering the undead into piles of shredded body parts.

In previous months, Proteus had satisfied his literal bloodlust by preying on one to three human criminals every couple of days, draining their bodies of life-preserving blood and fueling his own depleting energies. The swarm of his being could be arranged in such a manner as to duplicate the appearance of any person or creature, making him the ultimate master of disguise. Here though, battling large numbers, he felt no need of subterfuge, for this macabre altercation was all too familiar to him. Most perceived him as a swirling cloud of reflective even fiery insects, but the power of his form was more like a huge school of piranha fish. And though the degenerate matter that made up these undead forms was disgusting to digest, feast on their rotting juices he did, as he had no other choice and no other way to replenish his resources.

Ten thousand years ago Proteus had been at the vanguard of an invading army from a distant Hell dimension. It had been at the time of the previous *Sha'Daa*, that once every ten-millennium mother of all apocalypses that had regularly struck the Earth since the very creation of the solar system itself and which was recurring right now. Memories of that last epic ever so slowly flooded his mind.

Proteus was born of a distant dimensional hell, given mighty powers and abilities so that he could scout out the Earth upon arrival, spying out defenses and finding the most populated centers for targeting. But on that day long ago, when his hell and dozens of others managed to breach their dimensional portals and spill out across this lush blue and green planet, there arose a mighty being, in the guise of a mortal human, but possessing terrible powers that were a match for every hell god and hell army he came upon.

At first Proteus thought there were a cadre of these humanoid destroyers, but over the course of a day he came to suspect that it was but one being, a fallen one from on high that had been expunged and now sought to vent his anger and rages upon all others. A being that could traverse time itself, and so appeared to be many places at once…The Destroyer.

By the end of two days that marked that Sha'Daa of long ago, every invader had been killed, and every portal closed. The Destroyer had saved Eighth Century B.C. humanity from total destruction.

Proteus, using all the stealthy powers at his command, somehow managed to hide from the slaughter, and after his own dimension's portal was destroyed, was trapped on Earth for the next ten thousand years…

Senses that he had not used in thousands of years suddenly began to awaken as Proteus left The Sheep Meadow as a cacophony of screams echoed from Strawberry Fields. The sun began to set when a bright flash of green light flooded across the park for a full two seconds. Some second nature biological mechanism in Proteus's alien DNA automatically activated and he felt his individual components violently vibrate for several seconds and then stop.

*A quantum flux*, Proteus thought in surprise. The tingling he felt throughout the cloud of dots that comprised his being was something not experienced since he had passed through a magical portal that bridged his home dimension with that of Earth ten millennium ago. As he continued to levitate toward the portion of Central Park named after the slain John Lennon's song, a realization seared through Proteus's mind, *when the green light flashed I moved between dimensions.*

He reached Strawberry Fields but found nothing. The screaming had stopped. The grounds appeared undisturbed and there were no signs of humans, zombies, or anything else in sight. The surroundings appeared very familiar.

*This new dimension*, he thought, *it is almost a duplicate of the last. But something in the air warned Proteus that all was not as it seemed...So strange...*

Screams followed by five terrified teenagers exploded from the tree-line up ahead. A moment later what could only be described as two huge zombi-fied mastodons smashed through three large American Elm trees like they were made of cardboard. Proteus saw that the teens, two boys and three girls, were about to be trampled, and he shot forward to intervene.

As the lead mastodon was about to stomp on the blonde boy who had tripped, fallen, and was standing back up, Proteus shaped his particulates into that of a large rapidly spinning tube that struck the four-footed monstrosity in the side, instantly stopping it in its tracks, and burrowing a three-foot diameter hole straight through it. The beast screamed a death knell and fell over sideways, make the ground shake when it struck Earth.

The second monstrosity charged Proteus whose form scattered in every direction when two huge tusks raked and stabbed the air where he had just gathered. A moment later he reintegrated into another spinning and sparking shape not unlike a wine barrel with neither lid nor bottom. Two seconds later he drilled a large hole straight through the side the monster, popping out a huge beer can-shaped chunk of flesh, organs, and bones as he'd done with the other one. This was instantly followed by a second earth-shaking vibration.

Proteus, suddenly noticing that the five teens had stopped running thirty feet away, rearticulated himself into the very realistic looking shell of a tall, middle-aged man with light brown hair, dark rimmed glasses, and wearing an expensive white suit.

"Mister," one of the teen girls, an attractive slim brunette wearing cut-off jeans and a red t-shirt with the words Frakk You, Adama in out-of-date Pandora font scrawled just above her breasts yelled out, "how did you do that? Are you a super-hero like the Gold Avenger?"

Proteus strode toward the youngster and frowned at these last words. He was more than familiar with the former military human Burt Buchowski. He'd crossed paths with the unusual human-insect hybrid in previous weeks, though always beneath notice of the amber humanoid's attention as in each case he was disguised as a frail child, innocent youngster, or dispersed to the point of being invisible to most mortals. Buchowski had seemed as intent on punishing rapists and murderers in Central Park recently as Proteus had been for over three centuries. It disturbed him that the new vigilante had allowed himself to be seen and identified on more than one occasion, but he appeared to be new to the cause and was probably just inexperienced, and then the recent Sha'Daa had started.

"Are there more of these…giant creatures around?" Proteus asked.

The girl who had first spoken stepped forward without fear.

"I dunno," she said, "maybe…but that's not the worst of it!"

"What then?" Proteus replied.

"Lots of people, hundreds of them, they're like, all hypnotized or something," she shouted.

"Yeah man," a black teenage boy wearing a white t-shirt and torn blue jeans and kicks stepped forward, "at the Central Park Carousel! They're marching to that thing and disappearing. I think they're being killed! A bunch of our friends joined the lines and wouldn't listen to us and fought us off when we tried to drag them away."

"Yeah," the first girl added, "we freaked and ran and then those two giant hairy elephants started chasing us!"

"Mastodons," Proteus mumbled and turned his head toward the south and nodded for a moment, before snapping it back.

"Run. Now. Get the hell out of the park and head straight home," Proteus said to them with ferocity, "move it before something even worse comes along to chomp the five of you up."

This was all the kids needed to hear as they turned around and began running.

When they were out of sight, Proteus's form dissipated, rose into the air, and flew south as fast as a strong wind.

Even though the moon had dropped behind a green cloud, Proteus could see the Carousel, lit up, and spinning wildly a hundred yards away and closing with what appeared to be hundreds of human beings in long lines waiting to board it, and it was just at that point that a bright flash of green filled the air, then disappeared.

Proteus continued moving forward, but the Carousel had stopped moving. Just ten feet from it he scanned the area but found no one. The lights had gone out and not a single human being was in sight. He dropped to the ground and coalesced back into the semblance of the white suited man he had used earlier.

*I've transitioned into another duplicate reality of the park,* he thought, *I wonder what surprises await me here…*

In answer to his thought, three ten-foot-tall zombified dinosaurs walked onto the grass from behind some trees.

*Dilophosaurus*, Proteus mused, remembering them from having watched *Jurassic Park* on the big screen decades ago.

The three carnivores sprinted directly at him with their clawed fore-limbs raised.

"Well fuck me…," he said aloud.

CHAPTER THREE

# Curtain Call

### by Jason Cordova

*"We all have a dinosaur deep within us trying to get out."* — Colin Mochrie

## PART ONE

SERGEANT JULIA RUSSO, NYPD AND member of Strategic Response Group Six, rolled her shoulders and sighed as she peeled off her sweat-soaked undershirt. It had been a long day and the only thing on her mind was a hot shower and luke-warm coffee, a particular quirk of hers which had caused many of her fellow police officers to give her some grief. Caffeine was caffeine, she figured. There was no reason to scald the roof of her mouth in order to imbibe in her favorite non-alcoholic beverage. She sniffed and wiped her nose with her forearm as the unpleasant aroma of unwashed uniforms assaulted her.

The women's locker room at the Twenty-Eighth Precinct wasn't horrible, but it wasn't as nice as her old home at the First Precinct near Wall Street. Still, the promotion to the Special Response Group had been a welcome change, all things considered. However, it meant her normal days of patrolling the neighborhood and being bored were a thing of the past. Being a part of the SRG meant more responsibilities, more challenges to her everyday duties. Especially when the G-7 Summit was currently being held at the Apollo Theatre in Harlem.

An odd location at first glance, but not completely unexpected one. The Apollo was historical, and offered security concerns, true. It also was easier to lock down, and the streets were simpler to clear of the roving bands of protestors who spoke out against what they viewed as global cronyism. Plus, it amused her to watch the wealthy elite kids from Connecticut look around in fear as the decidedly non-white residents of Harlem watched them protest the wealth of nations. Julia, having grown up in Brooklyn, could only laugh at their unease and dawning realization they were not protesting on the *mean streets of Greenwich, Connecticut.*

After a quick shower, she pulled on clean clothes and got back into uniform. The protests which had plagued the morning seemingly eased off, though she had heard rumblings of *something weird* going on near Central Park. Despite a childhood in Brooklyn, she'd only been in the lush park in the middle of Manhattan once in her teen years for a softball tournament. Still, weird things in Central Park weren't all too uncommon. After all, every summer it seemed the homeless and the crazies congregated there. Especially during the night. Back when she was at the First Precinct she would listen to the radio chatter from the officers on the Central Park Precinct and their calls when it was slow. Weird was the norm. She would have been far more concerned if the calls coming in indicated all was quiet.

"Sergeant Russo?" a voice called into the locker room. She glanced over and saw one of the SRG's senior officers, Captain Tish Groller, looking her way.

"Yes, Captain?"

"SRG is mobilizing again," Captain Groller announced without preamble. A tough-as-nails fourteen-year veteran originally from Queens, she had been recruited into the SRG after assisting with a drug lord's takedown. It had also led to a few officers in that precinct being forced into early retirement after it had come to light aforementioned officers were on the take from local crime bosses. Even though it was universally accepted that Captain Groller was not a rat, it had still earned her the ire of a few of her fellow officers. A change of scenery had led to her rapid rise in the Special Response Group. "Your team, along with the Mounted Unit, are going to the north side of Central Park. We've had multiple reports of a 10-51 moving through the park, estimated numbers is between two and three dozen."

"The Mounted Unit as well?" Julia asked, surprised. She glanced at the clock on the wall and saw it was almost midnight. "I thought they'd be in their beds and asleep already."

"Your disdain of equine creatures and their riders is noted," Captain Groller smirked. "Standard loadout. Take extra zip-cuffs. I want these little *pleasant individuals* resting comfortably in our cells here for the next 72 hours in relatively good health."

"Yes ma'am," Julia nodded, understanding the captain's subtle nuances perfectly. "Relative being the operative word."

"Sergeant, there is a sadistic streak in you that I sometimes wonder about," Captain Groller chuckled darkly as she placed her pointer finger in the end of her nose. Her gray eyes twinkled. "Bullpen in fifteen."

"Got it, ma'am."

*Damn it,* Julia didn't say out loud. She had really been looking forward to a quick nap and some food. Though only halfway through her shift, it had already been an eventful one. Then again, she knew — as every member of her SRG team did — the protests always brought out the crazies. Even those who were only peripherally aware of what precisely they were protesting oftentimes became the most worked up over trivial things. Mob mentality, she guessed.

Throwing her still-damp body armor on top of a clean shirt, she began the long process of gearing up. Uniform pants were tactical in design and made to withstand the wear and tear which would normally destroy the normal police uniform slipped over her hips, while her steel-toe boots were worn with extra-thick socks. Despite the summer heat, experience had long taught Julia the value of having comfortable footwear. Her pants were folded into her boots to provide a little extra security, as well as to deny any protester a piece of loose clothing to drag her off the line should violence occur. Given the history of protests the G-7 summit tended to bring, SRG 6 was expecting it.

The final item of her gear was more of a ritual than a necessity. Her nana's broken watch, which she'd been gifted upon her grandmother's death years before, went into her pocket. The hands rested on the two and the seven still, which marked the exact moment her grandmother had fallen down the stairs and died. Julia, for some reason she could never explain to anyone else in the family, had never gotten it fixed, preferring the broken watch face with the time marked forever. It had helped her though thick and thin, through the good times and the very bad. Just knowing her nana was looking down on her every time she looked at the broken watch had kept her going.

"Hey sergeant," a familiar voice called out. She tucked the watch away in her pocket. After finishing her last button on her uniform blouse Julia looked up. She grimaced internally as she recognized the speaker.

"Lopez," Julia nodded in reply. The young patrol officer had only recently been assigned to SRG 6, and Julia had quickly come to despise her. The rumor mill surrounding the men and women in SRG 6 was that Eva Lopez's assigning to their team was nothing more than a public relations stunt, given her youth and relative inexperience. Seeking to have an attractive and energetic face to be the new brand of SRG was an astute political move, Julia was forced to admit. It did not mean she had to like it, only to deal with it.

"I overhead the captain," Lopez continued, her dyed blonde hair bouncing up and down animatedly as she talked. "Is the entire team deploying this time?"

Julia sighed. She had tried to keep Lopez from being deployed in crowd dispersion exercises, preferring the perky young woman to assist with crowd control events, such as parades and public gatherings like the Cinco de Mayo festivities. Julia was a short but stocky woman, with years of weight training to help bulk her up. Officer Lopez was almost waif-like in appearance, barely meeting both the height and weight standards of the NYPD. The last thing Julia wanted was for the young woman to get crushed by a non-compliant protestor. Or worse, dragged out of a line and unable to resist properly due to being out massed. It was a danger to the rest of the team if the gap was exploited, as well as the obvious need to rush in and subdue those who would take Officer Lopez from the line.

"Appears so," Julia confirmed after a brief pause. She knew she couldn't hide the young woman from harm forever, despite the top brass of the NYPD's desire to do just that. "Get your armor back on and be in the bullpen in ten."

"Yes!" Lopez pumped her fist and disappeared, leaving Julia alone and feeling very tired.

"I'm getting too old for this crap," the thirty-year-old woman muttered under her breath. The young officer's excitement was not contagious, as most veterans of SRG 6 hated dealing with the anarchists masquerading within the groups of protestors. Still, Julia knew the possibility of taking her frustrations out on the protestors would be bad publicity for both the NYPD and SRG, both of which were already under close scrutiny simply due to campaign promises of men and women far more crooked than any cop on the beat could ever be.

Was there ever a time she looked forward to doing crowd dispersion as much as Officer Lopez did? Perhaps, a long time ago. Back during her heady days within the First Precinct, when she had been a young, hotshot rookie fresh out of the Academy and ready to take on the world. To protect and to serve and be a police officer in one of the finest organizations in the world.

Before all of that had been stripped away by one man.

*DeAndre.*

She shivered uncontrollably. Even to this day his name brought both fear and excitement to her. Danger was a strange allure. Fear and desire entwined into one smoldering emotion. Her lips curved upwards into a smile as she thought about the past. For a brief moment she luxuriated in the good, pushing aside her exhaustion and frustration.

"No," she told herself. The bad memories came flooding back. The lies and manipulations, and the eventual truth of her being nothing more than a tool for her former love. A useful tool, but nothing more. She shoved the memory of DeAndre's chiseled physique from her mind and remembered the sense of abandonment when she'd discovered the truth. There was a time and place to stroll down Memory Lane. It was called The Pub and typically involved multiple shots of tequila.

Unable to do anything about her damp hair, she made her way to the bullpen. Long experience told her the briefing would be short and to the point, which was a good thing. The last thing any of them needed before going back out to handle a bunch of protestors was a laundry list of do's and don'ts from some officious ass. If anything, Captain Groller was the complete opposite. It was one of the many reasons Julie loved this precinct and believed she could become so much more with a fresh start.

Julia looked around the crowded room and inwardly smiled. Every single one of her team was there and looked ready to roll. They were steady and reliable, known quantities in an otherwise chaotic situation. *They will do a fine job*, she thought as her eyes took each and every one of them in. *They always do.*

"Good evening," Captain Groller said as the last few stragglers from the Mounted Unit made their way into the room. They lined up against the wall near the door and stood, eyeing their counterparts. The Mounted Unit was a vital piece of crowd control exercises, and even Julia had to admit the sheer weight and size of the horses came in handy. She simply didn't like their penchant for getting all of the press. Granted, SRG didn't need any press, but it was disheartening for Julia sometimes to see the positive public opinion of the Mounted Unit when compared to the coverage SRG received.

The lights dimmed and an overhead projector came on. Everyone could see the layout of the northern edge of Central Park, along with the southern border of Harlem. There were four individual units marked on the map, as well as a general direction arrow leaving from a red mass near the Duke Ellington statue. Inelegant, perhaps, but Julia was familiar with Captain Groller's briefings. Less showy, more information.

"We've rehearsed this for weeks now, so you all know your positions and duties," Captain Groller continued after a long pause to allow the latecomers to get settled. "There's been a slight change to deployment zones, but the plan remains the same. We have been provided a detailed description of the planned route for the protestors. Truth be told, it's a dream come true. They won't be protesting directly at the Apollo but instead are massing at the Duke Ellington statue in Central Park before coming to One Hundred Tenth Street Station. They'll hit the Two and Three lines to ride north. I don't want them getting into the station and the Transit Authority has agreed to shut down both lines running into Harlem for the evening, citing repair work. Make them march north through Harlem to protest, I don't care. But they will not enter the station. Sergeant Russo?"

"Teams One and Three will coalesce near Lennox and Central Park," Russo said as she stepped up to the dais. Her laser pointed circled two areas in particular. "Group denial and active dispersion. Team Two will be held in reserve at Fifth and One Hundred Fifteenth. Team Two will also be with the Mounted Unit to help drive the protestors towards Lennox and hopefully, push them down into Central Park proper. Let them deal with the crazies in there. It's dark. Maybe they'll get lost? Don't know, don't care. Larkins will lead Team One, and Mejia will be with Team Three. I will be leading Team Two."

There were a few chuckles at this. Central Park might have been situated in the middle of the most populated city in North America, but it was still one of the spookier places after the sun set. Darkness always brought out the strange in New York, and in the blazing misery of the summer heat it only grew worse. There was history as old as the earth in the park, and at night it sometimes felt the ghosts came out to play. The ominous feeling often chased out the typical casual tourists and allowed the NYPD to keep crime there more or less under control.

"Homeland Security will also be assisting with identifying and detaining known agitators with radical ties," Captain Groller added as she resumed her position at the dais, allowing Julie to slink off to the side where she was far more comfortable. There were a few groans in the bullpen at this revelation. Nobody liked working with the feds. They had a bad habit of stomping all over jurisdictions and ignoring the carefully laid out plans of the NYPD. Homeland Security was the worst, though, since they did not need to even charge those they arrested due to *national security*. They rushed in like a bull into a crowd, gored and stomped on whoever they felt like, then wandered away and wondered why nobody was grateful.

Julia was torn by this. On one hand, it would make dealing with the low-level drug dealers of the city easier to hold, especially if they could be held indefinitely. On the other, well, there were rights for a reason.

"You have your orders," Captain Groller said as she killed the projector and the lights came back up. Julia blinked at the sudden brightness. SRG and the Mounted Unit members stood and began filing out of the bullpen. Julia stopped as she heard Groller's voice. "Sergeant Russo?"

"Ma'am?" Julia's head snapped up and looked at her commander. Captain Groller's smile was wicked.

"I don't want any of those punks setting their eyes on that subway station," she said in a cold tone. "You understand? Make sure your team, and Sergeant Alexander's, understand this."

"Yes ma'am!"

"Well then, get your ass out there," the captain ordered. "Contrary to popular belief, taxpayers are not covering your paychecks so you can sit in a comfy room eating doughnuts all day."

"Not even the chocolate sprinkles, Captain?"

"Well, maybe one…"

# PART TWO

One thing Julia was thankful for was the late hour. Most of traffic in lower Harlem had been redirected around the Duke Ellington statue outwards of three blocks, and quite a few of those who lived there were wisely staying off the streets and out of the police eye. Every resident knew the NYPD were looking for a reason to arrest people, and the prevailing thought was to allow the protestors to be the ones wearing zip cuffs while they stayed indoors and watched. Julia couldn't blame them. The NYPD had a bad reputation in this part of the city, and SRG was the boogeyman, despite the outreach programs.

Still though, she had been expecting some sort of crowd when her small team from SRG 6 descended upon the area where the protestors had been reputedly congregating at. Instead of a teeming mass of humanity angrily hurtling whatever they could fit into their hands at the police, there was silence. For Julia, born and raised in New York City, the silence was louder than anything she had heard in her life.

There was a street vendor near their position who appeared to be selling gyros, and a solitary man in a fedora and trench coat buying one. This seemed odd because summers in New York were usually miserably hot, even after nightfall. However, this individual did not seem to mind and Julia quickly forgot about him as Teams One and Three moved off to One Hundred Fifteenth Street subway station, leaving Julia, Team Two, and the Mounted Unit alone to protect...nothing.

The circular street around the statue provided the police with a central elevated control point, since the protestors were nowhere to be found. Most of the police bands were quiet as well, which was unusual. Normal radio traffic for their precinct alone was constant on the usual hot summer evening. Tonight, though, there was a distinct subtle threat in the air, one which seemed to have driven even the most diehard of drug dealers and petty criminals into the safety of their homes.

Once a cordon was established preventing anyone else from moving along the street of Central Park North, Julia decided it was time for both the food vendor and anyone else not police associated to vacate the premises. She motioned for Officer Lopez to come over.

"Tell the vendor to relocate, and anyone else in the area," Julia ordered the young woman. Lopez nodded and moved away while Julia quickly scanned the area south of the statue. Goosebumps rose along her arms and she shivered in spite of the warmth. She looked up at the statue of Duke Ellington standing next to his piano and shook her head.

"Weird night, Duke," she muttered quietly. There was no other way to put it. Something in the air simply felt…*off*. She couldn't explain it, but the evening did not feel normal. Her eyes drifted further into Central Park and saw, much to her surprise, a heavy fog was forming over the expansive open space. It seemed to be forming just south of the lake. This would be normal… in December. She sighed and shivered. "Very weird night."

The Mounted Unit was moving in the middle of the circular drive, keeping their horses within the confines of Fifth Avenue. Being atop their horses gave them a better vantage point in a crowd normally. However, the elevated rise of the area around the statue brought her to nearly eye level with the lead rider. Julia waved at their commander, Sergeant Jasper Alexander. Using his knees, he guided his horse over to her, stopping just at the bottom of the brick steps.

"This seem weird to you?" She asked him in a quiet tone. Her hand waved around the quiet circle. "I've never seen Harlem this quiet."

"The horses are spooked about something," Sergeant Alexander admitted as he patted his mount on the neck. The chestnut brown horse shook his mane at his partner's touch. "Bolero here isn't bothered by much but look at his ears. He's not happy about something. Could be this silence, I don't know."

The horse's ears were turned back, though not flattened against his skull as she had seen in movies. Glancing at the other three horses she saw their ears in similar positions and their riders sharing uneasy glances. They were all disturbed. Something was definitely up, but for the life of her she had no idea what it was.

"Sergeant?" Officer Lopez had returned and sounded irritated. Julia hid her smile and turned to look at the diminutive officer.

"Yes?"

"The vendor packed it in and moved on," Lopez reported. She did appear to look bothered by something, which was unlike her normal personality. *Damn it all to hell, Julia thought as the faint vestiges of humor vanished. Is everything going to crap tonight?*

"And?" Julia prodded, reminding herself of the relative youth and inexperience Lopez had.

"There's this weird guy in a fedora and trench coat asking to speak with you," Lopez finished. "He's rather insistent about it."

"What, he asked to speak to the officer in charge?" Julia asked. Lopez might be new but even she understood the rules in SRG — do not identify the leader while in public. "What did you tell him?"

"No ma'am, he asked for you, Sergeant Julia Russo," Lopez stated. She pointed towards the entrance to Central Park. "He's over there by the trees next to the wall, ma'am. Want me to come with and provide backup, sergeant?"

"No, I've got this. We really don't have time for any distractions right now," Julia muttered but wandered over in the direction Lopez pointed anyway. She did have a few moments to spare, though the chances of anyone knowing her unit had been deployed to the area was almost nil. *Unless they know about DeAndre*, she thought. Her ex-boyfriend and father of her daughter probably had connections within many precincts around the boroughs, even while in jail serving time for distribution.

The thought almost made her pause and reconsider. She'd threatened DeAndre the last time she saw him, two weeks before he was picked up over near the Third Precinct. In an attempt to extort her for protection, he had tried to use their daughter as a point of leverage against her. Enraged, she had threatened to beat him senseless then report him for resisting arrest. He had laughed it off, but his words had lingered in the back of her mind.

What if this mysterious individual had been sent by DeAndre to remind her, even at Riker's Island, he could reach her anytime he wanted? It was a realistic question to ask. She'd run into a few members of his crew over the past few months. They hadn't said anything to her, but they didn't need to. Everyone knew what had happened between her and DeAndre. More than one was probably convinced she had something to do with his arrest.

*I can't hide the past forever*, Julia reminded herself and continued her walk, her right-hand drifting down to the collapsible baton on her utility belt. If this mysterious individual tried anything funny, it would be Julia with the last laugh.

As she moved under the trees, the shade they cast made the evening air a little cooler. Not great, but enough for Julia to not want to beat someone's head in if they looked at her funny. Summers in New York City were brutal, and with her riot gear on it was ten times worse.

*Why can't the spoiled rich kids protest capitalism in the fall?* She wondered as she spotted the most unusual individual waiting for her.

Despite the heat of the evening, the man was wearing a trench coat and a fedora. He was cleanshaven, which was something of a surprise given the outfit. She had him pegged as someone who was religious with the outfit in question. His pants were creased and he even had a suit vest on beneath the coat. He was certainly not what she expected.

*Maybe he's from Internal Affairs*, a voice whispered in the back of her mind. This thought caused her heart to seize a little. She knew she wasn't crooked, but there had been times in the past where she'd looked the other way. This didn't make her a crook. She was clean. She'd never taken money and never committed a crime while wearing he badge.

The voice, however, was insistent. *You helped DeAndre many times... telling him where Narcotics liked to stake out the most, and where his rivals have been pegged dealing from. Who knows what he did with all that information? You have your suspicions. Why do you ignore them so?*

"Sergeant Russo," the man removed his fedora and smiled as she approached. He had a gold tooth featured prominently on one side, where his incisor lay. Julia felt her guard go back up. *No, he's definitely not IA, she decided. Maybe mob?*

"Look, I don't have a lot of time right now," she said tiredly, though her eyes continued to sweep the man for any sign of a weapon. He looked clean but the trench coat was excellent for concealing many weapons, ranging in size from a pistol all the way up to a rifle. "What did you need?"

"My name is Johnny the Salesman," he introduced himself. He was finishing off what looked like a gyro. Suddenly she recalled seeing him when they had first arrived. "These gyros are great. Can I get you one? Oh, never mind. He's moved on. A shame. The lamb is quite good."

*Yep, this guy's with one of the families*, she decided. "Nice to meet you. Go tell your boss, whoever he is, that I'm not interested."

"My boss?" Johnny looked at her with some confusion before he seemed to understand. "Oh no, I'm not with any of the organized crime families. I'm not even with DeAndre. Or associated with Marcus, for that matter."

She froze as an icy rage she'd forgotten she had bubbled to the surface. He knew about Marcus, her ex-husband and former high school sweetheart. The man who had come within inches of ending her life with a gun and had, according to official reports, subsequently disappeared that very night. It was years in the past, and he'd been officially declared dead two years prior. He was gone, forgotten by almost everyone, and she was thankful for that.

"You say that name again, and you're going to need an orthodontist to give you more gold teeth," she promised him. The man held up both hands and shook his head.

"I'm sorry, my apologies," he said. He shot her a look. "You really do have striking eyes when you're angry. Has anyone ever told you that?"

"I'm about three seconds away from showing you just what I think of the word 'striking' being used in conjunction with me," she warned as her fingertips brushed the collapsible baton. It was a clear warning which even the dumbest criminal could understand. "Now what do you want?"

"I want to trade," Johnny said, his smile returning. "Not blackmail, so please quit touching your baton. It's making me mildly uncomfortable."

"You have information," she nodded, mildly relieved. He was a rat and was only trying to impress her by his knowledge. It was classic informant behavior — show the PO just how smart they were, and how invaluable they were to their boss, and in exchange they'd get paid or even relocated to a better life once they helped bring down the big boss. They all dealt with the same four reasons why they'd betray their boss.

*MICE.*

Everyone who'd ever run a confidential informant knew the acronym's meaning. Money, which was pretty obvious and the majority of the lower-levels of CIs who worked with the NYPD. These criminals were the ones who were out to make a quick buck, usually a junkie needing a fix and willing to snitch out a dealer. The reliability of these types was wishy washy at best, and every CI who did it for money was usually picked up in the end.

Ideology was the next, and these were usually the crooks who have had a sudden change of heart and began questioning their life choices. These were oftentimes the best sources, but also the worst because their newfound sense of guilt and justice often overrode their common sense. Too often these informants were found dead after a few deaths of their former accomplices. However, these types could bring down empires…when handled correctly.

The next was Julia's least favorite, coercion. Extorting an informant to gather information put the CI on the defensive, and once one applies the pressure the feeling of resentment never truly goes away. The CI will look to undermine the investigator any way they can, and sometimes to the police officer's detriment. These types often weren't even criminals, merely people who worked in proximity or even unwittingly for the main target of the investigation. Unreliable didn't even begin to describe the information an investigator attained from this sort of source, yet many others swore by it. Julia didn't understand their approach, which is partly why she decided not to pursue a detective path in her career.

Lastly, ego. Julia liked these CIs because they were doing it for their own reasons. Their boss had slighted them and wanted revenge, all the while calling it justice. The best part about dealing with egocentric CIs is eventually they would be investigated as a known quantity, since a wise detective always kept a separate file on the CI while working on the investigation. The time would eventually come when the snitch would become the arrested, and all would be right in the world. Invariably the informant slipped up and was caught by his crew before he could turn all of the evidence they had, but once in a while the NYPD got lucky. Perhaps her night wasn't going to be so bad after all.

"Of sorts," Johnny agreed. "I trade items."

"Even better," she smiled. He'd brought evidence on the first meet? Even the guys over at Organized Crime Control Bureau didn't get this lucky. Her crappy night was definitely looking up. "What have you got?"

"This." With a great flourish he pulled out a small pocketknife roughly the size of her palm. It was closed, but the handle was inlaid with what appeared to be silver or steel, she wasn't certain. The rest of the handle was an unusual colored wood unlike anything she had seen before. It was rather pretty, she thought, though she didn't understand how it tied-in to a mob boss this potential informant wanted to rat on. *Unless it was used in a murder or assault of some kind by one of the so-called untouchables*, she thought as Johnny continued. "The handle is from an English whitebeam tree, the same which was harvested by King Brian Boru himself to make his mighty sword lost upon his death at the Battle of Clontarf. A friend of mine had it in her shop in Ireland and made a trade for it, and now I am offering it in trade to you."

"That's nice," she grunted and pointed at the closed knife. "Who'd he stick with it?"

"Huh?"

"The knife, your boss," Julia clarified. "What'd you say his name was, Brian? Is there DNA on there we can use? Who'd he knife? Who's your boss? Did he wipe the prints off before you snagged it? Who else has touched it?"

"Oh, no, that's not what I'm here about," Johnny said and chuckled. "I'm simply here to trade you this knife because you're going to need it. I'm not in the mob or anything of that sort. Well, not in the manner you're thinking of, in any case."

"Look, buddy–"

"Johnny."

"Yeah, sure, Johnny," Julia pinched the bridge of her nose as a fresh wave of exhaustion rolled over her. Once hopeful, she could see her dreams of a peaceful night of bashing in the skulls of protestors quickly disappearing as her frustration grew. "It's been a very long day. I've been on the beat since this morning, and I won't get to go home to my kid until tomorrow at the earliest. God knows how my mother is dealing with her or what stories she's filling her head with. So either explain what you're trying to sell me, or beat it."

"The *Amhrán na Breoiteachta* is an ancient weapon of evil used to fight evil," Johnny explained. Julia's weariness grew with each passing word from the man. It was as if he didn't understand anything what Julia saying. Or, more than likely, simply didn't care. She'd seen men like this before and did not like them. They were too one-minded and wouldn't consider anything or anyone else once they had set themselves upon a certain path. For this Johnny character, it was clear to Julia his desire to trade was overriding all sense of self-preservation. Why he kept insisting he had nothing to do with the mafia, however, was a mystery to her.

"Okay, fine," Julia sighed. She understood now why he was called the Salesman. Persistent *and* annoying. "What are you looking for? Immunity? I can put you in touch with some people…"

"This isn't going the way I thought it would," Johnny stated, sounding mildly perturbed to Julia's ears. He tilted back his fedora and raised an eyebrow slightly. "Let me start over. I, Johnny the Salesman, am trading you, Sergeant Julia Russo of the NYPD, the *Amhrán na Breoiteachta* in exchange for…the broken watch in your pocket. Your good luck charm."

Julia recoiled as if slapped. Only three people knew about the watch, and one of them was back at the precinct, one in lockdown on Riker's Island, and the third was her mother. There should have been absolutely no way anyone other than the three could know about the watch. Yet this Johnny character not only knew about the watch, he'd known about Marcus as well. Her eyes narrowed as she looked at the man in a new light. Clearly this wasn't just some mob flunky.

"You're making a face," Johnny said, raising his hands to placate her. "A face which suggests I'm about to get my face smashed in with a collapsible riot baton."

"You're not wrong," Julia growled. "Who told you about the watch? How'd you know about Marcus?"

"Look, sergeant, I'm just trying to make a trade," Johnny said. "It's the Sha'Daa. The forces of evil are gathering to break through the barrier into this world. Close the gap with big red, fight off invaders, and all that jazz. The forces of good are rallying to their banners to protect the world. I am a neutral party forbidden from partaking, but I am allowed to make trades. Call it a legal loophole if you want. But time is short, sergeant. Before the sun rises tomorrow Earth will either be ravaged and destroyed or saved by the valiant few. This knife could turn the tide, one way or the other, if used at the right time. In exchange for your broken watch, a pithy trade. Worst case scenario? Nothing happens, you have the knife, and you can sell it to some hobbyist for a lot of money. Best case? Well…the best-case scenario is a bit wibbly-wobbly at the moment, what with everything hanging in the balance. Time is not on your side. But you must decide now, Julia."

Instead of reacting the way she wanted to — which was to smash the man's face with her baton — Julia paused. There was a ring of truth in the man's voice. The night felt odd, and she'd been expecting something bad to happen in the midst of the silence. This Johnny character might be crazy, and even might really be with the mob, but she felt the same conviction in his voice as she had in her nana's while growing up.

"It's just a watch, *dolcezza*," her grandmother's voice echoed in her head. A memory from Julia's childhood came to mind, when she had dropped the watch on the floor when her nana had let her hold it. She'd cried for hours, terrified she had broken something so valuable. But her grandmother had simply kissed her head, told her it was just a thing, and made her a batch of crostoli. The smells and the warmth of the kitchen were some of her fondest memories from her childhood. Before her world had gone sideways and best choices had led to…DeAndre.

"Can I trade it back later?" She asked. Johnny smiled and shrugged.

"Tell you what," Johnny said as he adjusted the fedora ever-so-slightly, lowering it back over to cast a shadow upon his features. "We survive the Sha'Daa and I'll entertain the offer. You might not want it back, though."

"I'm pretty sure I will," Julia countered.

"I don't know…"

"I will."

"Okay, fine," Johnny's disarming smile returned. "Let's say you will want to trade it back. If we all survive, I'll find you and we can make another trade."

"Fine," she said before cocking her head and giving him an unusual look. "What the hell is a Sha'Daa?"

"Well…*The Sha'Daa!*"

"Are you high right now?"

"No, I don't think so."

"Then start explaining…"

"I can't. Not enough time. Plus, I need to be off to a tattoo parlor soon."

"Can you summarize it?"

"Already did." Johnny smiled annoyingly and his gold tooth flashed. "I can offer one final parting word of advice, sergeant."

"What's that?"

"Keep an open mind."

# PART THREE

Julia wandered back to where SRG had established their base of operations, her mind lost. Johnny had sounded insane but the more she listened, the saner he became. The knife in her pocket was heavy, bulkier than the small watch had been. Feeling a little stupid about it, since she was pretty sure folding blades weren't around a thousand years or so ago, she pushed her doubts away and focused on the task at hand. The SRG still had protestors they needed to deal with.

*If they ever showed up*, she thought as she waved at Lopez. The young woman came running over the moment she saw Julia wave at her.

"Still no protestors, I take it?" Julia asked her.

"No sergeant, not yet," Lopez replied. "You think it was cancelled?"

"Doubt it," she shook her head. "Round up the team and have them meet here. We're going to reexamine our options and go from there."

"What about the Mounted Unit?" Lopez asked.

Julia sighed. *Rookies…* "Yes, them too."

Lopez nodded and turned away, clicking her radio to give the word. Meanwhile, Julia meandered over towards the Ellington statue, where the mobile headquarters had just finished being assembled. Large barricades blocked the roundabout's entrance onto One Hundred Tenth Street, forcing all vehicles to travel up into Harlem via Fifth Avenue. Two bored-looking patrol officers stood at the barricades with their vehicle.

There were no signs of any of the protestors. Julia began to feel a little put-off. Even traffic being diverted around was almost zero. It was very unlike the city of New York which she knew and loved. While she was certain traffic had been like this in the past, she couldn't recall it ever being so sparse. This was what she'd imagined like in the countryside would be like—quiet, no traffic, and lots of trees.

Her eyes drifted back towards the park. Through the trees she could clearly see the Harlem Meer, the large pond which a lot of hiking and jogging paths followed the shoreline of. While not the largest lake in the park — this honor fell to the Jackie O. Reservoir near the middle of the enormous plot of land — it was possibly the most frequented due to its proximity to Harlem, as well being close to Lasker Rink. In the winter, the New York Rangers often-times held their practices there, which was always a good show for civilians and police alike.

She looked out across the pond and spotted Nutter's Battery. Even in the dark the large hill was clearly noticeable, lit by the lampposts lining the concrete walkway surrounding it. Trees obscured much of the hill from her side but there was a break in them looking out towards the Dana Center. She'd never been to either place, but it was on her list of locations to take her daughter to once work calmed down a little.

She blinked as a weird trick of lighting changed the perspective of the area just a bit. The Meer looked different tonight. Julia couldn't explain it but combined with the odd feeling which permeated the air, it was enough to set her teeth on edge. A chill washed over her and she could feel goosebumps rising on her forearms. New York City was never, ever this silent. Not even in the worst of winter blizzards. Even then, some enterprising young idiot would be out and about, yelling at someone to move their car. This silence was unnatural.

Julia's eyes were drawn back to the Meer. There was something strange about it, yet she could not put her finger on it. Though it was very dark she could still see quite a bit, and the large island off to the far side near Lasker Rink was especially noticeable for an unexplained reason. The water seemed different, though. She blinked.

"What the fuck?" Julia muttered as she realized the reason the Meer looked different. It was because the was no water in the pond. It was gone, leaving behind only a dry, smooth pond bed and a few plants which looked oddly out of place. Somehow in the span of a few minutes the Harlem Meer had been drained of almost all its water. Over sixteen million gallons of water, gone.

Reaching for her radio, Julia paused as a bright green light flashed across the entirety of Central Park. Somewhere, a bird shrilled loudly and just as quickly, fell silent. The unnatural hush she had noticed before became oppressive and overwhelming. Her hands grew clammy inside her gloves. Nervous tension caused her to sweat. The already humid summer air was growing thicker with each passed moment.

"Team Three, this is Team Two Lead," Julia said to the members of her team. "Anybody else hear or see that?"

"Negative, sergeant," came a reply from Sergeant Mejia, who was with his team a few blocks away along One Hundred Fifteenth Street. "I didn't see–"

"Sergeant?" Julia asked as she checker her radio. "Team Three, come in. Comms check. Shit. Team One, Team Two Lead. I've lost contact with Team Three. Larkins? Sergeant Larkins, come in, over."

"Team Two reads you five by five, sergeant," Officer Patrick LeJuk responded over the radio. Julie nodded to herself. LeJuk was one of her more reliable team members, a steadfast veteran in SRG 6.

"Team Two, comms check," Julia decided. "Sound off."

"Silva, check."

"Lopez, comms check."

On and on they went until all twelve members of Team Two checked in. Julia was confused but also relieved. The comms issues were with both Teams One and Three. This was problematic, since there was no way Team Two would be able to reinforce either should an emergency arrive. However, since SRG 6 also had three other teams on standby to assist, Julia was confident in their ability to manage without Team Two rushing in.

"Mounted Unit?" Julia asked next as she stared at the muscular back of Sergeant Alexander from afar.

"Five by five, sergeant," came Alexander's reply. "I'm getting nothing else on the bands, though. Flipped through three different frequencies, nothing. Not even the emergency bands are up in this area."

"Local blockers," Julia muttered. She'd heard about them from veterans of both Afghanistan and other wars. Jamming a radio was pretty easy, all things considered. It simply took a little bit of knowledge and some electricity. Directional jamming was also a possibility but not something a police officer in New York City would anticipate handling. Not even one as trained in crowd control as Julia was. She glanced back at the Meer. Still empty, but instead of darkness throughout where the pond once lay a sickly chartreuse light seemed to be beckoning.

"Team Two, form up," Julia ordered over her radio. "We're entering the park."

"With all due respect, sergeant, not in our mission parameters," someone's voice came over the radio. She wasn't certain who spoke, but Julia felt fairly confident it was Officer Palmeira.

"We're NYPD first and foremost," she reminded them all. "Our mission parameters are fluid. There's something in the park, and it could relate to our objectives. Comms are down outside of the immediate area, so we can't call Park Precinct to ask them to investigate. So, we take point on this and can deal with the fallout later. What if the protestors are already in the park, en masse, and destroying property?"

Within moments her twelve person SRG team had formed up at her position. Julia weighed her options and after a moment, she motioned for Lopez to come over. The young officer quickly responded.

"Grab three and go get our gas launchers," she ordered Lopez. "Just in case there's a crowd in the park."

"Yes sergeant," Lopez nodded.

Julia waited as Lopez wisely grabbed three of the shortest officers to accompany her. *There just may be hope for you yet*, rookie, she thought as she turned back to look at the rest of her team.

"I don't know what we're going to face in there, so masks up in case any of those little fuckers has a camera," Julia said. The others all nodded in agreement. It was par for the course but being reminded never hurt. Plus, it was also a not-to-subtle prompt for them to be aware of their actions. Video evidence had a bad tendency to be selectively edited when it made it onto the news, and the last thing they needed was for an SRG officer to be identified by the seething masses for a public hanging.

Once they had pulled their masks up, she continued. "Flex cuffs and batons. Like the captain said, nobody makes it to the station."

"Holding pit?" someone else asked.

"Hogtie 'em with flex cuffs and leave them," Julia decided, considering. "Lopez and her team will take custody of them once the shield line moves on."

"Fuck," Lopez complained as she continued loading the converted grenade launcher with gas cannisters. "Anyone over two-fifty is getting their fat ass left there."

"Fair enough," Julia chuckled. "Make sure they don't aspirate on their own vomit though. Roll them onto their side or something."

"Got it," Lopez nodded. "They're adorable when they're cuffed and trying to throw up, though."

"You're a bloodthirsty little bitch…" Julia whispered admirably. She coughed, cleared her throat, and continued to new mission briefing. "Subdue, detain, move on. Don't dwell on anyone, try not to get carried away. We're on our own and no way to radio for backup, so if it's a huge crowd then we fall back to higher ground. Probably Fort Clinton but be ready for an audible."

"Sergeant?" a voice called from behind her. Turning, she spotted Sergeant Alexander and his Mounted Unit. "We'll be on your right, supporting. We can keep them from spilling onto One Hundred Tenth Street and out of Frederick Douglas Circle."

"Good idea," she nodded. "I'd normally be on board with that except, well, have you looked at the Meer?"

"What about it?" Alexander asked.

"There's no water in it," Julia pointed out. This got all of the officer's attention and they turned to see what their team lead was talking about. Excited and confused murmurs filled the stifling air. She waited for them to calm down before continuing. "We've all seen it low before, people."

"Yeah, but not empty," Lopez stated.

"I see where you're going with this," Alexander grunted after looking at the pond. "Yeah, you're right. Looks dry, too. We can probably take the horses out on it. I don't see a lot of large rocks for them to hurt themselves on, either."

"Let's get to it then," Julia ordered and the SRG lined up two abreast. The largest and burliest of the team, Silva and Mendoza, were in the front. It was a psychological trick used to put protestors off-guard. Having the largest officers dressed in all black and carrying ballistic shields and collapsible batons in front always gave even the most determined of protestors pause.

They moved as one down the sidewalk and into the park proper. Julia couldn't help but notice the air growing thicker once they actually crossed the barrier of Central Park. It was as though the park was a separate entity upon itself, not connected to reality of New York City for that matter.

"What the…?" Lopez's voice trailed off. "Sergeant, look! The fog!"

Julia glanced behind them. Following Lopez's outstretched hand, she quickly realized a thick fog obscured the rest of the city from the park. The unusually quiet night grew worse as all lights and sounds from the city ceased to be. To Julia, it felt that only SRG, the Mounted Unit, and Central Park existed in the world. The outside had ceased. Nothing remained.

The earth trembled and Julia almost staggered. An earthquake, in New York? While not the most common occurrence, she knew they did occasionally happen. Rarely, sure, but not impossible. Hurricanes hitting the city were far more common than an earthquake, even though she'd read somewhere the city was due for a big one.

*They always say that*, she thought as she grabbed hold of Lopez to help steady the young officer. The rest of her team appeared fine, though she could hear the horses from the Mounted Unit not enjoying the brief earthquake one bit. She turned her head to look over and see how they were doing but a cry of alarm brought her attention back to the drained Meer.

There was a large crack in the Meer. The disappearance of the pond's water made sense now, though why the pond wasn't a muck-filled mire was something she didn't understand. She was clearly looking at a sinkhole of some sort, dangerous but not normally fatal in a city like the Big Apple. Worst case scenario, Central Park North Station was now flooded with knee-high water and the Three Line would be shut down for some time. Irritating, sure, but the New York City Transit Authority was used to this during hurricane season. There were quite a few bilge pumps located in the subway system to assist should flooding occur.

*It should be fine*, Julia thought. Until it suddenly wasn't.

The earth shook a second time and the crack in the Meer grew larger. A putrid green light emanated from within, and an unearthly cry rolled across the entire northern end of Central Park. The shrieking sound was loud enough for all of the SRG members to slap their hands over their ears. The horses screamed in response and it was only due to the skill of their riders the horses didn't bolt. Something large and dark flew out of the chasm. Julia had the fleeting impression of a winged creature but she quickly gave herself a mental shake.

*Dragons aren't real*, she thought. *But that sure as hell looked like one.*

"Shields and batons!" Julia shouted at her Strategic Response Group team. In spite of the chaos raging before them, the well-trained and highly disciplined riot squad formed a solid shield wall immediately. Every one of their shields overlapped, braced by their left arms while their right held their baton. They were considered non-lethal weapons but any officer experienced with crowd control knew the batons could pack one hell of a wallop. Each collapsible baton snapped open loudly as everyone prepared to meet what was to come.

The first identifiable creature crawled out of the gap and stood. Julia had no idea what the hell it was, only that it needed to go back into the hole from which it came. It was shorter than a man but seemed heavier, squat. Muscular long arms featured long, claw-like blades instead of hands. The head was twisted and demonic, with glowing red eyes sunken in the thing's skull. Two tusks protruded out from the being's jaw.

Credit to the officers under her command, they stood firm and did not falter as the horrific visage of the demonic entity filled their gazes. Julia could see their hands tremble slightly while holding their batons, but they did not take a single step break. Nobody broke the wall. If she had anything to do with it, none of the eight would. Behind them, the second line knelt down and prepared to deliver pain of a different type.

"Humans," the demonic being hissed loudly. "Bow down and welcome your new ruler."

"Shaddup, asshole!" Julia shouted back, sarcastic instinct overriding common sense for a moment. "We're fucking New Yorkers! We don't bow down to shit!"

As one, the wall of shields took one step closer towards the demonic being. The creature blinked, clearly confused by the sight. The Class III ballistic shields were clear, allowing the officers wielding them to see through them while still offering protection against most projectiles thrown at them. Julia smirked as the demon took a hesitant step back.

*Just like the yuppies over in Manhattan*, she thought, amused. *Big and tough until we start walking forward to meet them. Then it turns into a bunch of scared kids throwing rocks from halfway down the block while recording how badass they are on their smartphones. Every fucking time.*

"Legions, come forth! Destroy these pissants!" the demonic being cried out as he spread his arms out wide. The earth shook a final time. The gap in the Meer grew and creatures began to pour forth. They were ancient, primal beings of unknown origin. Not the largest, but Julia was well-versed with the theory of death by a thousand papercuts.

"Hold the line!" Julia said as darkly colored beings charged across the open grass between the SRG's position and the chasm in the ground. It was a surreal sight to see anywhere, much less in the middle of what had been Harlem Meer only moments before. She had no idea where the water went, since there was no sign of it being drained into the gap, and the ground wasn't muddy in the slightest. She pushed the thought out of her mind. "Second line, ready gas!"

*Are those fucking dinosaurs? Holy balls, those are fucking dinosaurs!* Without much time to consider her options, Julia leaned heavily on her specialized training.

"Fire gas!" Julia shouted and four tear gas canisters *thumped!* out from the CCS-40B anti-riot launchers behind the line. The aluminum canisters landed roughly fifty feet in front of the line and began spewing white gas into the area. Designed for riot control over one hundred years before, the gas incapacitated almost everyone who inhaled it or got into their eyes. It worked very well against humans, disrupting a violent protest and scattering crowds when need be.

Apparently, it worked even better against dinosaurs because the tiny, feathered lizards streaking across the dried pond bed began to stumble as the cloud of CS gas enveloped them. They made odd little squawking sounds as they cough and lifted their feet to try and scratch at their eyes and nostrils. No longer moving as quickly as they had before, Julia was able to get a good look at them for the first time.

Her daughter was the dinosaur expert and probably would have identified it rather quickly. For Julia, however, it simply resembled a slightly overgrown rainbow chicken with claws on the end of the feathered arms instead of normal ones. A large ridge ran down their backs but this was coated with feathers as well, albeit darker ones. While the creatures had a beak, inside their mouths were tiny, razor-sharp fangs.

*A dinosaur isn't anything but a chicken on meth*, she decided. "Front line, advance!"

With practiced ease the line of officers began moving forward, taking slow and steady steps while ensuring the shield wall remained up and in a defensive position. Each time they passed one of the incapacitated hell-chickens—*I can't call them dinosaurs because dinosaurs don't exist but then again neither do demons*, Julia mentally argued with herself—a baton would snap down, crushing the skull of the creature. There was no blood, however, simply a disgusting black ooze which would trickle out of the destroyed cranium.

"Sergeant!" a voice shouted from her right. Turning, Julia saw Lopez kneeling down next to one of the dead creatures. The young SRG member picked it up by its leg and grimaced. "Looks like some sort of zombie dinosaur. What the hell is going on?"

*Like I have any fucking clue, rook*, Julia mentally groused. Instead, she pointed her baton at the muscular red demon standing in front of the mysterious gap. "Make him suck gas!"

Lopez reloaded her gas grenade launcher and fired a second time. This one landed at the feet of the demonic being, who looked down at it in annoyance before it began spewing noxious gas. Gagging as the harsh chemical reaction interfered with its olfactory system, the creature kicked the can away as it struggled to breathe. The can bounced away a few feet, ejecting CS gas the entire time.

"Foul humans!" the being shouted, his red skin almost glowing in the darkness. Part of the look Julia chalked up to the strange gap in the ground. "You cannot harm Carrog Cŭ Síth the Eternal! Long have my armies waited to do battle against Earth. I am mighty Carrog, son of—hey, knock it off! What is this foul stuff? What…Argh! It burns! The pain! What is it doing to my eyes?!"

Behind her mask Julia grinned. Lopez had nailed the creature square in the chest with another gas cannister. The demonic being was so busy mono-loguing he had missed the CS grenade launch. Her daughter would have been very proud of her, knowing mommy had caught the bad guy monologuing. More of the noxious tear gas flooded Carrog's immediate area and the demon stepped back, gagging and rubbing at his eyes.

*Oh yeah, that shit sucks, don't it?* Julia thought as the line moved forward another few steps, the entire unit moving as one. Julia and the other three offi-cers of the second line began peppering the area around the gap with more CS gas, creating a small corridor where there was only two ways for the hordes to run—directly into the shield wall, or back into the gap.

The demon must have realized this as well. He half-turned and hunched over, straining mightily. Two large wings suddenly unfurled from his back and they stretched outwards. Wider than multiple cars when lined up, the wings began to slowly flap in the night air. Fanning the grounds, the CS gas began to drift away as the wind from the wings grew in intensity.

*Well, fuck,* Julia thought as the last of the gas dispersed into the breeze. She glanced back at Lopez, who shook her head. They were already out of tear gas.

A sudden, thunderously loud trumpet sounded nearby. Julia blinked and looked in the direction it came from. Lumbering along the jogging trail in Central Park was…a woolly mammoth? She placed the back of her wrist against her eyes and rubbed them before looking a second time. The woolly mammoths were still there, their shaggy heads swinging back and forth as they walked along. They looked similar in condition to the weird little dino-saurs which had come from the gap, though these weren't in nearly as rough shape as the much smaller dinosaurs.

"What the fuck is going on?" Julia asked. It was as though every crea-ture in the history of New York was emerging from within Central Park. She looked around the small wall which bordered their area and saw the fog was just as impermeable as before, blocking even the tallest of buildings in the area from view. Whatever was happening, it appeared to be confined strictly to Central Park.

*For now,* she thought as the herd moved on towards Nutter's Battery, a nearby stone and concrete circle on a slightly raised hill. Julia looked it over for a moment before realizing it would make an excellent vantage point for recon, as well as a defensible position should it come to it. The demon being was still having issues with wrangling his dinosaur minions, and the arrival of the woolly mammoths seem to have thrown him off his game just a bit. It caused Julia to wonder if the demon Carrog was fully in charge of this. What-ever *this* was.

"First line! Fall back to Nutter's Battery!" she called out. One or two glanced back, confused, but the line pivoted and kept their shields between them and the zombie chicken dinosaurs as they slowly began walking back towards the raised barriers of the outlook. It took careful navigation and treading for them to make it up the rocky, grass-covered banks of the steep hill.

"Not McGowan's, Sergeant?" Lopez asked as she sidled up next to her. The young rookie officer didn't appear flustered in the least by the demon's giant wings, nor the woolly mammoths which were now munching on some of the local vegetation. Or the tiny dinosaurs for that matter. Either Lopez was jaded by it all, or in shock.

"Can't see the gap thing from there," Julia pointed out. McGowan's Redoubt would normally be an excellent vantage point except the tree growth of the area prohibited anyone from being able to see the part of the Harlem Meer where the gap was located. In addition, it was almost too far away. If Carrog or any of his legion decided to make a break for Harlem, then there was nothing the SRG could do to stop him from up there. At least at Nutter's they had a chance to intercept, however small.

"I just noticed the position of the gap is where that tiny island used to be," Lopez said. "You know, where the little ferry used to be?"

Julia blinked, surprised. *How had I missed that?*

"Good eye," Julia stated as they began to slowly make their way to Nutter's Battery. It was a steep climb up the hill, which made Julia's decision seem even smarter than before. If they were having problems with it, then the zombie dinosaurs shouldn't find it any easier to traverse. She glanced back over at the woolly mammoths, who seemed to be pointedly ignoring everything going on around them. *They could probably make it,* she thought with a nervous titter. *That would make for a bad day.*

"Sergeant!" one of her SRG team members shouted. She glanced over and saw Officer LeJuk approaching. Intense blue eyes peered out from his half-mask. He pulled down the mask, exposing his face for a moment. "Not McGowan's?"

"Can't see the gap from there," Julia said, glad she wasn't the only person who was considering the redoubt. If they survived this, Officer LeJuk had all the makings of an excellent sergeant one day.

"Fuck, didn't think of that," Pat muttered. "I was just thinking of a defensible position, you know?"

"Yeah, I considered it," Julia said before an ear-shattering screech interrupted them. Julia slapped her hands over her ears as something *enormous* flew overhead. She saw nothing but a dark, winged shape against the fog before a huge gust of wind blew over them. It stank of rotted flesh. Julia's eyes watered. "Dragon? Fuck...you don't see that every day."

"Eh," Pat shrugged his broad shoulders. "I saw an eagle almost take off with a little kid last summer when I went down to Australia on vacation. That was some shit right there. Almost got the kid, too. Eagle lost its grip on the kid's jacket."

The glowing gap in the dried pond bed dimmed as they moved further away. Carrog, still flapping his wings to disperse the tear gas, made no move to follow them up the hill. Instead the demon seemed to be attempting to marshal his forces, with minimal success. The smaller dinosaurs still struggling with the CS gas were flopping around on the ground, making unnatural noises as they scratched at their non-existent eyes. Julia had no idea what was going on with them, but she wasn't going to complain. While they were only the size of a medium sized dog, her years working on the force had shown just how much damage a single dog could do to someone caught unawares. When she'd been a regular patrol officer she couldn't remember the number of times she'd been called to a scene involving a dog bite. Chihuahuas were especially bad. Tiny little terrorists wearing pink rhinestone collars. After a brief comparison of the hellspawn called chihuahuas to the little creatures coming out of the gap, she didn't want the small dinosaurs anywhere near them.

"Still, it's not every day you see fucking demons and dinosaurs in Central Park," Officer LeJuk continued after a moment.

"Don't forget the woolly mammoths," Lopez added as she climbed over the low wall. She set her grenade launcher down had pulled her mask low. "And whatever the hell that was up in the sky."

"Everyone okay?" Julia asked as the last of her unit made it safely over the wall. Glancing around, she spotted the Mounted Unit moving along a different path to their position. She didn't envy Sergeant Alexander and his team trying to navigate the trails. While she was pretty sure Central Park Precinct had officers on horseback for patrols and navigated the trails frequently, SRG typically had no business in the park proper. Riots rarely, if ever, actually happened in the park itself. Then again, nobody had anticipated an anti-summit protest and riot breaking out in the middle of Harlem, either. The summer heat did weird things to an average New Yorker. Tourists were even worse.

Taking a quick headcount, Julia was pleased to see all twelve of the unit had safely arrived without any damage. Lopez had easily taken control of the second line, which surprised Julia a bit. She hadn't thought much of the young officer initially and had made it clear to Captain Groller her opinion of the matter, but Lopez had surprised her. She was showing an unexpected leadership quality Julia hadn't seen coming.

The Mounted Unit arrived last. Jasper Alexander and his three other officers looked irritated. Then again, Julia was fairly certain this was the standard look for the men under his command. While nominally operating within the umbrella of the Strategic Response Group, the Mounted Unit oftentimes found themselves working in groups of two during parades and whatnot.

"Picked a hell of a spot, Russo," Alexander grunted as he guided his horse up the grassy embankment. He could have led his horse up the stairs but that would have been an unnecessary risk. "Good spot, but hard on the horses."

"Yeah, wasn't thinking about the horses," Julia pointed out. She pointed towards Harlem Meer — or rather, what *had* been the little pond. Without the typical algae-filled water the Meer was looking a little strange. "We can see the gap thing from up here and keep tabs on everything else. It's why I picked it."

"Radios are down," Alexander said as he looked down at her. "Well, frequencies outside the park are down. I can still get your squad's. Not getting anything else though."

"The fog," Julia stated with absolute certainty. It hadn't looked natural when settling over the park and had mysteriously grown thicker as the two units had been towards the pond to when the pulsing green light had first begun. She continued. "It's masking everything. The sky, the city, comms… everything. Bet you can't get cell coverage."

Alexander reached into a vest pocket and pulled out his phone. Holding it aloft, he rotated his horse around as he searched for a signal. After a few moments of this fruitless endeavor, he pocketed his phone. He shook his head.

"Yep, no service."

"I'll be honest with you," Julia said as she looked back towards Harlem Meer. The eerily pulsing light remained, but it seemed to be growing ever so slightly brighter with each passing minute. She couldn't be certain without investigating. This was something she really didn't want to do at the moment. "This? It freaks me out a bit."

"I about lost my shit when I saw the mastodons," Alexander admitted with a dry chuckle. Taking off his helmet, he wiped the sweat off his forehead before continuing. "I saw them in the museum once…they didn't look nearly as big there as they do in person."

"Mastodons…oh, the woolly mammoths," Julia realized what he was talking about and nodded in agreement. "Or whatever that big thing was that flew overhead. Not sure what it was."

"Considering everything else we've seen?" Alexander paused, contemplative. "A fucking dragon."

"Yeah, that's what I thought, too," she said. "Got a plan yet?"

"Against zombie dinosaurs?" Alexander laughed. "Fuck no. You?"

"Fuck no."

"Open to ideas," he said as he gave the horse a little rein. The large animal dipped its head and began munching on some clover growing in the cracks of the concrete.

"That demon guy? Carrog?" Julia's expression became thoughtful as she turned to look at Harlem Meer. "He's in charge of this…is it an invasion? Yeah, fuck it. He's leading the invasion. If we can kill him, it might stop them."

"Think we could arrest him for disturbing the peace?" Alexander joked.

"Well then, he's going to get beat hard for resisting arrest," Julia said, smiling. "It's one of those rare instances where I agree that the more force applied, the better the result."

"You were always a weird one, sergeant" Alexander stated as he put his helmet back on and fastened his chin strap. "I have a plan for us, but it's going to involve doing what horses do best — staying mobile."

"Gonna let me in on the plan or am I just going to have to guess?" Julia asked as she pulled her mask back up.

"I'm going to take the guys around the side and see if we can get a shot at that demon thing," Alexander answered as he pulled the reins back in. His horse, irritated his snack had been taken away, instantly went alert. The shift was palpable even for Julia to see. The mounted officer continued. "Barring that, we can at least secure a flank so you can take your squad and drive him back into the gap. Hell, if I were more religious, I'd hit that little demon fucker with some holy water to see if it might help."

"I was raised Catholic, but that was a long time ago," Julia admitted sheepishly. "Besides, I think you need a priest to bless the water."

"Eh, it was an idea," Alexander said. "Otherwise I'd be on the horn with Ladder Twenty-Six. They could shoot holy water out of their fire hose. Demon or not, he'd feel that."

Julia laughed in spite herself. "God, that'd be a sight."

"Five hundred gallons a minute, three hundred pounds of pressure per square inch," Alexander chuckled and brought his shoulder radio to his mouth. "Radio check one, two."

"Loud and clear," Julia responded through her radio. She released the button and looked up at the rider. "Be careful out there."

"You too," Alexander told her. The Mounted Unit turned and left Nutter's Battery. At the end of the path they angled slightly right and continued on towards Lasker Rink. In a matter of moments the group had disappeared, leaving the SRG alone once more.

*That departure felt a little final,* Julia thought as she turned back to organize her team.

# PART FOUR

"Okay, so we don't really have a plan for dealing with dinosaurs and demons in the department guidelines," Julia said as she leaned against one of the metal benches atop Nutter's Battery. The rest of the SRG gathered around her. Taking a moment to gauge the mood of the group, she quickly determined they were in relatively high spirits in spite of the unearthly forces arrayed against them. "I'm going to be honest with you and admit I have no idea what to do. I'm open to suggestions here, people."

She was met with silence. Not that Julia had been expecting anything, really. She'd been a little hopeful one of them would have something, anything which could trigger an avalanche of ideas to follow. Still, there were some good minds in the group. She knew this from past experience. They would normally have some sort of oddball suggestion. It would be laughed off but would set something else in motion.

"No?" She asked them. Lopez tentatively raised her hand.

"You mentioned to Sergeant Alexander that the gap thing might close if the demon is knocked inside, right?" Lopez asked. "Sorry, sergeant. I overheard a little bit."

"It's fine, go on," Julia said as she waved for the young SRG member to continue.

"Well, I saw a movie once where they used a bunch of woolly mammoths to cause a stampede," Lopez said, looking around at the rest of the group. "Stupid movie, but it had that cool part where the mammoths were charging down a ramp and knocking the enemy soldiers around?"

"Okay, we get it, Lopez," Julia smiled. "Get to the point."

"Well, most of the dinosaur things we've seen are small, right?" Lopez asked. Seeing everyone nod in affirmation, she continued. "We should try to guide the mammoth things towards the gap and get them to charge forward. They'll squish everything in their path, and then the demon thing might get close enough to the gap to be pushed back inside. That should end the Sha'Daa."

"The..." Julia blinked, confused. She'd heard that word before, and recently, but from where?

"So how do we herd a bunch of supposedly extinct animals where we want them to go?" Officer LeJuk interrupted them. He pulled down his mask and took a sip from his canteen. He offered it to Lopez, who shook her head. LeJuk shrugged. "I don't know about you, but the only thing I've ever seen like them was when I went to the Bronx Zoo as a kid."

"Loud noises? I don't know," Lopez admitted sheepishly. "It was just an idea."

"It's not a bad one," Julia said. "We just need something loud and a way to direct them at that Carrog guy."

"Too bad we don't have any flashbangs," Officer Darren Silva said in a wistful voice. "I miss the old days. Protestors? Flashbangs. Crack house? Flashbangs. No-knock raid? Flashbangs."

"You're the reason we had to stop using them, remember?" Julia reminded him. "Mister 'hey a yorkie, I need a flash bang'…seriously, a fucking puppy?"

"I felt I was in danger…"

"Save it," Julia snapped. "You know how hard it was to explain to my daughter that someone on my team flash banged a fucking dog?"

"Guys," Lopez interrupted them. "Focus."

"Right," Julia nodded, giving Silva a final dirty look before settling back against the bench. "So, we get them charging towards demon asshole."

"What about the dragon thing?" someone else asked. Julia recognized the speaker, though she was a bit surprised he spoke up. Todd Haus was not one of the natural leaders in her team, and typically preferred to do as told.

"There's no such thing–" Silva said but Haus interrupted him.

"–as dragons?" Haus laughed sardonically at Silva. "Man, I watched you beat a fucking dinosaur to death with a baton. You're gonna try to tell me in the middle of all this weird shit that dragons aren't real? Go fuck yourself, Silva."

"Okay, enough." Julia was glad her mask was up. There was no way anyone could see her smiling. "Let's not worry about the dragon. Let's focus on the dinosaurs and Carrog."

"Two teams," Lopez suggested. "Each to a side of the mammoths. Just kinda herd them along, right? With the Meer dry they'll stampede right over there. The only problem is getting them to stop before they hit Harlem. That… would be bad."

"Sounds like a plan," Julia nodded. "LeJuk? Take Mendoza, Thompson, Bonucci, Palmeira, and Haus as your team. You guys hold here and wait for our signal. I'll take Lopez, Silva, Nicely, Bowland, and Monson. We'll take that trail around East Drive and head towards Huddlestone Arch before coming around the other side. I'll radio you and then we can try to herd them towards the Meer."

"What should we do if we run into any dinosaurs?" LeJuk asked before shaking his head. "That's something I never thought I'd ask out loud."

"If they're not bothering you, don't bother them," Julia answered. "If you see any civilians around, get them out of the park if you can, or else have them find one of the bathrooms and shelter in place."

Nodding, LeJuk and his team moved out of their way. Julia and her team grabbed their shields and batons. She debated taking some of the gas launchers before deciding against it. They were out of CS cannisters anyway, so taking them would merely be added weight. She led her group down the same path the Mounted Unit had, quickly leaving Nutter's Battery behind.

It was like stepping into an entirely different world, Julia realized as they moved deeper into the park and towards the Ravine. It was officially marked as a forest sanctuary in the middle of Central Park, but Julia had always heard other things about it. More than once she'd heard stories about what it was like back in the day, before it became a tourist haven. Robberies and grand larceny were a common occurrence still, but a murder was rare enough. They were more likely to stumble upon a couple of individuals romantically involved than a dead body.

She wound her way through the trail, for a moment actually forgetting why she was in the park. It was really nice here, even if it was dark and foreboding. Other than a few trips upstate and a vacation to the Outer Banks as a kid, Julia really had never left New York City. She had never really had a desire to see nature, being too busy with her career and later, raising her daughter as a single mom.

There was something primal about being in the middle of nowhere all alone, she realized.

"Sergeant?" a voice asked from behind her

*No, not alone, just isolated,* Julia corrected as she paused and looked at Lopez. The young officer, along with the rest of the group she'd had remain behind with her, were following her along the path faithfully. Lopez, along with Officers Silva, Bowland, Monson, and Nicely, were dependent upon her for orders. This was not in the mission parameters but Julia was known for creative problem solving amongst the rest of the SRG.

"Yes?" Julia asked the young officer.

"Maybe we shouldn't cut through the Ravine," Lopez suggested. "It's really dark in there at night."

"How dark are we talking?" Julia asked her. Lopez gave her a strange look. Julia sighed. "I don't come to the park often. Okay, I never come here."

"Really?" Lopez looked surprised. "Don't you live five blocks from here?"

"Those are really big blocks and I don't have a lot of downtime," Julia stated.

"Well, there's a couple of lights, but the trees block out the moonlight," Lopez explained, blushing slightly. "A couple of years ago, I was in high school and a boy brought me out here…"

"I see," Julia sighed. For a moment she'd forgotten just how young Lopez was. Julia didn't want to be the old grizzled veteran who looked at all the younger officers with disdain. *That's the captain's job, she thought. I'm barely thirty!*

She glanced at the others who were lined up behind Lopez. They fidgeted nervously. Sitting around and waiting was not something the SRG was asked to do often. When protests went bad, or needed a particular bad element dealt with without instigating the rest of the people in the crowd, the SRG was the best option. What they were being asked to do now was well outside their norm. As well trained as they were, even the best got jitters when there was nothing to do but sit around and dwell on the fact there were dinosaurs in Central Park.

"Anybody got any jokes?" Silva asked in an attempt to lighten the mood.

Julia inwardly groaned. Silva was the self-proclaimed king of dad jokes. More than once a fellow officer had to be held back from strangling the Puerto Rican. They weren't necessarily bad, merely irritating and stupid. After a few dozen of them, the novelty wore thin and it became more akin to psychological warfare than joking. Even she had been tempted to take baton to face on multiple occasions.

"No," Lopez answered for the entire group. "I have mace."

"Ahhh…" Silva let the word hang in the air for a long moment before chuckling. "Okay, fine. But the silence is creepy."

He had a point. The thick fog which seemed to encircle the entire park was doing a terrific job at isolating them from the outside world. Not only could they not see the nearby Heritage apartment building, but the usual noises of New York City were non-existent. Julia had noticed this earlier, before the fog and the strange glowing gap to hell but had forgotten about it when Carrog and the dinosaurs had appeared.

"Ever get the feeling you're being watched?" Lopez asked the group in a quiet voice as she looked around.

"You get used to it," Julia told her. "One thing about being in the NYPD is you're always under scrutiny. It's why you should try to stay aware of the public eye when making decisions. Isn't that right, *Silva*?"

"With all due respect, sergeant, fuck off."

"You're the one with a flashbang hardon," Julia reminded him.

"They're handy!" Silva protested. "Stun, disorient…"

"Kill puppies?"

"Bite me!"

"In your dreams."

"Sergeant?" Lopez interrupted the bickering duo. "Uh…where's Monson?"

Julia blinked and looked back at her SRG team. She counted heads. *One, two, three, four…where was Officer Monson?* She tried looking around the bend to see if he'd fallen behind but the tall, skinny officer was nowhere in sight. Her right hand instinctively fell to where her gun holster would be but stopped halfway there.

"Shields," she called out and instantly the other four officers brought their riot shields up in preparation. All of their bickering and arguments disappeared once there was a perceived threat. Raising her own shield, she slowly advanced towards the bend in the trail. Behind her she could hear batons snapping out into place.

Rounding the corner, she expected to see something standing over the body of her fellow officer. Shifting her grip on the baton, she angled her shield so she could see the area better. Her eyes scanned the dirt covered path for any sign of the missing police officer. Instead, all she saw was forest and shadows. The path was clear. There was no sign of Monson anywhere.

"Where'd he go?" Lopez asked in a hushed voice as she took her position on Julia's left.

"I don't know," Julia admitted quietly. "It's not like him to wander off."

"Maybe he had to use the bathroom?"

"I doubt it," Julia replied. "He's an experienced officer. He knows when to go to the bathroom. It's not while we're in movement. No, I think it's something worse. I think something else is out here."

"Wall?" Lopez asked, her shield shifting slightly as the young woman readjusted her grip. Julia shook her head.

"No, too many angles," Julia answered as she thought about their position. "We're exposed with multiple avenues of entry. Silva, you and Nicely take point. Stay together."

"Got it," Silva said, his previous joking manner set aside. He then cursed. "Nicely's gone."

"What?" Julia asked, shocked. She turned her head to look back at Silva. "He was right there a second ago!"

Julia quickly did a head count. Besides herself, there was Lopez, Silva, and Bowland. Not only had Monson disappeared, but Nicely had vanished along with him when the group stopped a few moments before.

Her heart hammered in her chest. In all her months in the SRG she had never once imagined a scenario where there was something in the wooded areas of Central Park hunting her team members. It was mindboggling, straight out of a horror movie, yet here it was. In the real and now. The mystery and terror which loomed over her and the rest of the team was physical. Grown men had disappeared without so much as a cry of warning.

"Double time, let's move," Julia ordered. Silva and Bowland nodded, partnering up and jogging ahead along the trail. Lopez and Julia quickly followed, their feet pounding along the train in sync as they tried to keep up with the taller men. Julia grunted as she slipped on a small stone, then winced as her supposedly supportive boots let her ankle roll. Swearing, she stopped and began hobbling.

"Sergeant?" Lopez stopped and hurried back. "You hurt?'

"The hell do you think?" Julia ground out through clenched teeth. "I rolled my ankle."

"Sorry, wasn't thinking," Lopez apologized. "How bad?"

"I don't know," Julia admitted as she tested her weight on it. There was some pain but she found it manageable. "Not too bad. Don't know if I can run, though."

"Need help?" Lopez asked.

"No, I'm good," Julia said and tried walking a few steps. What had been a sharp pain quickly lessened to a dull, throbbing sensation. Yeah, she could still do her job. She looked at Lopez. "Where'd Silva and Bowland go?"

"I, uh…shit," Lopez looked further down the trail. It was pitch black. "Looks like they kept going."

"Or got taken," Julia offered. She shook her head. "Damn it. What the fuck is out there?"

"I saw…something," Lopez admitted. "It was dark but I thought I saw something that looked like an overgrown monkey."

"Not funny," Julia said.

"I'm serious," Lopez reaffirmed. Julia looked the younger woman over for a moment before deciding she might not be lying. Even in the dark Julia could see the young woman's face was earnest.

"Okay, so you saw overgrown monkeys," Julia said. "Maybe. Still doesn't make any sense. Monkeys can't take down a full-grown man, right?"

"Chimps can," Lopez stated. "Saw it on TV once. They're strong."

"Oh."

Something moved in the brush to their right. Julia's shield immediately came up and she pressed her back against Lopez's. The young SRG member did likewise, and together the two women stared out into the dark woods surrounding their position. Another rustling of leaves to their left drew Julia's attention. She shifted her grip on her baton and waited.

"Move," Julia ordered. "Back to back, watch the bushes. Is there anything around here where we can fortify the position?"

"Huddleston Arch," Lopez answered immediately. "It's where we used to go…well, it's a pretty good spot. Right next to Lasker Rink and East Drive."

"How far?"

"Maybe a hundred feet, I don't know," Lopez admitted. Julia grunted. It would have to do. They didn't have many options, really. Whatever was hunting them was faster in the dark and seemed to be at home in the woods.

"Which way?" Julia asked.

"Down this trail," Lopez said and used her baton to point. "We were already headed in that direction."

"On my cue, we make a break for it," Julia said. "Shield up but if I fall, keep going."

"Fuck that," Lopez snarled. "I'm staying with you."

"I'm injured, you're not," Julia reminded her as the two began shuffling down the trail, their backs still pressed against one another. "I need you to take down the red guy, Carrog, if I don't make it."

"That's not my..." Lopez's voice trailed off.

"What?" Julia asked.

"Nothing."

"C'mon, what were you going to say?"

"Just repeating what some weirdo told me on the street," Lopez said. "Okay, ready to run?"

"No, but here goes nothing." Julia took a deep breath and exhaled slowly. Her next words were barely above a whisper. "Okay, now."

The duo bolted down the path, their footsteps pounding loudly through the otherwise silent forest. Something large screeched and followed them, staying just out of sight as it moved along next to them. An answering cry rang out in Julia's ear to her left but she didn't look. She didn't dare. A dark, furry claw reached out from a bush to grab her. Julia saw it just in time and lashed out with her baton. The creature squealed in pain and the claw retracted abruptly.

Lopez stumbled and fell behind. Julia stopped and turned, but Lopez was already battling against two more of the beings hunting them. Her shield was protecting her side but one of the beings had managed to grab hold of her baton. Julia gasped as she caught sight of what was hunting them for the very first time.

They were indeed very large chimpanzees, she recognized as they fought with the young officer. Their faces were unlike anything she'd ever seen on a monkey, however. They stank of a warm corpse left out to ripen in the middle of summer, something Julia always associated with the worst parts of Hell's Kitchen. Wielding makeshift weapons, they were trying to break through Lopez's defenses. Missing her baton, it was only a matter of time before they overwhelmed her.

Julia ran back and entered the fray, her baton being put to good use as she quickly equaled the playing field. She bashed one of the chimp things in the face with her shield, which elicited a painful squeal from the creature. She quickly followed this with a sharp strike of her baton across the creature's temple. It dropped Lopez's stolen baton and stumbled back, clearly dazed.

"Go!" Julia shouted and Lopez disengaged from the second creature, running further down the trail and away from danger. Julia's baton strikes were made with deadly intent now. Officers were in danger and without a firearm, the best weapon she had for melee was her baton. Blow after blow rained down on the creature's arms and head. It cowered meekly and tried to crawl away. Enraged, Julia continued to beat the creature until it stopped moving. Panting heavily she looked back at the first creature. Unsurprisingly, it did not want anything more to do with the clearly agitated NYPD officer and was making a hasty retreat.

Turning, she jogged down the trail, trying to follow where Lopez had gone through the darkness. Unable to see and not familiar with the path, however, Julia quickly found herself off the normal path and looking at a creek. Glancing around, she couldn't see anything that looked like an arch. There was a large pile of boulders nearby which had a tunnel leading through them, but no sign of any architectural structure.

Considering how quiet the rest of the park had been, the bubbling little brook nearby seemed almost obscenely loud to Julia. Cautiously she approached the tunnel but there didn't appear to be any sign of the creatures around. Nor could she see any trace of Lopez. Frowning, Julia rested her hand on one of the larger boulders and looked around. Other than the nearby creek and her own breathing, there was no other noise.

Suddenly exhausted, Julia leaned back against the rock and tried to catch her breath. Whatever was in the dense wood was hunting her people, taking them one by one without any warning. It was terrifying, but she'd proven they can be beaten with the proper application of force.

Branches snapped slightly to her right and above. She barely had time to register the sudden noise before a second officer, in armor, but sans helmet crashed to the ground just outside the entrance to her tunnel. Julia almost lashed out with her baton but held back as she recognized Lopez. The young officer was missing her shield as well and appeared to be worse for wear.

Kneeling down to check on Lopez, Julia was surprised to see Lopez was almost smiling.

"Oh good, you found the arch."

"This shit?" Julia asked, surprised. "It's a tunnel."

"Yeah," Lopez grunted as she sat up and pushed back against the tunnel's wall. "This runs beneath East Drive. This is Huddlestone Arch."

"Looks more like a pile of rocks with a hole in it," Julia hissed. Lopez shrugged.

"Eh."

"What the fuck is out there?" Julia asked as she pulled down her baton and helped the fallen officer to her feet.

"No idea, but it's fast," Lopez replied as she pulled out her canteen and took a quick swig from it. She passed it over to Julia, who accepted gratefully.

"They're not monkeys, I think. They're like skinny Neanderthals. Can't be certain."

"Dinosaurs, woolly mammoths, and now fucking ninja Neanderthals?" Julia said after taking a drink from Lopez's canteen. "Thanks, by the way."

"Least I could do," Lopez said as Julia passed the small container back over. "They're fast and strong, whoever they are."

"Well, we've seen dinosaurs already," Julia sighed. "Why not some Neanderthal ninjas?"

"You're being ridiculous now," Lopez chuckled darkly. "I doubt ancient ninjas would be as fast as these guys are, apparently."

"Ninja dinosaurs?"

"Too obvious."

"Maybe the rest of SRG just called it a night and went home?"

"Oh, I wish we could," Lopez sighed. "That would make things so much easier."

"Definitely easier than fighting a demon with a fucking dinosaur army and Neanderthals acting like fucking ninjas in the middle of Central Park," Julia grunted. "This is not how I saw my night going."

"I was excited," Lopez admitted as she put her canteen away. The young officer looked at Julia earnestly. "Not about what's happening, but about being deployed with SRG. I really thought joining SRG would let me keep the city safe, you know? But everyone pawns me off for PR shit because I'm 'cute and non-threatening'. What kind of bullshit it that?"

"Well, you kinda are," Julia proclaimed. She held up a gloved hand to forestall the expected protest. "You are. You're young, perky, not jaded or been on the job too long, and there isn't a whiff of corruption on you. You're ideal to be the face of SRG, especially when we're trying to revamp our image with civilians and the fucking press."

"Well, why not someone like you then?" Lopez asked, clearly exasperated by Julia's remarks.

"Oh, Captain Groller explored the idea a few months back, before you joined." Julia admitted after a moment. "But once they dug into my past… yeah, you're a much better option."

"What?" Lopez leaned closer to her, surprise etched all across her features. "You're the type of officer all woman should be! Single mom, a badass, sergeant in her first ten years, worked in multiple precincts and have glowing reviews from them all and from what I hear, up for lieutenant next year."

"Yeah, that's not going to happen," Julia said. Her head dipped to her chest and she sighed wearily. "They'll talk about it, but it won't happen. I have…horrible taste in men. When I mean horrible, I mean so fucking bad every guy I date should have a warning label tattooed to his forehead."

"We've all made choices we regret," Lopez pointed out. Reasonable enough, Julia knew, all things considered. Still, the young officer had no idea just what the other officer meant. Not exactly. Lopez continued. "Do you know how many others are on like their third marriages?"

"I was married once," Julia said quietly. She shook her head. "I don't know why I'm telling you this. I haven't told anybody about Marcus."

"You don't have to…" Lopez's voice trailed off. Julia could tell the other woman was curious. She couldn't blame her. Julia was notorious for not sharing much about her personal life. Hell, only a few knew her daughter's name.

"I know," Julia acknowledged. "Still, if we're going to die, I should come clean about some of the shit I've done. I'm Catholic — lapsed, but still…Father Smith always said that confession was good for the soul."

"I smoked pot once," Lopez admitted before grinning. "Okay, more than once. But hey, it was high school. We all did crazy shit back then."

"I was married right out of high school," Julia murmured as she stared off into the distance, her mind drifting to the past. "I was going to be a good housewife. I mean, we had our hopes and dreams, and Marcus had a great job. We had a cute little apartment and everything. I got pregnant. Life looked amazing."

"So…what happened?" Lopez asked.

"I don't know," Julia admitted after a deep sigh. "No, I do know. Marcus started going out with his friends. Started coming home drunk. He wasn't a mean drunk. No, never a mean drunk. We had a few arguments but nothing serious. Make up sex is the best, by the way. I wanted him to come home earlier. I mean, I was five months pregnant at that point. I was a moody mess and wanted my husband. He thought I was being overly clingy. Okay, I might have been needy, but damn it, I was fucking pregnant. I had a reason.

"One night he came home with a black eye and bloody lip. He and his boys had gotten into a fight with some other guys. He was ranting and raving about how they had jumped him when he'd gotten separated from the others and he was going to make them pay. He went into the closet in the bedroom and grabbed the gun from his shoebox. I knew he had it but didn't really say anything because it was supposed to be in case someone broke in. I tried to stop him from going back out there. I didn't want my baby daddy to be locked up on Riker's for the rest of his life for murder. We started to argue, and he slapped me. I hit him back, and then he pointed the gun at my head.

"I swear to God I thought I was going to die. But…I stepped closer. I don't know why. The cold metal from the barrel on my forehead is something I will never, ever forget. I told him to pull the trigger because if he went out there, I would die. I told him to choose. His family, or his revenge. He… moved the gun off my forehead and I think I peed myself a little.

"Then the gun went off by accident. I fucking felt it go through my hair. I screamed and he dropped the gun. Marcus run out the apartment and…I went into premature labor. Right there in the bathroom. I don't remember much, except for the pain. And blood. God, it was so bright. Went to the ER. They didn't save the baby, but they did save me, so there's that. My mother arrived and we talked. I told her about what Marcus had done. I was high on pain meds, so I didn't think anything of it. My grandmother is old world, and she raised my mom just like that, so my mother…had connections is the best way to explain it. Marcus disappeared and nobody'd seen him since. Officially, a few years back I became a widow because it had been seven years since he was last seen."

"Holy shit," Lopez breathed. "Your mother was in the mob?"

"No, I don't think so," Julia admitted. "I think she was owed a favor or something. Or she knew a guy who knew a guy…I don't know. I didn't ask."

"Well…that's not really that bad," Lopez decided after a brief pause. Julia scoffed and rolled her eyes.

"Oh, it gets better," Julia promised as she peered out into the dark surroundings. "I started dating a guy named DeAndre right after I got out of the Academy. Sweet guy, a little flashy, always tried to take care of me. Swept me right off my feet. This was two years after Marcus, and I was ready to start dating again and this guy just fell on my lap. It was great.

"Then it stopped. I noticed weird things around the apartment. He had some friends come over once and I was pretty sure I'd seen one or two of them down at the precinct getting booked. His work hours were weird. I tried to ignore the vibes I was getting. He treated me well. I got pregnant and he was ecstatic. He started making plans to move all of us into a bigger apartment. He even mentioned marriage. Then…he got a promotion or something, because his attitude changed. He went from curious about my job to almost predatory. Like he was looking for weaknesses in the precinct and the NYPD.

"Like I said, I felt something was off but…he was so sweet and kind to me. Fuck. I should have seen it. I heard from Narcotics that their normal players were getting better about figuring out the patrol patterns of cops, and that a few CI's had gone missing. It was like the major distributors had a mole in the precinct. I didn't think anything of it. I mean, someone would have to be a fucking idiot to not be able to spot a mole, right?

"Then DeAndre got picked up and it all fell into place. He'd been using me, and four other female officers around the city, to spy on the NYPD. I was the lucky one because I was the only one who didn't know what the fuck was going on. I was his 'baby', his new recruit. The others had been doing it for years. He'd ease them into it, slowly at first but with growing frequency, until they were his insiders. The other four were charged and had to resign. I was offered a change of precincts and a new job. Since the SRG never comes into contact with narcotics, my old captain decided to transfer me over here, and that was that."

"Wait…DeAndre Parker? The Big D?" Lopez's eyes were wide. "Holy shit, I heard about that! That was like seven years ago, right?"

"Almost, yeah," Julia nodded and sighed again. "Our daughter is eight now. She doesn't know him, never will. IA came sniffing around right after everything went down, but I didn't admit to shit because it wasn't my fault. Well, it might have been a little. I don't know. God, I don't know why I'm telling you all this shit. The only people who know are my old captain at 1st Precinct, and Captain Groller."

"Damn," Lopez whistled softly. She shook her head. "I'm no rat, but you should at least come clean with the rest of the guys in SRG. They whisper a bit whenever you're not around."

"I know they do," Julia replied. "I'm stupid with men, not about everything. I just work hard, try to keep my nose clean, and everything will work itself out, one way or the other."

"Until tonight happened," Lopez pointed out. Julia laughed harshly.

"Yeah, until tonight," the sergeant agreed. "I don't know what the fuck is going on anymore. Like, am I losing my mind?"

"I don't know if you are," Lopez said as she pulled her mask back up and reaffixed her chin strap for her helmet. "But I really am ready to knock this demon asshole back to hell now. How about you?"

"Fuck it," Julia shrugged. "If I'm going to die tonight, might as well save the city while I'm at it."

"That's the spirit," Lopez smiled at her. "So how do we do this, boss?"

"Carrog," Julia said as she pulled her own mask up over her face. "The demon asshole. He's gotta be the key somehow. We get in close, introduce his face to our batons, and get him back into that hole."

"It's that simple," Lopez agreed. "That weird guy said…never mind. You're right about Carrog."

Julia looked at the younger officer, curious. "You know something I don't?"

"Not really," Lopez said after a moment. "Just a gut feeling."

"Right."

"Seriously, Carrog, batons, face, into the hole," Lopez affirmed. "Sounds simple."

"Unit Six, this is Alexander," Sergeant Alexander's voice crackled over their radios. "Come in Unit Six."

"Holy shit, I forgot about those guys!" Lopez exclaimed. "They're alive! Wow!"

"Shh…what's up, Jasper?" Julia asked as she pressed the transmit button on her radio.

"There are some fucking *zombies* running around here!"

"Say again?" Julia stared out into the darkness. "Did you say zombies?"

"Yeah, but they're not like normal zombies, like in the fucking movies," Alexander clarified, his voice sounding a little strained to Julia. "These look like what would happen if you crossed some Neanderthals with monkeys, then made zombies out of them."

"The *fuck*?" Julia looked at Lopez, who appeared to be almost excited about the prospect of zombie hunting. Julia mouthed *you're fucking weird* at Lopez, who nodded without any hesitation.

"My thoughts exactly," Alexander replied. "That glowing gap in the ground is getting bigger, too. That little demon fucker is guarding it, from the look of things. I've got a plan."

"Let's hear it," Julia said.

"We're going to charge these fucking zombie things and push them away. You and your team will have a straight shot at the demon guy."

"Yeah, if I had my team still," Julia muttered without transmitting. Lopez nodded in agreement. Julia considered for a moment before deciding it was the best plan she'd heard so far. She keyed the radio. "Sounds good. Be careful, Jasper. We'll try to hit that winged bastard hard."

"Stay safe, Six."

"Watch your ass, cowboy."

"Just because we ride horses doesn't make us cowboys," Alexander reminded her, humor evident through the radio. "But…if we live through this? You and me? We need to go get a coffee together."

"Are…are you asking me out, sergeant?" Julia blinked. Surprised couldn't even begin to describe the whirlwind of emotions going through her. She was trying to keep her team in one piece and alive, and this man wanted to ask her out? During the apocalypse?

"She'd love it!" Lopez answered over the radio for her. Julia gasped and tried to grab the young officer's radio but Lopez leaned back and away. "Just gotta find a babysitter first. No, wait…she has one. I'll do it. Good luck, Sergeant Alexander. Stay alive!"

"Copy that, Six."

"Are you fucking *insane*?!" Julia hissed as soon as the radio went silent. Lopez smiled at her.

"I don't believe in bad luck or karma, sergeant," Lopez said. "He seems nice."

"Oh my God," Julia rolled her eyes. "I'm going to fucking kill you!"

"Kill me after we save the city, sergeant. Oh my God, my brother would be so jealous. I get to kill some fucking zombies!"

"I swear to God, kids these days…" Julia sighed and hefted her riot shield. She looked at the younger SRG officer before motioning for her to follow. "Fine. Let's go save the city."

"Then coffee with hunky sergeant from the Mounted Unit?" Lopez asked, smiling. Her grin suddenly widened and she giggled softly. "I just thought of something funny."

"If you make any sort of mounted joke, I *will* beat your face in with my baton."

"Never mind. It wasn't as funny as I thought it would be. Let's just go and save the city."

"Smart girl."

# PART FIVE

Julia and Lopez crept through the tunnel and came out near Lasker Rink. Once more Julia found herself impressed with the young officer's knowledge of the park's layout. More at home within the steel jungles of the inner city than a park, Julia could have wandered around inside the park forever and not found her way. Lopez seemed to have an innate sense of direction Julia found odd. For her, directions usually involved the words "towards Jersey" or one of the boroughs.

Passing Lasker Rink, they found themselves on the opposite side of where the small island in Harlem Meer once lie. The giant gap which had replaced it was still there, and the green glowing light was brighter than ever. Deep inside was a myriad of shapeless forms which caused Julia to feel sick the longer she stared. Turning away, she spotted four large shapes near the edge of the Meer on the opposite bank. She quickly identified Sergeant Alexander and his Mounted Unit.

"Jasper, what are you doing?" Julia asked into her radio as she stared out from the heavy brush. "Jasper? Sergeant Alexander, reply."

"You wanted a window to get at big red, sergeant," the Mounted Unit officer replied. "Me and the boys are gonna give it to you. Do me a favor?"

"No, you stubborn asshole," Julia said, voice catching in her throat. "I'm not saying any goodbyes for you."

"Tell Jacob I love him."

"Fuck you, asshole," Julia said. "Tell him your own damn self…wait. You're gay? You're gay and you're deciding to come out *now*?! What the fuck is wrong with you? You asked me out for coffee! What the fuck?"

"Jacob's my son, Sergeant Russo. It's just the two of us."

"I…I didn't know you had a son."

"You can be friends with other cops, Julia," chuckled Alexander. "Get big red. We'll take care of the zombies for you. Oh, and sergeant?"

"Yeah?"

"I'm totally not gay. Getting coffee is a euphemism. Just thought you should know."

Sergeant Alexander and his three Mounted Officers lined their horses up along the pavement. For a moment Julia wasn't certain what they were doing until she saw what the four officers were all fixated on — a large cluster of the zombie creatures were shambling along the dry bed near Lasker Rink, near the gap. Also, very close to where Carrog stood. While they weren't wearing shiny metal armor and wielded batons instead of lances, Julia saw it for what it was. She swallowed and silently wished her knights in blue good luck.

Across the dried pond bed they charged, the four Mounted Officers wielding their batons and shielded only by their courage and body armor. Their horses screaming defiantly as their hooves thundered and the ground shook. The zombies might have been unfeeling and not very aware, but even they noticed the charging beasts. Batons snapped open as one and the four horses crashed into the crowd of zombies. Well-trained at crowd control and not panicking when someone grabs at them, the horses expertly pivoted and pushed the large zombie horde into smaller groups, all the while delivering the occasional kick when one got too close from behind.

Meanwhile, batons flashed out as Alexander and his three men worked the zombies over, delivering skull-splattering blows. They were all skilled at riot control, having dealt with the many protests over the years which invariably turned violent. The zombies dropped like flies as the Mounted Unit worked them over. They might be undead horrors but like the movies, a head shot would take them out. It didn't seem to matter if it was a horse hoof or a riot baton, either. Both did the trick.

However, numbers were not on the Alexander's side. The zombies were finally able to gain purchase with their clawing and the horses began screaming. Sergeant Alexander and his men fought harder as their horses began to falter. The momentum of their charge broken it quickly became a desperate fight for survival — one which the NYPD Mounted Unit appeared destined to lose.

Julia had no other options besides Lopez, and she was unarmed. All the others had disappeared into the fog one by one, taken by whatever lurked in the horrid darkness. She had no idea where they had gone and could only hope they were still alive. They were her responsibility at the end of the day and if anything had truly happened to them, she would never be able to live with herself.

Hoisting her shield, she made a choice. Her baton was slippery in her grasp, the rubber grip feeling odd. Perhaps it was coming loose, she wasn't sure. It didn't matter. This was her moment, the one chance she had to save someone other than herself. As much as she disliked horses, she respected the officers who rode them. Much like the K-9 officers at the Twenty-Sixth Precinct, the Mounted Unit viewed the horses they rode as their partners. Therefore, it wasn't four officers of the NYPD who were in danger, but eight.

"Stay here," she ordered Lopez. Before the young officer could protest, Julia explained. "You're unarmed and exposed. Just…stay here and keep your radio open."

"Sergeant?" Lopez tentatively reached out for her, but Julia pulled away.

"No sentimentalities," Julia told her. "Follow orders and do your job."

Julia began to walk across the open grassy knoll near Lasker Rink, a rhythmic beat in her head. Her baton began to tap the edge of her riot shield in time with each step. *Tap. Tap. Tap.* Each impact of the baton on shield slightly louder than the last. She began to hum under her breath as her mind drifted to the face of her daughter. Mia was the one good thing in her life which came from the failed relationship with DeAndre. She owed her child a better legacy than what DeAndre offered. Hell, what she herself was leaving behind.

The strange-looking zombies all looked towards the sound of Julia marching towards them. Beyond she could see the pulsing green light from the gap in the ground. The original plan remained the same, even though she was on her own now. Get Carrog into the gap. Julia didn't know why this was so important, but her gut told her it was the key to it all.

*Get big red into the gap,* a voice from recent memory whispered in her ear. She shook her head and increased the tempo of her banging. All of the zombies were looking at her now and the Mounted Unit was able to break contact. Spinning their horses around, Sergeant Alexander and his team galloped towards Nutter's Battery to regroup. While it saved the riders and their horses it also left Julia alone to face the remainder of the zombies…and the demon, Carrog.

*Shit,* she thought as she watched the Mounted Unit disappear. *I didn't plan on that happening.*

Intentional or not, she was now all alone in the middle of the park with a horde of zombies bearing down on her. She breathed in the thick, humid summer air and exhaled slowly. Her grip flexed slightly as she repositioned the baton in her palm as the first zombie shambled up to her, rotting hands reaching out towards her. Using the shield as a weapon she bashed the arms aside. One of them broke clean off while the other hung limply by a single rotted tendon. Shifting her stance, Julia lashed out with the baton and split the skull of the zombie apart like an overripe melon. The zombie dropped like a sack of potatoes.

Tactics, technique, and planning quickly devolved into a deadly game of whack-a-mole with Julia fighting for her life. They tried to surround her, but the woman remained mobile, dancing through and around the brainless creatures with surprising agility before delivering a crushing blow to one of the undead. For every zombie which was felled by her hand, it seemed two more would appear. Her swinging arm quickly began to tire yet there was no end to the zombies in sight.

Filth and blood splattered against her helmet's face shield. Instead of wiping the disgusting material away she ignored it, braining every zombie which came within reach and using her shield to keep the ones she wasn't ready for at bay. While her right arm tired which every swing, her shield remained up and steady, keeping her left side well protected. If she could hold out, perhaps Carrog would quit sending zombies out and come for her himself?

The zombies faltered in their approach. She felt a small twinge of hope. Was this the turning point of the battle? Instead of mindlessly attacking her they began to back off. A surge of fierce satisfaction washed over her. She'd done it. She had survived the horde. Shifting her gaze, Julia locked eyes with Carrog. The demon, however, was not quite looking at her.

An earth-shattering roar directly behind her caused the woman to instinctively drop to a crouch. Ears ringing, she pivoted and brought her shield up protectively as she tried to see what the new threat was. She blinked, mildly dazed. The roar had been louder than anything she had heard in her life. Julia's gaze went up…and continued up, almost twenty feet into the air, as the found herself staring face-to-face with a Tyrannosaurus Rex.

"Fuck me," she whispered as the dinosaur roared a second time. The ringing in her ears grew worse. Even if she survived the night, a small part of her brain was happy to inform her that her hearing would never be the same again.

Something moved on the back of the massive beast. Julia blinked as the dinosaur's hot breath washed over her. Rank and putrid, it reminded her of the breeze from Trenton in summertime. Instead of worrying about being eaten, though, Julia was very curious to see just what was on the Tyrannosaur's back. She knew she was about to die yet fear no longer held her. Like the cat, curiosity would be the true culprit of her eventual demise.

A very human face looked down at her from behind the dinosaur's head. Straddling the back of the T-Rex was a man in traditional Native American garb, replete with the headdress of a war chief of some kind. He pointed a finger at her and shouted something. Julia, ears still ringing, couldn't hear whatever he yelled. She didn't know what else to do at this point, so she flipped him the bird. Taken aback slightly, the war chief seemed to ponder her gesture. The T-Rex beneath him remained under his control…for the moment, at least.

The beast bellowed again, challengingly. Julia, who was almost certain she would never be able to hear again, screamed back anyway. The massive beast turned away from her suddenly. Julia had zero notice before the heavy tail of the lumbering dinosaur slammed into her shield. The heavy impact tossed her to the ground, shattering her shield in the process as she managed to use it to absorb her impact on the packed dirt which had once been the Meer. The shield did its job, however. While her left arm tingled, it wasn't broken.

The Montauk riding the Tyrannosaurus Rex—*how do I know that's one of those Montauk Indians from Long Island*, she wondered—seemed to shout something at the dinosaur, which seemed properly cowed by the great war chief. For some reason it reminded Julia of a dog which had just been caught chewing up some expensive shoes. Using his knees, the Montauk war chief guided the zombie dinosaur away from Julia and back into the forested area leading to the Ravine. She briefly head Lopez cry out in alarm but then the young officer started cursing, telling Julia she was still alive.

"Ouch," Julia grunted as she struggled to pick herself up and out of the dirt. Her left arm was still tingling, and her ears were ringing but otherwise she felt okay. Nearly exhausted, beaten, bruised, bloodied, and sore, she rolled onto her knees. At least she was still breathing. She glanced up and was surprised to see that the demon Carrog had suddenly moved within two feet of her.

A mixture of panic, fear, and anger flooded into her veins and Julia jumped to her feet and swung her right hand in a tight horizontal arc. Her baton made a solid connection with Carrog's left tusk, clearly catching him off guard. This stopped him in his tracks and Julia hit his right tusk with a backhand thrust instantly followed up by a devastating overhand strike to the creature's head which split skin, crunched bone, and elicited the loudest of beautiful ear-splitting howls.

Carrog suddenly flung his right claw forward and struck Julia's chest, spinning her around one hundred and eighty-degrees, barely managing to stay on her feet.

A fresh wave of pain crashed over her and Julia ended up on her face. She coughed and inhaled a cloud of dust, which set off more wheezing as she struggled to regain her breath. Using the last of her strength, she managed to roll onto her back. Above her, a familiar red face could be seen.

Carrog looked down at her, amused. Never before had she felt the desire to plant her boot squarely in someone's face as strongly as she did right then and there. Julia's best efforts had fallen short and now, the sacrifice the SRG and Mounted Units had made to give her a shot at the demon prince was all for naught. She had failed them. He nudged her with a clawed foot, which elicited another groan of pain as his toe caught her ribs. If not for the body armor she would probably be dead, courtesy of the rampaging tyrannosaurus rex. Even in her pain-induced haze she found the idea of a T-Rex in Central Park to be more than a little odd. But then, this night hadn't even been remotely close to normal.

"Nothing can defeat me!" Carrog screamed into Julia's face after kneeling down next to her. His hot, rancid breath stung her skin. His tusks were cracked from the impacts of her baton, but they still looked sharp enough to damage her. "I am Carrog Cǔ Síth the Eternal! I have slain gods at their mightiest! Humans I have crushed by the thousands with but a single snap of my fingers! You, pathetic morsel of a creature, do not have the strength stand up and face my full might! Cower and die, mortal, like all your kind do!"

Carrog stood up and walked back to the gap to Hell. He'd won, and he knew it. The rest of his army would come shortly, and Julia was out of energy, men, and time. Broken, Julia stayed down. Her arm still hurt from where the Tyrannosaurus Rex had hit her with its tail, and her cracked shield lay nearby. She had no idea where her baton went. Everything after the giant dinosaur was a bit of a blur. Why there had been a Native American riding the thing like a horse she had no clue, but it did remind her that the Mounted Unit was still out there, somewhere. At least, last thing she remembered they were. Or had they followed the SRG towards the Ravine and the stone tunnel there? Julia couldn't remember.

*Weapons*…Julia tried to do a mental inventory of everything on she still had on hand but was drawing a blank. She didn't know what the hell happened to her mace. Shield? Broken. *Thanks, stupid dinosaur*, she thought. Collapsible baton? Nearby but out of reach. Carrog would be able to easily stop her from reaching it if she made a move in that direction. Flexicuffs? She doubted her hand-to-hand skills against a stronger, fresher opponent. She might have been a little taller than the demon but he out massed her almost two to one. There was no way she could take him and get the flexicuffs on his wrists. Plus, what was she supposed to do with the demon if she did manage to get him in cuffs, take him to processing? That would go over well.

Almost all of what had managed to come through the chasm created by the demonic Carrog had been smaller dinosaurs, most of which had been in the New York region millions upon millions of years before. Except for the T-Rex, at least. She had no idea where that bastard had come from. Or why the Montauk war chief had been riding it, for that matter. The only thing she was certain was the Native American on the back of the dinosaur had been Montauk because her daughter had a school project about them not too long ago.

Julia rolled onto her stomach and felt something solid on her upper thigh. She blinked, confused. Had she rolled onto a rock? Given her recent string of bad luck she wouldn't be surprised if a broken shard of one stabbed her thigh. Reaching down to move the offending stone she realized it was not on the ground but in her pocket.

*Johnny's strange little knife*, she realized. The smooth handle was poking her in the thigh, not some random rock. She tried to remember what the irritating man had told her about it when they'd made the trade. *Evil to defeat evil, or something like that*, she recalled. Still, considering the weapons at hand—or lack thereof—it would have to do. If she was going to die for her city, then she was taking some cocky asshole demon with her.

Carrog was showboating, clearly enjoying his apparent victory. Julia, a lifelong Knicks fan, knew just how dangerous celebrating before the final whistle sounded could be. It would simply be a matter of timing on her part, and overconfidence on his. He had plenty of this, Julia knew, and tried to not to feel too hopeful. Carrog was about to be her Knicks and the knife, Michael Jordan.

*I need a better analogy*, Julia complained silently as she slowly picked herself up off the ground. *I'll be damned if I let Michael fucking Jordan be the hero of this piece.*

"Ah, the human is defeated and yet believes she can still fight," Carrog chortled. He waved for her to approach him. "Please do give it your best efforts. I want my conquest of this squalid land to be entertaining at least."

Julia managed to get back to her feet and spit blood onto the grass. One of her teeth had been knocked loose but she wasn't too worried. The NYPD offered excellent dental plans. No, she was more concerned about the broken rib which was stabbing her in the back. She'd dealt with pain in the past, but nothing could have prepared her for this level of sheer agony. She never thought breathing would hurt. Even while screaming and cursing at the attending physician during childbirth she hadn't struggled to breath.

"No witty rejoinder? Nothing?" Carrog clucked his tongue at her. "Just give me something to work with, mortal."

"You…you come into *my* town," Julia wheezed, one hand clutching her ribs while the other remained at her side, resting partially inside the pocket of her utility pants. "Who do you think you are? Fuck you. Fuck your ratty ass tyrannosaurus rex. Fuck your broke ass gap to Hell and fuck your whole fuckin' existence. You come to my town actin' all nasty, you can get in fuckin' line, get a fuckin' permit, and open your own goddam business like everybody else! What a fucking asshole."

"Eh? Excuse me?" Carrog looked at her, clearly confused. "I'm here to conquer, to enslave, not open a business. Did you hit your head or something?"

"Unless your name is Jordan or Martinez, New Yorkers are gonna forget you the moment you leave," she continued, the pain growing worse as she limped towards the short demon. "Enslave us? Conquer us? If being an Islanders fan can't kill you, some punk ass demon doesn't have a chance here. You say you're from Hell? Try growing up in Hell's Kitchen. Punk ass wannabe *bitch…*"

Julia's fingertips brushed the knife handle in her pocket. As Carrog leaned back and roared in amusement, she pulled it out of her pocket and quickly snapped the knife open. She lunged, aiming for where she supposed the demon's heart would be. Assuming he had one, that is. She had no idea where his internal organs were, or if he even had any.

Three inches from his chest and Carrog's clawed hand stopped her by simply grabbing her wrist. He was much stronger than she was and the force she'd put behind the blow was the last ounce of strength she had. It wasn't enough. Carrog began chuckling as he glanced at the knife before looking at Julia. Yellow glowing eyes stared directly into hers. His chuckled quickly grew as the demon's personal amusement grew with each moment.

"A folding knife? You bring a folding knife to a world-ending apocalypse? You fool!" Carrog roared with laughter as he released his grip on her wrist. He stuck his chest out at her. "What idiot brings a knife to a world-ending fight? No, please, go ahead and stab me. Maybe I'll feel it. Come on, little girl. Do your worst."

"Why don't you go back to fucking Boston like all the other assholes," she hissed and stabbed the demon square in the chest with all her might.

Carrog cried out in surprise and shock. The demon stumbled back, clearly pained by the knife. He looked down at the blade and tried to really inspect it for the first time. Black blood flowed steadily from the wound. Escaping air hissed around the knife as the demon's essence began to pour forth. It was clearly a killing blow. Recognition came over him the longer he stared at his chest. Or more importantly, the knife embedded in his breast.

"You have *Amhrán na Breoiteachta*?" he asked and dropped to one knee. His clawed hand reached up and tried to pull the knife from the wound. His strength failing, it remained firmly lodged in his chest. "How?"

"Some mafia guy named Johnny," Julia said as she slowly made her way closer to the dying demon. She paused within an arm-length of Carrog but he did not try to reach out for her. It was clear the wound had greatly weakened him. "Now fucking die already."

Julia snap-kicked the demon square in the tusks and Carrog fell backwards into the gap to Hell. The sickly greenish light glowed brightly, and

Julia thought the world was really going to end. Carrog's scream reverberated across Central Park.

A bizarre vortex of green-tinted wind began whirling around her, and in a few moments she realized that it had begun pulling everything in the vicinity into the huge gap.

Dozens, hundreds, then thousands of zombie corpses and body parts skidded across the ground and swooshed through the air. Human shapes, large primates, mammoths, and all manner of dinosaurs. Julia had to duck the flying decaying flesh, drop to the ground and fiercely crawl away, hugging grass like a desperate snail. She was sure she would not be able to resist the roaring winds all around her that were pulling everything into the evil pit.

*Not everything*, she suddenly realized. Only the macabre and outrageous things and creatures that the demon had created when he originally pushed through to the surface of Central Park from some nether realm. Nothing else was being disturbed. Trash cans, park benches, statues, flags, no not even a blade of grass seemed to stir as waves of eldritch debris was sucked out of existence. Julia continued crawling and when she'd crept about fifty yards she felt the sudden urge to lift her head and look back.

The last thing pulled into the pit was the zombie T-Rex with the zombie Montauk Warrior riding atop it. The dinosaur had dug his large foot claws deeply into the turf and leaned away from the massive hole, the warrior fiercely holding onto its neck. Still, inch by inch the two were slowly sliding backwards.

"Ashawagh, Kìzis, Tibik-kìzis, Nibì!" the Montauk Native-American zombie screamed aloud, "Madjashin!"

Both mount and rider turned at the very last moment and the T-Rex leaped forward and into the pit feet-first without hesitation. The warrior struck his decaying right arm straight up and his hand closed into a bony fist right before he completely disappeared from sight.

With a final loud popping sound, the gap to Hell closed. The green light quickly disappeared. The dense fog which had surrounded the border of Central Park very slowly began lifting.

In the distance, police, fire truck, and ambulance sirens became perceptible. As more fog fled the area, Julia spotted the Duke Ellington statue looking none the worse for wear. There wasn't any sign of the SRG or Mounted Unit around. Broken masonry appeared throughout the surrounding landscape around Laskin Rink and the destroyed park benches.

Something flashed, catching her eye, and she reluctantly stood up and staggered back to what she had just fled. Again, something shined briefly on the ground near the edge of where the hell-gap had been. Julia continued limping forward then knelt on the beginning of the large circular perimeter of wet grass. It was *Amhrán na Breoiteachta*, she recognized immediately, only the blade had broken off when she had stabbed Carrog. Only the handle remained intact, though there were scratches all across the face of the wood. Even the silver was tarnished and damaged.

She sighed, dropped back onto her butt, and rolled onto her back. The pain along her spine was excruciating but, surprisingly, began to fade. Shock, or perhaps the wound wasn't as bad as originally believed. Julia tried to check the blood loss with her hand but was simply too tired to do anything more than stare up at the graying sky. It should have been long past dawn at this point and yet the impermeable mist which clung to the park had kept everything in a pre-dawn gloom.

A narrow splinter of light finally broke through and her face was bathed in the warm glow. She sighed a second time. The distant sound of sirens grew louder. Desperately needing a nap, she closed her eyes. Just a quick, hard-earned respite from it all. A few minutes, tops. It was all she would need.

The ground beneath her shook once, twice, then a third time, like minor aftershocks after a large earthquake.

"Probably magical post-tremors," Julia mumbled to herself, trying to calm herself down for a couple of minutes of blessed unconsciousness…and afterwards she would return to the precinct and file off the report (assuming this blasted Sha'Daa was actually finally complete and over) which should be a snap. Damning and career-ending, sure, but it was necessary. Everything would need to come out. Her relationship with DeAndre. The past instances where she had looked the other way. Even Marcus, and everything she knew about his mysterious disappearance. All of it, in the open, the ugly truth to be seen by all. The innocents deserved justice at the least. Her daughter deserved better. Julia owed her that much.

First, though, she would rest.

A sudden thought snapped into her head.

*I'll never get my nana's watch back now*, she realized as she looked back at the broken knife in her hand. It was worthless now, ruined. There was no way Johnny would trade back the watch now, not after what she had done to his knife. Life just wasn't fair sometimes.

*Damn it.*

A flash of brilliant green light shot through Julia's eyelids which flew open in shock.

"What the fu…"

The ground suddenly shook harder than ever…then millions of tons of dirt exploded up into the air.

# Afterburn

## by Michael H. Hanson

*"Fire is never a gentle master."* — *Proverb*

**A**AGNEY, THE ANCIENT, SENTIENT ELEMENTAL Avatar of Fire, hovered above the Atlantic Ocean just over ten miles away from the coast of Manhattan island. As powerful and destructive as Aagney was, his purpose and intents were not the destruction of humanity and all life on the Earth. Unlike the majority of macabre powers that were struggling to break through hell portals spread across the planet, Aagney's mission was one of protection.

Though he had no eyes, his mystical perceptions could peer into reality far beyond the limits of a mortal human, and as he approached Manhattan, he beheld a wonder. Two wonders in fact.

First, he saw that the area known as Central Park, in the heart of Manhattan, was actually *three separate entities*. Not living beings, no, but three separate dimensional realities, near complete copies of each other partitioned by only the thinnest of quantum veils.

Each Park suffered the atrocities of The Sha'Daa and the same hell portal that was breaching into the fabric of them all, though this dark penetration appeared to be manifesting in wildly different manners in each variation of the park.

Aagney also quickly surmised that this *tripling* of the park had occurred only recently, probably at the outset of The Sha'Daa, and was inherently unstable.

Then came the second wonder…as all three realities suddenly merged.

An explosion of chartreuse light, brighter than a dozen suns flooded the air and temporarily blinded several million people who were unlucky enough to be awake and outdoors in an eight hundred-mile radius of New York City.

In the full breadth of a mere two seconds, three separate realities were forcefully integrated into one, and the results were nearly inconceivable.

People who had died horribly in the park in one or two realities, but whose duplicates survived in a third, instantly found themselves overwhelmed by the horrific memories of their doppelganger's tortures and deaths, leading many to collapse in outright madness.

Simultaneously, the multitude of damages to structures and soil in one or two of the realities was seemingly healed, as any and all surviving buildings, sidewalks, benches, statues, etc. from a third reality were fully incorporated into the final reintegrated version of the park.

For a glorious moment it looked like all of the disturbing physical manifestations of The Sha'Daa had been permanently wiped away.

Dozens of ambulances, fire trucks, police and state trooper vehicles, and the National Guard itself converged on Central Park from all directions as the last of the mystical, impenetrable, fog-like barrier dissipated.

Immediately following this quantum reunification, a massive hole, over a full mile in circumference, appeared in the heart of Central Park as unimaginable tons of rock and soil exploded upward thousands of feet into the air.

The few hundred people in the immediate vicinity who had somehow managed to survive the events of the past forty some hours in one or more of the three realities, were killed, instantly, their luck having finally run out.

Huge plumes of green, oily smoke and mist began pouring up from this gargantuan five-mile-deep wound in the park, rapidly spreading outward and towards the surrounding Manhattan skyline.

Aagney rushed forward to embrace his destiny.

Jabru, the Hell God of Death and Resurrection, slowly left his home dimension, crossing through the flickering portal between realms, and rose up through the five-mile high vertical tunnel that bridged his vile kingdom with that of Urath. Following him closely and climbing rapidly were millions of his slaves and worshippers, horrific creatures filled with the unquenchable desire for blood and flesh. In moments, he would release them upon this green and blue jewel in the heavens. As he crested the rim of the massive mouth of this gigantic hole, Jabru suddenly stopped his massive glowing green amoeba-like form which was roughly five times the size of a Mack truck.

Hovering just one hundred feet away was a brilliant red and gold globe, no larger than a human head, but emanating great heat and gravity waves not that much weaker than a miniature spacetime singularity. The air around this perfectly circular object crackled and burned and tiny bolts of multi-colored energy could be seen tracing a ten-foot spherical area surrounding this abomination to nature.

"Foolish humans," Jabru thought, "do you think your simple magics and sciences are a match for my deific power?"

"I am not human," Aagney, the burning globe that Jabru confronted, replied with his own non-spoken thoughts, "nor am I a creation of mortal science or magic."

Jabru's legions stopped just below him, rapidly filling up and crowding the five-mile-long tunnel beneath.

"Competition then," Jabru laughed, "no need to be greedy. Surely there is enough meat on this world for two hell dimensions to share?"

Aagney hovered closer by three feet.

"I am no petty interdimensional interloper like you," Aagney thought with great anger, "I am Aagney, the Avatar of all Fire. I burst into existence upon this world before men could speak or leave the safety of trees. I claim ownership of this planet over all my kin elementals of water, air, and earth, for I am the strongest, and most powerful, and none but me will decide the ultimate fate of humanity and all other life upon this lush body."

Jabru continued hovering, letting his armies below grow angry, and hungry, knowing this would just fuel their lust that much more.

"Considering the destruction of all that preceded you into this locale," Aagney thought, "I'm surprised that you are so eager to follow their example."

"Bah," Jabru laughed disdainfully, "those hordes of wastrels were the merest wisps born of stray power. The first energies emanating from my opening portal lent your planet's dead some moments of rebirth, life, and the feeblest of magics, but they were unaccounted for anomalies and in no way part of my great invasion. True, there were a few fallen buried hell-lords my eldritch powers resurrected, but their inevitable destruction has granted humanity no more than the smallest of respites."

Jabru studied Aagney with all of his arcane senses, and in moments a smile grew within the mind of his bulging and partly incorporeal being.

"I see weariness within you, Aagney," Jabru thought, "and yes, I can also see that you are still incredibly powerful. However, you have fought long and hard these two days of The Sha'Daa, and much of the energies that once burned in you are gone. You are far from your peak powers. Why waste yourself in this futile effort? I have no qualms with a fellow immortal like yourself. Do not be greedy. Let us share this world. I and my armies wish you no ill will."

Anger bubbled and boiled within Aagney. The hell god's words had struck to the heart of things. Aagney had fought and defeated several hell armies and more than a few hell gods during the past forty hours. It was an epic effort whose details could fill an entire tome, assuming any human or humans existed who had the imagination and wit to write of it.

"What do you think, Proteus?" Jabru suddenly turned his giant bulk in a new direction and spoke mentally to what appeared to be an empty swath of air, "don't you consider my offer a fair one? Come now, surely you know I can clearly see you hovering so closely nearby. Now is not the time for your subterfuge."

What Aagney had spied earlier as an insignificant swarm of insects all drew together and settled upon the ground directly between him and Jabru. In seconds the particulates formed into the perfect shell of a man wearing a white suit.

"Ten thousand years since I first sent you here," Jabru laughed, "and I thought you were eliminated by The Destroyer. Such a nuisance that one. I hear his deific punishment was to witness this new Sha'Daa with all his powers shackled and unable to directly interfere in my planned rape of this world. I so hope he is watching us now. Tell me, have you done your best to prepare this fresh planetary fruit for my conquering armies?"

"I did," Proteus said, walking forward to within a dozen feet of the hovering mass that was Jabru, "for several thousand years…but then something changed in me, and I found a new purpose."

"New purpose!" Jabru shouted in his thoughts, "what new purpose could supersede my desires? I created you, molded you from pure hate and eldritch fire to be my ultimate spy and terrorist. What riches were offered you to entice you off my righteous path?"

"Nothing you could understand in a million years…"

"What!" Jabru's thoughts screamed painfully, "answer me, slave! I demand it!"

"Love," Proteus replied, then exploded into a cloud of particulates that flew directly at the hell god. Caught off guard by the effrontery, Jabru had no time to react as his one-time servant tore into his master's flesh with terrible abandon. Jabru's mental screams of pain were awful as Proteus cut and ripped swaths of green living tissue as large as small cars from the hell god's levitating form. This commenced for a full minute before the hell god exuded a massive blast of hundreds of red lightning bolts that ripped through Proteus's swarm, destroying over half of the demon-spy's mass.

"Enough!" Jabru thought, mental waves of pain still emanating from him, "this ends now. Beg for my forgiveness, and I will give you an impossible task to complete in another universe. If you survive that, I will consider leniency."

Proteus managed to re-form his middle-aged man in a white suit persona and stretched his mouth into a wide grin.

"Can you see the *fuck you* in my smile?"

Jabru screamed and unleashed a second wave of red lighting that completely obliterated the hell-spawned Proteus, one-time demon spy, and more recently one of Central Park's most effective reformed vigilantes.

"For a hell god your wounds look quite mortal," Aagney thought aloud.

"This?" Jabru laughed, "please. I am a being of eldritch energies. I wear this flesh shell so that more primitive beings can actually see me and quake in terror at my approach. It is but a meaningless shroud, though perhaps one I should not have allowed myself to become so attuned to. I plan to spare a few million of these humans so that they may worship me for several hundred years before I tire of them. I'm sure they will find this shape quite pleasing."

Aagney quickly noticed the vicious wounds in Jabru's gargantuan form heal almost instantly.

"You, though, do not need any more battles today. I know you are tired, my friend," Jabru said.

Aagney had closed and destroyed several dozen hell portals over the last forty hours, never once admitting defeat, and here he now hovered, possessing only fifty percent of the incendiary powers he had possessed a mere two days ago.

Reaching with his own senses deep into the massive hole, Aagney quickly comprehended the full extent of the forces that Jabru was set to unleash on the Earth. For a moment, he hesitated, seeing that this might very well be beyond his full capabilities.

"I sense a change in you, Aagney," Jabru spouted in his thoughts, "you agree with me. I know it. Very well, let us begin joint efforts, my friend. Pray move aside and let my minions pass."

It was this last request, made with the force of smug demand, that pushed Aagney over the edge.

"No," Aagney said with deadly finality.

Overwhelming rage filled Jabru who simultaneously exulted the thought "attack" to his underlings while exuding a purple force-bolt of unimaginable feral energies at Earth's Avatar of Fire.

Aagney deflected most of, and absorbed the rest, of Jabru's lethal power.

Hundreds, thousands, then hundreds of thousands of monstrosities started pouring out of the hole.

The Avatar of Fire deflected three more massive purple bolts of power from the hell god, one which shot towards the heavens and turned the International Space Station Two into orbiting slag instantly killing all one hundred crew persons aboard, one which shot into the Atlantic Ocean instantly frying the very last Pod of Mesoplodon Traversi (the spade-toothed whale) sending the species into permanent extinction, and the third of the hell god's deflected power bolts struck the center of One World Trade Center, cutting it in half, and killing six thousand innocent civilians as the top half of the structure tilted over and crashed into the crowded streets below.

Aagney rose up a quarter of a mile into the air.

Jabru laughed within his mind, sure that the Fire Avatar had grown weaker still under attack and was running away to lick his wounds.

The legions of monstrosities poured outward in all directions, tearing through the thick green smoke that now covered most of the park, and in moments were within several hundred feet of the surrounding human rescue forces that were on the verge of entering the park proper.

"Fýrr!" Aagney screamed within his own mind and let loose the full force of all his powers downward.

Jabru barely had time to look upward and grasp the nature of his doom as it arrived.

An unending holocaust of pure white fire flooded down upon Central Park in wave, after wave, after wave, burning, and melting, and ultimately disintegrating everything in its path. No building, statue, stone, tree or metal remained intact for more than seconds as all was reduced to ash.

The terrifying swells of flame poured outward after hitting the ground, catching up to and overwhelming all the hellspawn that Jabru had released, and killing them.

Standing at the front of a crowd of New York's finest within Hunter's Gate at Eighty-First Street and Central Park West was the Gold Avenger, humanoid in shape, but hairless with skin that looked like dense, glowing amber. Sharp barbs covered his fists, forearms, elbows, knees and ankles. He was naked, though no visible genitalia could be seen between his legs. His face was handsome and his eyes glowed yellow. Long thick cracks he had acquired during two days of battle covered his entire body, but he held himself upright, preparing to fight to the death any creature or monster that dared to try to leave the park.

Just as the white flames reached the full perimeter of the park itself, they slowed, then stopped. One small wave of fire flowed up to Avenger's clawed toes, then shot up his body, engulfing him in flames. The police behind him stepped back in shock as all of the magical white fire immediately receded back towards the giant hole. The miles of green oily fog that had enveloped the park had completely burned away.

The flames died out across the Avenger's body and officers broke free from their surprise to attend to him. Their mouths dropped open in shock as they beheld not the wondrous gold-colored mutant they had met mere minutes ago, but an ordinary and healthy-looking naked man in his early thirties. Someone rushed forward with a green blanket and threw it around him as he stood up and saluted an NYC Police Captain.

"Sergeant Burt Buchowski," he said, "United States Marine Corps. Reporting for duty, sir!"

Up in the sky, Aagney continued to exude more floods of destructive fire, draining off every single photon of his existence, forcing it down into the five-mile deep tunnel, killing the millions of marauders within, until his power reached the hell portal itself, and utterly destroyed it in a single massive eruption of heretical annihilation.

The explosion made the gigantic vertical tunnel collapse into itself. The resulting shockwave made cars bounce a full foot into the air and knocked people off of their feet as far away as ten miles.

It took time for the wind to clear away the dust, and smoke, and floating ashes, but a full twenty minutes later the shocked and dazed rescuers on the periphery of the deific battle started walking through the twenty entrances to central park…and then they stopped.

All that was left of the once lush eight hundred and forty-three acres of meadows, reservoirs, forests, statues, and buildings was a six-mile perimeter of Central Park North, Central Park West, Central Park South, and Fiftieth Avenue surrounding a massive stretch of smoking grey ash. All else was gone.

Floating down from the sky was a small burning spark that looked not unlike a blinking firefly, only it was still day and this strange thing was bright enough to be easily seen beneath the blazing summer sun.

A short while later it settled down upon the empty sidewalk of East One Hundred Eighth Street. A moment later a shiny black leather shoe appeared beside it. Next, a broad hand with long fingers picked up the flashing spark of material that looked no larger than a pea.

"Aagney," a rich, mellifluous voice spoke gently, "it is me, Johnny The Salesman. Do not exert yourself. No matter how weak and feeble your thoughts, I will hear them clearly."

Aagney, exhausted and filled with pain, struggled to focus his mind.

"I am a great flame reduced to but a fraction of my one-time glory," Aagney's weak thoughts came forth, "I would not have you witness my shame and doom, salesman."

Though Aagney's perception had dimmed tremendously, he knew he now rested in the upward facing right palm of Johnny. Even at this tiny size, stripped of most of his heat, he would have burned right through a human hand in but a moment. Johnny was far from human, though, so Aagney was not surprised.

"Believe me, Mighty Aagney," Johnny said kindly, "of all the beings that ever existed in the universe, I alone know exactly how you feel."

"Enough," Aagney thought, "I am about to embrace eternity. What is it you want, other than to gloat over my demise?"

Aagney sensed that Johnny was now walking.

"I am here to make a trade, what else?" Johnny asked, "The Sha'Daa has six more hours to dispense before its conclusion, and the odds of humanity surviving to the end is still very small. I have a vial of a most precious substance that can revive you. Simply grant me but a single promise and you can have it right now."

Johnny's movement told Aagney that the supernatural being had walked a block, turned down a side street, and was striding down a sudden decline.

"What promise?" Aagney thought, "that I will never ever harm a single one of your precious human beings for the rest of my existence? No more fanning the flames of catastrophic wildfires in California, the Amazon, and Central Africa? No more feeding the devastating purifying blazes spreading through overpacked slums in large cities? Bah! You are so pathetically predictable, trickster! I would die a thousand deaths before slaving myself to your will. Save your dog collar for another, and to hell with your trades!"

"Well then," Johnny said, disrespectfully tossing the flickering spark that was Aagney the Avatar of Fire over his shoulder, "all bets are off, I guess."

Aagney floated down in a series of sideways back and forth movements until landing on the sidewalk. He sensed the abominable salesman striding away and steeled himself for the final extinguishment of his existence. A couple of moments later, though, and he weakly sensed something approaching him rapidly…a vague, snakelike form slithering closer and closer.

Johnny glanced over his shoulder and his eyes focused for a moment on a large gasoline tanker truck that had fallen onto its side about thirty yards uphill from where he had tossed the weak and withering Aagney. A release valve on the rear of the main tank was bent out of shape and a moment later internal pressure caused a small rent in the metal to appear, and eleven thousand six hundred gallons of gasoline began pouring out onto the sidewalk. It quickly formed into a quick moving stream that followed the path of gravity downhill.

"Well well well," Johnny mumbled to himself, smiling as he turned back around and walked away, "now what are the odds of that happening at just this moment?"

*The explosion was a terrifying primal birth scream of overwhelming agony and ecstatic joy!*

—The End—

www.ingramcontent.com/pod-product-compliance
Lightning Source LLC
Chambersburg PA
CBHW070457260626
47161CB00004B/1341